Where's My *Wife?*

CLARK SELBY

STRATTON
—PRESS—
Publishing Life

WHERE'S MY WIFE?
Copyright © 2018 **Clark Selby**

All rights reserved. No part of this book may be used or reproduced by any means, graphic, electronic, or mechanical, including photocopying, recording, taping or by information storage and retrieval system without the written permission of the author except in the case of brief quotations embodied in critical articles and reviews.

Stratton Press, LLC
1603 Capitol Ave, Suite 310,
Cheyenne, WY 82001
www.stratton-press.com
1-888-323-7009

Because of the dynamic nature of the Internet, any web addresses or links contained in this book may have changed since publication and may no longer be valid. The views expressed in the work are solely those of the author and do not necessarily reflect the views of the publisher, and the publisher hereby disclaims any responsibility for them.

ISBN (Paperback): 978-1-948654-14-2
ISBN (Ebook): 978-1-64345-068-1

Printed in the United States of America

CHAPTER ONE

Taking a Trip up the Mississippi

Rocky Stone and his wife, Latesha, boarded the riverboat *The Pride of St. Louis* in New Orleans en route to St. Louis to meet with his publisher, Bobby Longstreet, to discuss Rocky's latest novel, *Six Guns of Wichita*.

Rocky and Latesha had been traveling for several weeks now, first to Louisville to visit old friends and then to New Orleans so Latesha could buy some new clothes coming in from Paris.

St. Louis would be their last stop before traveling home to Boonville, Missouri. It wasn't a very big town, but they loved having their home overlooking the Missouri River because it was always such a pleasure watching the changes in the river during the different seasons of the year. There was always something new to look at on their river. They loved it.

Besides, Rocky was a big deal in Boonville with all his success writing his dime novels. He enjoyed belonging to the local writers club. Most of the writers were very different than Rocky. They were either in the newspaper business, or they wrote textbooks, so he was the odd one out by writing dime novels.

The truth was most of the members were jealous of Rocky's success because they had the education and the training to be writers and all Rocky had was the experience and the ability to make up stories and sell thousands of those little dime novels.

Rocky and Latesha were well known to most of the riverboat captains who plied the Missouri and Mississippi Rivers, as was

Captain Don Jones of *The Pride of St. Louis*. Over the years, he had become a very good friend of theirs.

Captain Jones met them as they boarded the boat, and he personally showed them to their cabin.

Latesha was very fond of Don because he always saw that they had the best cabin on the boat and that they were very well taken care on their trips with him.

After the porters delivered their luggage and all of Latesha's packages to their cabin, Rocky thought their cabin looked like they were either moving or that Christmas must be just around the corner.

Captain Jones asked Rocky if he would like to get a drink and give Latesha some time to get things straightened up in their cabin and for her to have some time to herself before dinner.

Rocky thought he should stay and help Latesha, but she told him, no, to go ahead and have a little drink while she arranged things in their rooms the way she wanted them.

Captain Jones said, "Rocky, can't you see your wife wants to have a little time by herself without you hovering over her all the time?"

Latesha replied, "Go ahead and have a drink with the captain while I get some of our things put away."

Rocky could see the two of them were ganging up on him so he said, "Okay, I give up. I'll go have a drink with you, Captain."

Captain Jones and Rocky walked to the bar and sat down at a corner table away from the noise made by all the preparation needed to get the riverboat underway and away from the dock.

Rocky said, "Captain, don't you need to be directing your crew to get started on our way to St. Louis?"

"Not anymore. I got a great first mate working for me on this trip. His name is Dan White, and he can handle it all by himself. Besides, this is going to be my last trip because after this trip, I'm moving into the home office in St. Louis as the director of operations for the St. Louis & New Orleans Shipping Lines.

"Dan White will be taking over the helm of *The Pride of St. Louis* when we reach St. Louis. This is kind of his test trip."

"Well, I'm sorry to hear you won't be captain on our trips anymore, but I sure wish you good luck in your new job as director of operations."

"You know, Rocky, I'm going to miss talking to our passengers, but I'm going to be happier being home with my wife and kids instead of being gone all of the time."

"How many kids do you have, Captain Jones?"

"Six kids, three boys and three girls."

"Wow, six kids. You must have got home sometimes."

"Yeah, and it seems like every time I was home for a few weeks, the next time I got home I found out my wife was expecting a baby."

"How old are your kids?"

"Let's see, the youngest one is, golly, she's twelve now, and the oldest one is a boy, and he is twenty-two. We have twin girls. They're sixteen, and then our problem boys that are fourteen and seventeen."

"How come you say your fourteen- and seventeen-year-old boys are a problem?"

"Well, they don't want to mind their mother anymore, and they don't want to do their chores."

"Why do you think they are acting up?"

"Sorry to say it, but probably because I haven't been home with them enough and they're the in-between children. I'm sure they think they're not getting enough attention from their parents."

"I hope you being home with them will help change things for your wife for the better, because as they say, '*If mama ain't happy, nobody's happy.*'"

"Well, that's enough about my problems. I've always wanted to ask you how you ever got started writing those dime novels, so I will, how did you?"

"I'll tell you, Captain, most people don't know it, but I worked for the Texas Rangers for several years. In fact, before I quit I was the captain in charge of investigations. A lot of my books are from the different investigations of cases I worked, but of course I had to make my cases more dramatic in order to get my readers to buy my books. That's what you do if you really want to sell a lot of books."

"I'll be darned. I sure didn't know you used to be a Texas Ranger. Another question I always wanted to ask you, how tall are you anyway? Because you sure go up a long ways in the air."

"Captain, I used to be six five, but I don't know anymore. I've probably lost an inch or two. Age does that to you, you know."

"Rocky, I knew you were tall! Whew, six foot five."

"Well, I'm not really so tall. One of my great-grandfathers was seven foot two. Now that's tall."

"Seven foot two, that's really tall, Rocky!"

"I think I'm too tall. I don't want to even think about the problems he must have had with beds and everything else. I'm glad I never got that tall. I have enough trouble going through a lot of doors, and I can never find a bed long enough for me."

Rocky finished his drink and told the captain, "I think I better go back to my room to see how things are going with Latesha."

The captain said, "You go look after that beautiful wife of yours and tell her I'm expecting to host her for dinner. You tell her I have a couple of bottles of champagne cooling just for her."

Rocky shook hands with the captain and thanked him for the drink and told him they would see him later.

Rocky walked the few feet back to their room and found the door wasn't locked, which was very unusual because Rocky always wanted to be sure they kept doors locked.

When Rocky opened the door to their rooms, he didn't find anyone there and wondered where Latesha had gone. He was sure she would be back very soon.

Rocky looked around the rooms, and he could see Latesha didn't have many things put away, and that really surprised him. She was always one to have everything neat and tidy. Well, she must have had a good reason to leave the room without putting it in order.

Rocky decided he would lie down for a few minutes and wait for her to return. He thought she probably went out to watch their boat as it was leaving the port of New Orleans. He knew she always liked to hear the band playing as they left the port.

Rocky couldn't keep his eyes open, and he fell asleep. When he woke up, it was dark outside, and Latesha still wasn't back in their rooms. Everything was still just like it was; nothing had been put up since he went to sleep, so he was sure Latesha had never come back to their rooms.

Rocky wondered what in the world that girl could be doing since she hadn't returned to their rooms after all this time. She never strayed very far away from him since they had been married. They loved being together no matter what they were doing. They both loved that.

Finally, after waiting another ten minutes and Latesha hadn't returned, Rocky decided he had to go looking for her. She couldn't have gone very far because this boat wasn't that big.

Rocky left their cabin and began his search in the bar where he and the captain had their drink. He knew the bartender would recognize Latesha, so Rocky asked him if she had been in the bar looking for him, and the bartender told him she hadn't been there.

Rocky continued to walk around the boat, and when he went into the dining room, he saw the captain sitting at a table by himself.

The captain said, "Rocky, you're late for dinner. Where's Latesha?"

"I am trying to find her. I went back to our cabin, and she wasn't there. I don't know where in the hell she could be."

"That doesn't make much sense. She was going to be putting things up in your rooms when we left to have a drink this afternoon."

"Captain, you're telling me that it doesn't make any sense. I can't figure out where she could have gone."

"Take it easy, Rocky. She has to be on this boat somewhere. I know she was on it when we left New Orleans because they already had the gangplank up before we got to your cabin. We certainly haven't stopped at any ports since we left New Orleans.

"Rocky, I'll organize a search of the boat right away. We'll search every room on this boat because she has to be on here somewhere."

"Thanks, Captain Jones."

The captain told Rocky to come with him while he organized the search.

They walked to the wheelhouse, where he introduced Rocky to Dan White and explained to Dan that they needed to get the crew to search the entire boat until they found Latesha.

Dan told the man in the wheelhouse to take over steering while he got the crew together to search the entire boat.

Although Dan White didn't know Latesha, most of the crew did since she was a frequent passenger on the *Pride of St. Louis* and a very beautiful woman, about five foot six with beautiful brown eyes, long light brown hair, and a wonderful figure that women admired and men desired.

The crew members certainly all knew what Latesha looked like.

While other women walked, Latesha appeared to glide with her grace, poise, and elegance. Latesha was soft-spoken and, with her proper English, was fit to converse with kings, queens, or presidents, befitting her education, but she never talked down to anyone whether they were servants or a bum on the street.

Latesha could be at ease with her friends or kings and sometime even playful like a child if she made up her mind to.

Rocky had never known anyone like her. She was unbelievable, and he loved her so. Why or how she ever fell in love and married Rocky only God knew.

Dan got enough of the crew together to be able to search every inch of the boat beginning from the top to the bottom.

Two hours later, the crew reported back to Dan that they had searched every inch of the boat and found nothing of Latesha.

The crew had searched all the public rooms, the crew's quarters, the captain's quarters, the boiler room, every passenger's cabin, the lifeboats, and each one of them reported they couldn't find Latesha anywhere on the boat.

When Dan came back to the wheelhouse, he said, "Rocky, we have searched the entire boat and couldn't find your wife. I'm so sorry. I can't imagine what could have happened to your wife. All I know now is that your wife is not on this boat."

CHAPTER TWO

Circumstances Leading to the Crime

Charlie Christian had been trying for years to figure out how he could pay Rocky Stone back for all the pain he caused him, but couldn't decide how he could do it.

It was pretty funny to Charlie now just how a strange set of circumstances led him to the perfect opportunity to finally get even with Rocky Stone.

Charlie and his gang had pulled off three nice bank robberies in East Texas and had their pockets full of money, so Charlie decided the gang needed to lay low for a while.

Charlie really needed a woman. It had been far too long since he had a woman, and he had always wanted to go to New Orleans. He heard the French women in New Orleans were really hot lovers. So he told the gang they were all going to New Orleans, and they would stay there until they ran out of money.

When they arrived in New Orleans, he told the guys to be careful and not to be hanging around together all the time.

They all found rooms in different places in the Quarter, and Charlie found a very nice place to stay right in the middle of Bourbon Street; this was where all the action took place.

It didn't take long for Charlie to find the woman he was looking. She was working out of the Red Dog Saloon, and her name was Dotty Ferguson.

Dotty was a real looker, and the stories he had heard about the French women of New Orleans being hot were certainly true. Dotty was one hot lover.

Charlie and Dotty were having a great time. Dotty liked to eat in good restaurants, and Charlie didn't mind paying for them. Nor did he mind paying her very well for her company.

They were together for several days and nights, and one morning Dotty was looking in the *Picayune* newspaper and found something that really interested her. She said, "Charlie, do you think you could ever love me as much as this guy they're writing about in the paper? He brought his wife to New Orleans just to buy her some new gowns that just arrived from Paris."

"Sure, baby, I could love you that much. Where are they selling these gowns?"

"At Madam Desiree's Fine French Shoppe on Canal Street."

"What's the guy's name who brought his wife to New Orleans to buy her a dress anyway?"

"I don't know, Charlie. Just look at this article in the paper yourself."

Charlie took the newspaper from Dotty, and he began reading the story about this fellow who wrote dime novels.

His name was Rocky Stone, and his wife's name was Latesha. They came to New Orleans only to buy her some new gowns from Paris.

Charlie started to lay the newspaper down, and suddenly he stopped and reread the name again, Rocky Stone and his wife, Latesha.

The story went on to say they would be leaving New Orleans in four days to travel to St. Louis on the riverboat *The Pride of St. Louis*.

The wheels began turning in Charlie's head. Rocky Stone and his wife were right here in New Orleans. He and his men were right here in New Orleans.

Now Charlie knew how to cause pain to Rocky. Boy, it was going to be a great payback for all the pain Charlie suffered serving those two prison terms in Texas because of Rocky Stone.

Where's My Wife?

Charlie remembered Rocky's story *Kidnapped off the Mississippi Queen*, and Charlie planned to use Rocky's own plan to kidnap his wife, Latesha.

Charlie had to get to work quickly to be able to gather everything up they would need to make the kidnapping work.

They were going to need a warehouse to operate the kidnapping from and then to hold Rocky's wife after they grabbed her.

Charlie began to list all the things in his mind they would need to do the kidnapping exactly the way Rocky described it in his book.

They would need to buy a hammock like they used as beds for the crew on ships. This shouldn't be much of a problem in a port like New Orleans.

They had to have several ropes, long enough to lower Latesha down from the deck of the riverboat to a rowboat.

They would need a big bag, large enough to put Latesha into before putting her into the hammock.

Plus more rope to close the hammock up so Latesha didn't fall out as she was being lowered down to the rowboat.

Charlie would have three of his men buy tickets for passage on *The Pride of St. Louis* as deck passengers going to the first stop the boat made.

These men would be the ones who would actually do the kidnapping of Latesha and get her off the steamboat.

They would need something to knock Latesha out with, and he knew just the right thing to use.

The guards at the prison had these small clubs with steel pellets from shotguns shells sewed inside a leather case.

The guards used these to keep prisoners in line so it wouldn't leave marks on the men that they had been beating, unlike the wood night stick they carried.

The guards wanted to be sure the warden never saw any prisoners with big bruises on them so he would never know how bad the guards were abusing the prisoners.

Yes, they would need a rowboat, but Charlie decided it would be better to steal one of these instead of buying one. They could save money, and no one could say they sold a rowboat to any of his men.

Suddenly, Dotty said, "Charlie, what's happened to you? You act like you are somewhere else?"

Charlie replied, "Sorry, baby, I just had a great idea. Why don't we go down to that dress shop and let me buy you a new dress."

"Charlie, that's awful sweet of you, but those dresses from Paris cost hundreds of dollars, and I don't go anywhere where I would ever need a dress like that."

"Okay, baby, I tell you what. I'll give you fifty dollars, and you go out and buy yourself a complete new outfit so we can go out to dinner tonight at some really fancy restaurant."

"Oh, Charlie, you're the best."

Charlie gave Dotty fifty dollars, and she said, "Charlie, you're going to love me in my new outfit tonight."

"I'm sure I will, Dotty, but I'll like you better when I'm taking it off of you tonight. It will be like opening a wonderful present for myself."

"Oh, Charlie, you're so silly."

"Go on and find a new outfit. I can't wait to see it on you. Baby, I may be gone when you get back. I've got some business to attend to this afternoon, but I'll be back in time to take you to dinner."

Dotty left to search for her new outfit.

Charlie left a few minutes later to begin looking for his men.

It didn't take too long before he found the Barr brothers, Tom and Sandy. Charlie asked them to help him find the other members of his gang because he had a job to do right here in New Orleans.

Tom said, "I think we know where most of the fellows hang out, and we'll find them and let them know you've got a job for us. They will be thrilled to hear it because all of us are having a grand time in New Orleans. Charlie, where and what time do you want to meet?"

"Let's meet down by the steamboat docks tomorrow about ten o'clock in the morning, okay?"

Tom said, "Sounds good to me, boss, ten o'clock tomorrow at the steamboat docks."

Tom and Sandy left to see if they could find the other members of the gang, and Charlie started walking toward the riverfront looking for a warehouse.

It didn't take Tom and Sandy long to find three of the other gang members; they found Jack Robinson, Tony Caraway, and Ronnie Barnhill as they were walking down Bourbon Street.

Tom said, "Listen, fellows, the boss has a job for us here in New Orleans, and he wants to meet all of us tomorrow morning at ten o'clock at the steamboat docks, okay?"

Tony said, "Sure, we'll be there."

Sandy asked, "You guys know where you can find James and Billy Jack?"

Ronnie replied, "I know they were going over to Jackson Square a while ago."

Tom said, "Ronnie, would you mind seeing if you can find them and let them know about the meeting tomorrow."

"No problem, I'll find them. All I have to do is look wherever the girls are."

Tom laughed and said, "We sure like these New Orleans ladies with their French accents. They sound so sexy, it makes my hair curl."

All the other guys laughed at Tom's statement.

Finally Ronnie responded, "That's not what it does to me."

The laughter grew even louder with Ronnie's statement.

People walking down Bourbon Street looked at these five men and wondered what was so funny.

While Tom and Sandy were busy finding the other members of the gang, Charlie was looking at warehouses along the Mississippi River and found one that had a For Rent sign on it.

Charlie looked through the windows and could see the warehouse had an office area and what looked like some other partitioned-off rooms.

Charlie thought that would work well for what he wanted the building for. He made a note about the information of the rental agency handling the rental of the warehouse.

When Charlie returned to his room, he found Dotty had already made her purchases and was all dressed up for dinner in her new outfit.

Charlie said, "Baby, you look wonderful. I love your new outfit. It looks great on you."

Dotty grinned and put her arms around Charlie and said, "You know, Charlie, if you stayed around New Orleans very long, I could fall in love with you. You say the sweetest things to me, unlike the jokers I normally wind up with."

She kissed him hard on the lips, and Charlie said, "You know, Dotty, I might just stay here with you forever, but right now I think we should go to dinner so you can show off your new clothes."

They had a wonderful dinner and a great time back in Charlie's room, and sure enough, he enjoyed taking her new outfit off her.

The following morning Charlie asked, "Dotty, could you please do something for me?"

"Whatever you need, honey. You just tell me, and I will do it."

"Thanks, baby, this is a really special favor. I need you to go and see if you can rent a warehouse for me along the river for a month. My associates and I have a small cargo coming in very soon. I had planned to find and rent a warehouse earlier, even before we met, then I met you, and I couldn't think about anything else but you. We had so much fun together I completely forgot about doing it. I have a meeting this morning with my associates, and I don't want them to know I didn't do it."

"Sure, Charlie, I'd be glad to do it for you. How big of a warehouse do you need for your shipment?"

"While you were doing your shopping yesterday, I took a walk, and I think I found a warehouse that would work just fine for our shipment. I wrote down the information of the rental agent who's renting the building."

Charlie handed Dotty a piece of paper with the rental agency name and address on it.

Dotty looked at the name of the agency and said, "No problem, I even know some of the people who work there. Who should I say it is that wants to rent the building?"

"I think we should use our association's name instead of mine. Its name is *The Rocky Payback Company.*"

"Gee, that's a funny name for a company. What does it mean?"

"Dotty, it's a long story, but it comes from one of my competitors from years ago.

"His name was Rocky, and he kept beating us in business all the time, but I finally got the best of him, and he quit. So when he went out of my business. I decided to change the name of our company to *The Rocky Payback Company.*"

"That's a funny story, Charlie, you sound like you and your associates must really enjoy your business."

"Oh, we certainly do, we love it."

Charlie gave Dotty two hundred dollars to be sure she had enough money to pay for one month's rent on the warehouse. He didn't think it would be that much for one month's rent, but he wanted to be sure she had enough money with her to pay the rent. He certainly did not want to go down there himself.

Charlie and all his gang members met at the riverboat docks, and Charlie outlined his plan and assigned jobs to each of the men to buy or steal the items they would need to carry out Rocky's plan for kidnapping someone off a steamboat.

Charlie said, "Remember, everything has to happen fast because *The Pride of St. Louis* is leaving in three days, so everyone has to do their work, and everything has to work like clockwork to pull off this job. One slip and everyone's caught. I heard the prisons in Louisiana are worse than the ones in Texas, and I for one don't want to find out if that's true. The ones in Texas were enough for me."

Charlie gave out the assignments to his men.

Tom and Sandy Barr were to buy the hammock, ropes, and other assorted items they would need, plus buy or find someone who could make a small club using shotgun pellets wrapped inside a leather cover to knock out their victim

Charlie explained the way the kidnapping would go down and assigned Jack Robinson, Tony Caraway, and Ronnie Barnhill the job of buying deck passenger tickets for the riverboat.

They were to be on board the boat as soon as they let passengers on. It was important to be on the boat early so they could see which cabin Rocky and Latesha were assigned to.

When they found out when she was on board the boat, they were to make their way to Latesha's cabin when everyone was working on loading the boat and taking on passengers.

One of them was to knock on the door and tell them the captain needed to see Rocky right away because there was a problem with their tickets.

As soon as Rocky left to meet with the captain, they were to go directly back to her cabin and knock on the door. Then they were to knock her out, place her in the big bag they brought on board, place the bag in the hammock, and tie up the hammock so she couldn't fall out of it when they lowered it into a waiting rowboat.

Once Latesha was in the rowboat, they should climb down the ropes they used to lower the hammock into the rowboat and then proceed to the warehouse where Charlie would be waiting for them.

Charlie said, "It's important to be sure you fix the ropes so you can take the ropes with you, so no one knows how you got Latesha off the boat."

James Newton and Billy Jack Reynolds were to steal a rowboat, and they would be the ones who tied their rowboat up to the riverboat waiting for Latesha and their three friends to join them so they could all get away from the steamboat.

Charlie told Tom and Sandy they should position themselves along the Algiers side of the river and make sure no one was following the rowboat.

If they were, Tom or Sandy should fire two shots, and then the men in the rowboat were to throw Latesha into the river.

If the rowboat made it safely to the warehouse, they were to pull up next to the dock and unload their cargo as quickly they could and get her inside the warehouse.

The last thing for them to do was to set the rowboat free so it would float on down the river.

They were to be sure there was nothing left in the rowboat that wasn't in it when they stole it.

Charlie would be waiting for them at the warehouse.

Charlie returned to his room to wait for Dotty to come back from renting the warehouse for him.

He didn't have long to wait as Dotty came bursting into his room only ten minutes later and exclaimed, "Honey, I got the warehouse for thirty days for only thirty dollars."

Dotty held out the money left over from paying the one month's rent on the warehouse.

Charlie said, "Dotty, you're a marvel. Thank you so much for help me and keeping me out of trouble with my associates. Sweetheart, you just keep the one hundred seventy dollars for helping me out."

"Oh, Charlie, you don't have to pay me for doing that. I want to do it for you."

"I know, Dotty, but I really want you to have the money, okay?"

"Okay, if you insist."

"I do, baby. I insist."

CHAPTER THREE

Executing Rocky's Kidnapping Plan

Charlie told Dotty he was going to meet with his associates again this morning and he would be back as soon as he could.

Dotty, who was still in bed, said, "Charlie, I'm really tired, so I think I'm going to stay in bed this morning until you come back."

"Okay, baby, you just do that. I'll be back as soon as I can. Love you."

It didn't take long for Charlie to find all his men and tell them to come with him to the warehouse he rented for their job.

Arriving at the warehouse, he was pleased to find the key Dotty received from the rental agency worked fine.

When they got inside the warehouse, they were surprised to find whoever had the warehouse before had left several chairs, tables, and a desk, and one of the rooms they discovered had been used as a bedroom. It still had a bed and dresser in it.

Charlie said, "This is going to work out perfect for holding Rocky Stone's wife and a place we can all stay. When we finish this meeting, I want all of you to move all of your things into the warehouse, and if you had an assignment to buy things for the kidnapping get it moved in here as well."

All his men either said, "Yes, sir," or they nodded their head in an affirming manner.

Charlie next said, "I want to go over each one of your assignments for this job. Some of you were assigned to pick up certain items we would need for the job, so I'll start with Tom and Sandy. Were you able to get everything I asked you to get?"

Tom replied, "Yes, we got everything we were supposed to get: the hammock, ropes, and we even found a leather shop near Jackson Square that made the leather-bound club you wanted us to buy."

Charlie responded, "That's good. When we're finished here I want you to bring everything here along with your personal items."

Tom answered, "Yes, sir, Charlie, we'll get all of our things and the items we bought for the job moved in here."

Charlie asked, "Jack, did you pick up the three tickets for desk passengers yet?"

Jack said, "I got the three tickets yesterday to Portman's Landing. That's the first stop the boat makes after it leaves New Orleans."

Charlie said, "Okay, so how about James and Billy Jack? Were you able to steal a rowboat?"

James answered, "No, boss, we couldn't find any rowboats in the area around New Orleans. I think we will need to go outside New Orleans to find one we can steal, but we've got a problem besides not being able to find one."

Charlie asked, "What's your problem, James?"

"Billy Jack and I don't know anything about how you operate a rowboat."

Charlie asked, "Why didn't you say something yesterday about not knowing how to operate a rowboat?" He turned and looked at the group. "Okay, do we have anyone who knows how to handle a rowboat?"

For a little while no one said anything, but Tom finally said, "Sandy and I know how to use a rowboat. Our grandpapa taught us when he used to take us fishing for catfish on the White River in Arkansas."

Charlie said, "Good, you and Sandy are switching jobs with James and Billy Jack, so you need to find a rowboat to steal, and I think it would be a good idea to see if you remember how to use it and see if you can get it close enough to *The Pride of St. Louis* to be able to tie the rowboat up next to it."

Tom replied, "From what I've seen around New Orleans, I think James is right. We're going to need to get out of New Orleans to find a rowboat to steal."

Charlie said, "Okay, James, I want you and Billy Jack to rent a rig and drive Tom and Sandy out of New Orleans and help them find a rowboat. There's got to be some rowboats around here someplace."

James replied, "Okay, we'll rent a rig and take them out of New Orleans and help them find and steal a rowboat. If Billy Jack and I are changing assignments with Tom and Sandy, what were they supposed to do?"

Charlie said, "They were to position themselves across the river in Algiers and look to see if anyone was following the rowboat, and if there was someone following them, you are to fire two shots in the air, and they are to dump Latesha into the river."

James replied, "Okay, we got it. Billy Jack and I will go pick up a rig and be back here as soon as we can."

Charlie said, "The rest of you men pick up your belongings and bring them back to the warehouse while James and Billy Jack are getting a rig to take Tom and Sandy out to hunt for a rowboat."

All the men except James and Billy Jack, who had gone to rent a rig, left to pick up their gear. By the time they made it back to the warehouse, James and Billy Jack had returned with a rig.

As soon as Tom and Sandy dropped off their gear and the items they purchased for the job, they climbed into the rig behind James and Billy Jack.

James had talked to the man at the livery stable about where they could drive out of the city and still be by the river. They followed a road that took them into Jefferson Parish. They didn't have to go very far until they found several shanties with small docks with rowboats tied up to them.

James continued to drive along until he saw one shanty that was sitting all by itself, with a rowboat pulled up on the riverbank and with no one around.

James said, "Tom, I think that rowboat has your name on it."

James stopped the rig, and Tom and Sandy began walking toward the rowboat.

When they got to the rowboat, they saw it looked the worse for wear, but it had oars in it, so they pushed it off the bank and got inside.

Tom began rowing the rowboat out away from the shore and got the boat on the right side of the river and then started traveling downriver toward New Orleans. James was turning the rig around and began making his way back there, too.

It took them over an hour to make their way down the river to New Orleans, hugging the right bank of the river because they were so much slower than the rest of the traffic on the river. They had to stay out of the way of the bigger and faster boats.

When they approached the *Pride of St. Louis*, Tom turned the rowboat left to cross the river to the port side of the river where the steamboat was docked.

Tom found it very difficult to make the turn as the river kept pushing him further downriver away from *The Pride of St. Louis*.

Finally, he got the rowboat headed back in the direction of the steamboat and moved up next to it.

He was having a hard time keeping the rowboat next to the steamboat because of the current of the river. He told Sandy he was going to have to tie a rope onto the steamboat's anchor chain to hold them in position.

The only rope in the rowboat was attached to the front of the boat, so Sandy made his way around Tom, who had to continue rowing using all his strength to keep the rowboat next to the steamboat.

Sandy asked Tom if he could row them closer to the anchor chain so he could reach it to be able to tie onto the chain.

Tom continued to struggle trying to get the rowboat closer to the anchor chain, but finally he managed to inch the rowboat up close enough for Sandy to tie onto the chain.

After Sandy was able to tie the rope from the rowboat onto the anchor chain, Tom could relax as the rowboat stayed next to the steamboat.

Tom gave a huge sigh of relief because he thought for a while he wasn't going to be able to hold the rowboat next to the steamboat and then the kidnapping plan wasn't going to work.

Tom and Sandy learned a big lesson on what they had to do to be able to do their part in making the kidnapping a success.

They would have to leave much earlier than they had assumed they would before they actually tried to position and tie the rowboat up next to the steamboat—that is, if they were to have any chance of having the rowboat in position in time to take the victim and their three friends on board the rowboat.

Sandy unfastened the rope from the anchor chain, which he found very hard to do because Tom had to move the rowboat forward closer to the chain to take the pressure off of the rope before Sandy was able to untie the rope.

Another lesson learned. They decided they needed to have a knife with them to be able to cut the rope tomorrow since the extra load of people in the rowboat would make it even harder to get the rope slack enough for Sandy to untie it, so they decided they had to be able to cut the rope.

Tom let the rowboat slip on down the river using the river's current until he was past the steamboat, then he used his oars to turn the front of the rowboat downriver. Next, he had to cross to the other side of the river to be traveling on the right side of the river to be sure they didn't get run over by the bigger and faster boats.

It didn't take long to make their way downriver to be able to see the warehouse where they would be staying.

Tom made his way across the river and managed to bring the rowboat up next to the dock.

They took the oars out of the rowboat and took them inside the warehouse so no one would steal their boat and they would be ready to use it tomorrow.

That night Charlie went over the kidnapping plan again to be certain everyone knew their jobs, and when he was satisfied they did, he told them to get some rest and he would see them in the morning because he had some unfinished business to take care of.

Charlie and Dotty had another great night of lovemaking, and the next morning he told her he wanted to have her come with him to the warehouse and he would introduce her to his associates.

When they arrived at the warehouse, Charlie introduced Dotty to all his men, and then he told her he wanted to show her around the warehouse a little.

Charlie took her into the bedroom that they found in the warehouse and told her to try out the bed.

Dotty lay down on the bed when Charlie suddenly grabbed her by her neck and choked her to death. He went through her purse and took out all her money.

Before he left the room Charlie looked down at Dotty's limp body and said, "You know, Dotty, I really loved you, but I knew one day you would turn me in for the reward."

When Charlie got outside the bedroom door, Charlie yelled, "Billy Jack, come here!"

Billy Jack responded, "Okay, Charlie, I'm coming."

Charlie went back into the bedroom as Billy Jack followed him in.

Charlie said, "Billy Jack, I want you and James to take this woman and her purse and dump her and her purse into the river after the rest of us leave for our assignments, and then you can take the ferry over to Algiers to be our lookouts."

"Okay, boss. James and I will take care of her."

The time was about one o'clock in the afternoon, and *The Pride of St. Louis* was scheduled to leave port at 3:00 p.m. Passengers would be allowed to board at two o'clock, so Charlie told Jack, Tony, and Ronnie to get on board as soon as they would let them on.

The three of them left to make their way to the dock to be among the first ones to board. They took along all the equipment they needed to do the kidnapping and get Latesha off the steamboat.

Next, Charlie told Tom and Sandy they should be making their way up river now so they had a chance to get tied up to the steamboat in plenty of time to be ready to take on their passengers.

As soon as all the men left to do their jobs to kidnap Latesha and to get rid of Dotty's body, Charlie left the warehouse.

Billy Jack and James carried Dotty's body and her empty purse in a bag they found in the warehouse and carefully looked around to see if anyone was around who could see them, and they dumped her body into the river.

Charlie told them not to take her too far out in the river because he wanted them to be able to find her.

Billy Jack and James had no idea of why he wanted her body found, but knowing Charlie they knew he had a good reason, so they did as they were told.

At two o'clock the crew began allowing passengers on board *The Pride of St. Louis*, and Jack, Tony, and Ronnie were among the first ten passengers on board.

Boarding a steamboat in New Orleans was a wonderful experience.

Jack, Tony, and Ronnie could watch all the activities that were involved in making the boat ready to leave port.

At the front of the boat they were loading all types of cargo to be stored below while at the rear of the boat the passengers and their luggage were being loaded on.

Jack got himself in a good position near the man who was taking the passenger's tickets and checking them off his manifest of passengers.

Jack could hear the name of every passenger who boarded the boat. When he saw her, no one would have to read her name off for him to know that woman was Latesha Stone.

She was beautiful, dressed like she was a queen, dripping with jewels and carrying a beautiful woven travel bag.

No wonder her husband would pay lots of money to get her back. Jack had never seen a woman like her in his life.

The man handling the boarding process said, "Good afternoon, Mr. and Mrs. Stone."

Rocky replied, "How's it going with you today, Mr. Roberts?"

The man replied, "Just fine, sir, we're always glad to have you and Mrs. Stone onboard with us."

The captain of the boat met them and said, "How are you, Rocky? Welcome aboard."

"Good, Captain Jones, and it's always good to see you."

"How about you, Latesha? How was the shopping in New Orleans?"

"It was great as you can tell by the number of things the porters are carrying on for me."

The captain took a look at three porters carrying Mrs. Stone's packages and said, "Latesha, I think you did a great job this time. Come on and I'll show you to your suite."

The captain led the Stones along with the three porters carrying her packages to their cabin.

They went inside the cabin, and just a few minutes later the three porters came out of the cabin and left.

Jack, Tony, and Ronnie had their eyes glued to the Stone's cabin door.

Ten minutes went by, and the captain and Rocky Stone left the cabin, and they could see they went into the bar.

That was their cue that they had to get moving while Rocky was out of the cabin.

The three of them made their way up the stairway to the second floor, and Jack knocked on the cabin door.

Latesha opened the door and said, "May I help you?"

Jack pushed his way into the cabin with Tony and Ronnie right behind him, and as Latesha turned to get away from them, Tony struck her in the back of her head with the leather club.

Latesha began falling to the floor, but before she was down on the floor, Jack caught her, and Ronnie placed a black bag over her head as Jack laid her down on the floor and helped Ronnie pull the bag down over her body and her legs.

Tony had been busy undoing the hammock and had it lying ready on the floor for Jack and Ronnie to put her in it.

As soon as Jack and Ronnie had her inside the hammock, Tony started sewing the hammock closed. When the hammock was completely sewn closed, Jack and Ronnie picked Latesha up as Tony held the door open.

As soon as they went around to the river side of the steamboat, Tony checked to be sure they had taken everything they brought with them. He found the room was clear; they had left nothing behind, and Tony went around to the other side of the boat to help his comrades.

By the time Tony got there, Jack and Ronnie had set up ropes to lower Latesha down to the rowboat that was tied up waiting for them.

They had ropes tied on railings on the third deck and began lowing Latesha down with ropes tied to front of the hammock where her head was and at the bottom of the hammock where her feet were.

They slowly lowered her down, making sure they kept her level as she was lowered down to the waiting rowboat.

As soon as Tom and Sandy could get to her, they carefully placed her into the rowboat.

They untied the ropes, and the ropes were pulled back up by Jack and Ronnie.

Next, they untied the ropes from the third deck railings and doubled the ropes over the railings so when they were safely on the rowboat, it would allow them to let go of one end of the doubled rope. Then they could pull down the other half of the rope, leaving no ropes on the boat.

When all three of the men were in the rowboat with Tom, Sandy, and Latesha, Sandy cut the rope that he had tied to the anchor chain. He had tied it so it would allow the river current to free the rope from the chain, again leaving nothing on the ship.

The rowboat was being pushed down river away from *The Pride of St. Louis* as the band was playing a lovely, lively tune for the folks on the riverboat before it sailed away.

Even having the rowboat filled with people, Tom managed to guide the rowboat down to the warehouse easier than the day before.

When they got to the warehouse dock, Tom guided the rowboat onto the shore. They quickly unloaded everything except the oars and then shoved the rowboat out into the river current, which took it quickly downriver, away from the warehouse.

Charlie was there waiting as they carried Latesha into her bedroom, and they cut the ropes off the hammock and took Latesha out of the big bag and gently laid her on the bed.

Charlie took a long, longing look at Latesha and saw how beautiful she was and thought what an awful waste it was going to be when he killed her.

Charlie congratulated the men for the great job they done as he watched Latesha lying on her bed, still unconscious.

Then Charlie gave orders to all his men that they were not to feed her or give her more than two ounces of water a day.

He asked the men if they all understood his orders. Yes, they all certainly did.

Tom and Sandy didn't like the orders but knew better than to cross Charlie.

Charlie said, "You know, we should send a letter of congratulations to Rocky Stone for his wonderful plan on how to kidnap someone off of a riverboat."

CHAPTER FOUR

I Can't Believe My Wife Is Missing

Rocky said, "Captain, where in the hell is my wife? I can't believe my wife is missing! What in the world could have happened to her?"

"Rocky, have you and your wife been having marital problems?"

"I can't believe you would even ask a question like that. You know we're crazy about each other."

"Rocky, you never know what another person is thinking. Sometimes a husband thinks everything is just great, and the wife thinks her husband doesn't love her anymore or that her husband doesn't pay enough attention to her like he used to."

"I think you're wasting my time with questions like that. What we need to be doing is to be thinking about if she's not on this boat, where is she?"

"Rocky, what we do know for sure is she's not on this boat, and we haven't stopped at any port since we left New Orleans, so she either jumped off the boat or someone took her off, and if they did, how, where, and why would they take her?"

"Captain, I'm pretty sure we can forget about her jumping off the boat because she wouldn't go swimming because she's afraid of water, so she certainly wouldn't jump off the boat on her own accord."

"Well, that leaves the question of how did they get her off the boat without anyone seeing them or hearing them?"

"Captain, where are most of the crew when you are leaving port?"

"The crew would either be on the dock side of the ship, the boiler room, or the wheelhouse."

"I guess that leaves the river side of the boat for someone to get Latesha off the boat before it left the dock."

"Rocky, it's pretty hard to believe someone could act that quickly and have a boat on the river side of our boat just as we were leaving port."

"Maybe not, Captain, just think about it for a minute. All the action is going on the port side of your ship: loading supplies, luggage, passengers, and cargo. Everything that's happening is taking place on the port side of the boat.

"I think whoever did this planned it for some time. If I was going to try to take someone off of a riverboat, I would consider the easiest time to do it was when everyone was busy getting the boat ready to leave port. I would have a small boat tied up to your boat on the river side of the boat while you were getting the boat ready to leave.

"If I was doing it, I'd have someone waiting in the small boat so it was ready to push away from your boat as soon as I had my victim on board. I would probably have two people on the riverboat as passengers to capture the victim and to help get her loaded into my small boat.

"As soon as she was on board the small boat, we would push off and head downriver, away from the direction you would be traveling. Then I would go to a warehouse or someplace like that to hold my victim hostage and just wait for a ransom to be paid."

"Rocky, it sounds like you've spent a long time working out a lot of details to know how you could kidnap someone off of a riverboat without anyone seeing you do it."

"I have, Captain, it was in one of my books, *Kidnapped off the Mississippi Queen*. Some son of a bitch kidnapped my wife off your boat using my own plan."

"I'll be damned. You've got to be kidding."

"I'm not kidding. Let's check your passenger list and see if you have all the passengers you had booked for the trip."

The captain went to the purser to have him check to see how many passengers were booked for this trip, and then the captain asked the crew to find and bring all the passengers to the dining room.

After all the passengers had been brought into the dining room, the passengers who had cabins were accounted for; however, three of the deck passengers were missing.

After they checked out the destination of the three missing passengers, they found they were booked for the first river port north of New Orleans. It was a place called Portman's Landing, about five hours away from New Orleans.

Portman's Landing was not a regular stop. It was like a flag stop where they only stopped if they had passengers to drop off or pick up. It was also the least expensive trip a passenger could book from New Orleans.

Rocky thought they were pretty smart to not only pick the first potential stop that a boat ticket could be booked for, it was also the cheapest fare they could get and still be able to get on the boat.

Rocky felt he now knew how they got Latesha off the boat, but he also thought he knew why. They thought Rocky had lots of money to pay the ransom and wouldn't be one to go to the police.

On this point they were wrong. He planned to go back to New Orleans as soon as he could get there and not only go to the police and report Latesha's kidnapping but to have posters made up offering a reward for information on the people who kidnapped his wife.

He guessed they thought because they used his own plan to kidnap Latesha, he wouldn't want to go to the police and let people know he had by duped by his own ideas to kidnap his wife.

They were wrong, they were dead wrong because if he found them, they would be dead. Rocky had no qualms about killing the people who took his wife.

Rocky said, "Captain Jones, I want you to put me off at the first place you can stop and let me off so I can get back to New Orleans."

"Okay, Rocky, the first place we can get into is Portman's Landing, but I don't have any idea when you can get picked up to get back to New Orleans. What do you want me to do with all of your things?"

"Captain, can you please either have them stored in your baggage room in St. Louis or, better yet, if you can send them on to Boonville for me, I would appreciate it."

"Okay, Rocky, I can do that for you, I'll have them sent on to Boonville."

"I'll gather up the things I need in New Orleans and pack one bag to take with me. How soon, will we be in Portman's landing?"

"I'd say about an hour or sooner."

Rocky returned to his cabin and packed a bag with the clothes he thought he would need. He searched through his trunk and found his Colt .44 Peacemaker, his gun belt, and his holster.

Rocky changed from a suit into a western-style shirt, blue jeans, cowboy boots, and his leather vest.

Then he strapped on his gun belt, placed his loaded Colt in its holster, and put on his cowboy hat. He was ready to go to face whatever came his way in his search for Latesha.

When Rocky came down to the first deck carrying his valise, Captain Jones said, "Rocky, you look like you're ready for whatever kind of trouble you find."

"Captain Jones, I wasn't always one of those guys sitting at a desk stringing together a bunch of words to make up stories. I was the kind of guy those stories were written about, and it looks like I'm setting out to live out another big one while I'm finding my wife. I can tell you one thing, people are going to pay for taking Latesha."

"Damn if I don't believe you, Rocky. I hope you find her very soon, and I hope you take care of yourself doing it."

About that time the *The Pride of St. Louis* arrived at Portman's Landing, and the captain said, "Good luck, Rocky, I hope to see you soon."

They lowered the gangplank and let Rocky off, and as soon as he cleared the end of the gangplank, the gangplank was raised, and the steamboat was back on its way to St. Louis.

Rocky stood there on the shore watching as the lights of the steamboat disappeared into the darkness, and Rocky was left standing there alone.

CHAPTER FIVE

It's a Long Walk Back to New Orleans

Rocky started walking up the Portman's Landing Dock, and soon found he was off the ramp and onto some very muddy ground. It must have rained here only a short time ago. Just then it started raining again in earnest. Rocky found his slicker and put it on to keep off some of the rain, but the rain wasn't helping the mud he was sloshing around in.

His boots kept getting heavier and heavier. Cowboy boots are not designed for walking in mud as they picked up more mud with every step he took, and the more steps he took, the more mud his boots were carrying.

His legs begin to feel like they were made of lead. He knew he couldn't get very far walking on this type of terrain, so he had to come up with some other type of transportation.

Portman's Landing wasn't exactly a thriving community. He couldn't see a light of any kind in any of the few buildings he could make out in the dark.

He kept struggling on in the mud and rain until he came to one of the buildings, which turned out to be more of a lean-to than an actual building.

He thought it must be a place to store cotton bales since it had only three sides and a leaky roof.

Rocky was able to find a place where the roof was good enough to keep the rain off of his head and where he could lay down to get some rest until morning.

The rain continued all night long, with each raindrop playing a little tune on the tin roof. It wasn't the greatest night's rest Rocky had ever had. Plus, he spent the night worrying about how the people were treating Latesha.

God help them if they hurt Latesha in any way because He would be the only one who could when Rocky found them.

Rocky knew so many ways to kill a person in the slowest, most painful way possible.

He learned the many ways people tortured their victims before letting them die when he was in charge of investigations with the Texas Rangers.

Also, he had studied the types of torture some of the Indian tribes had used on their prisoners, and some of those were not only slow but so very hurtful. Rocky could hardly think about how awful the pain must have been.

God help the people holding Latesha because Rocky wouldn't be helping them.

The rain slowly stopped, and Rocky could begin to see some light coming up in the east; good, it was finally going to be morning.

He looked around for something to clean the mud from his boots and found a wide stick he could use to work on the boots. It took him almost thirty minutes to get most of the mud off his boots.

He thought maybe walking would get off what was left of the mud on them if the ground had dried up some.

By this time the sun was up enough for Rocky to see that some of the mud was beginning to dry up.

Whew, that was a relief. Maybe he would be able to walk without taking on a ton of mud with each step he took on his way back to New Orleans.

He gathered up his few belongings and started walking south, following the river the best he could. He had to get away from the river because the terrain was so rough, and with so much wild growth, he couldn't walk through it.

After walking for several hours, Rocky found a small road that seemed to be in use with some regularity, and he was happy to start following it.

The walking became somewhat easier walking along this road, and after about an hour, he came upon a very small old-looking house.

Arriving in front of the house, Rocky yelled out, "Anybody home?"

He was thrilled to hear a woman's voice reply, "Yeah, I'm home. What can I do for you?"

"I would like to get something to eat if you can spare anything."

"Well, come on up to the house, and don't pay no mind to the dog. He don't bite. He just growls a lot."

Rocky made his way toward the house, and then he saw and heard the dog the woman was telling him about.

The dog was a big German shepherd, as big a dog as he had ever seen. If he didn't bite you, he sure as the hell would scare you to death, growling and baring his teeth.

Rocky was taking his time walking up to the house with the dog staying less than two feet away from him.

Rocky wasn't so sure the dog wasn't going to attack him, so he kept his right hand on the butt of his Colt.

When Rocky got closer to the house, the woman shouted, "Nick, get away from that man and leave him alone."

The dog quit growling and slowly moved away from Rocky, all the while keeping an eye on him. Then he lay down right in the front of the door of the house, blocking Rocky's entrance to the house.

The woman opened the door, and when she saw where the dog was lying, she said, "Nick, would you get in the house and leave this man alone. Now go lay over by the fireplace and behave yourself."

Nick got up and went directly to the fireplace and lay down on a small rug in front of the fireplace.

The woman said, "Good boy."

Nick looked up at her wagged his tail and then put his head down between his paws.

The old lady said, "What you doing walking along the road? It ain't going to take you nowhere."

Rocky replied, "Ma'am, my name is Rocky Stone, and I'm trying to get to New Orleans."

"Well, I reckon you must have a powerful reason to want to get there to be trying to walk all that way."

"Yes, ma'am, I do, somebody has kidnapped my wife, and I think they are holding her there."

"Well, I ain't never heard about somebody kidnapping somebody's wife before. You sure she ain't just a run off with some other man?"

"I'm pretty sure she didn't leave me for some other man. We were on a riverboat leaving New Orleans, and I was away from our cabin for a few minutes talking with the captain. When I came back to our cabin, she was gone. All of her things, including her purse, were still in the cabin. She didn't go anywhere without her purse. She wouldn't hardly go to bed without it."

"How would somebody get a woman off a steamboat while it was moving on the river?"

"I believe she was taken off the boat before we left New Orleans."

"Okay, you said you were hungry. Would some bacon and eggs be all right to eat?"

"That would be wonderful, ma'am."

"You just sit down there in that chair at the table, and I'll fetch you some breakfast."

"Thank you, it would certainly be appreciated."

The old woman went to work prepare Rocky's breakfast.

First, she lit the wood she had put into her small iron cookstove, and after the fire was going, she put a small iron pan on the stove and placed five slices of hog fat in the skillet.

After she finished cooking the hog fat, she placed four eggs in the skillet and cooked them until she thought they looked done on that side, then carefully turned them over and finished cooking them on the other side.

Next, she placed the eggs on a plate where she had put the hog fat and had kept it on a corner of the stove, keeping the plate warm.

Then she sat the plate down in front of Rocky and reached for some freshly baked bread she had in her oven. She placed a bowl of butter and a jar of strawberry jam on the table for Rocky to go with his eggs and hog fat.

Rocky said, "Thank you, ma'am, it looks wonderful."

Then the old woman asked if Rocky would like to have some coffee.

Yes, he certainly would, so she poured his coffee in the biggest cup he had ever seen.

"That's sure a big cup of coffee."

"It were my late husband's cup, and he loved his coffee. He said he didn't want to be running back to get more coffee all the time."

"With this cup he shouldn't have had to go very often."

"No, usually one cup would do him to lunchtime."

Rocky finished his food and got down the last swallow of coffee and said, "I sure do appreciate you feeding me, ma'am. I would like to pay you for my food and your trouble."

"It weren't no trouble. I enjoyed having you here. It gets pretty lonesome with no one around here anymore."

"Just the same, I'd feel better if you let me give you something."

"No, sir, I was glad to have you here."

Rocky begin gathering up his belongings, and while the old lady was busy taking things off the table, he slipped two twenty-dollar gold pieces under his napkin.

As he began to walk toward the door, her dog got up and started toward him, and the old lady said, "Now, Nick, don't you be bothering Mr. Stone."

Nick just wagged his tail and rubbed up against Rocky's right leg, then looked up at Rocky like to say "Hey, aren't you going to pat me?"

Looking into those big brown eyes, Rocky felt compelled to reach down and give Nick a few pats, which he did, and Nick rubbed his leg with even more vigor.

Nick continued to follow Rocky as he was now on the road heading south toward New Orleans.

The old lady yelled, "Nick, you get back home."

Nick stopped and looked back at her and looked once more up at Rocky, and Rocky said, "You better go back home now, Nick."

Nick abruptly turned and started running back to the old lady who was waiting for him.

When Nick arrived back where the old lady was waiting for him, he almost jumped up into her arms, but instead, she put her arms around his neck and gave him a big hug.

Rocky watched as the old lady and Nick went back inside the house.

Entering the house, the old lady went back to finish cleaning up the kitchen table, and when she picked up Rocky's napkin, she found the two shiny twenty-dollar gold pieces Rocky left for her.

She said to Nick, "That there man must be really rich. He's done and left us more money than we ever had in my whole life. Praise God. I pray he soon finds his wife."

Rocky continued to walk down the small road, and occasionally he could catch a glimpse of the Mississippi River. At least he knew he was walking in the right direction.

After walking about four more hours, he came upon an old plantation, and he could see how bad it looked now after the Civil War.

Rocky thought at one time this home must have been beautiful. Now it looked about ready to fall down. He could see one side of the house had been burned.

He thought about walking up to the house to see if anyone still lived there when he heard someone yell out to him, "Hey, mister, where are you going?"

Rocky stopped and turned around and saw a young black man coming out of the part of the house that hadn't been burned.

Rocky said, "I'm going to New Orleans."

The young black man said, "You walking all the way there?"

"I'm afraid I am. I don't have any other way to get there."

"Would you like to buy a horse?"

Rocky asked, "Do you have a horse for sale?"

"No, sir, but my boss lady has some, and I know she would be happy to sell you one."

Rocky turned back toward the house and started walking up to the house and was quickly met by the young black man.

Rocky said, "Where is your boss lady?"

"She's in the house. I'll fetch her fur you."

The young man went back inside the house and returned with a middle-aged white woman he was pushing in a wheelchair.

Rocky said, "Good afternoon, ma'am. My name is Rocky Stone, and I understand you have a horse you might like to sell."

The lady in the wheelchair said, "I'm Rose Perkins, and I do have some horses I would love to sell. I would be glad to have Thomas show them to you if you're interested."

"That would be wonderful."

"Thomas, would you bring around Spring Rain to show to Mr. Stone."

"Yes, ma'am, I would be glad to."

Thomas left to bring the horse around to the front of the house, and Rocky walked over to where Mrs. Perkins was sitting.

Rocky said, "Your husband not around today?"

"I'm afraid you don't understand. I'm not married. This plantation belonged to my father, and he was killed during the war. I was caught inside the house when the Yankees set it on fire, and part of the house fell on me, causing me not to be able to walk. My intended was also killed in the war.

"So I'm afraid it's only Thomas, his mother, and me as the only ones left in this house, what's left of it. Thomas's father was also killed in the war. His family and mine have been together for three generations. We are all that's left after the war."

"I'm very sorry to hear about all of the folks you have lost. It must be very hard on you."

"If it wasn't for Thomas and his mother, Jane, I don't know what I would do."

About then Thomas returned with a magnificent-looking horse, much to the surprise of Rocky, who assumed the horses they had would look like the plantation.

Rocky said, "Spring Rain is a beautiful animal. How much do you want for him?"

Where's My Wife?

Rose said, "Spring Rain is one of the finest horses we have raised in the past few years. I need five hundred dollars for him."

Rocky asked, "Do you have a saddle and tack I would need to be able to ride him?"

Rose replied, "Thomas, do we have in a saddle left?"

"Miss Rose, we've got a western saddle you got in trade for the black horse we sold last year."

"Well, Mr. Stone, it seems we have a western saddle, and we can find you the rest of the tack you would need. For the horse, saddle, and tack it would be seven hundred and fifty dollars."

Rocky said, "Okay, Miss Rose. Seven hundred and fifty dollars. You've got a deal."

Rose said, "Thomas, would you go ahead and saddle up Spring Rain for Mr. Stone."

"Yes, ma'am."

Rocky opened up his case and took out his poke and counted out seven hundred and fifty dollars and was going to hand it to Miss Rose.

She said, "Please, just wait and pay Thomas when he returns."

Rocky replied, "Okay, Miss Rose."

Rocky looked at Rose sitting in the wheelchair and saw she had her hands under a shawl and wondered if she had any use of her hands.

Thomas returned with Spring Rain and had him saddled and ready to go for Rocky.

Rocky was pleased to see the western saddle looked like it was brand-new, and the rest of the tack looked good enough to him that he wouldn't have any problem with it either.

Rocky said, "Thomas, Miss Rose asked me to give you the seven hundred and fifty dollars."

Rocky held out his hand to Thomas to hand him the money, and Thomas opened up his right hand to accept the money.

After Thomas took the money, he counted it and told Miss Rose the money was correct.

Rose said, "I'll have Thomas get you a bill of sale for Spring Rain."

Rocky realized there was nothing wrong with Rose's hands. She was blind, and that's why she didn't want to take the money.

Soon Thomas came back with a bill of sale for Spring Rain all made out properly to Rocky Stone and signed by Thomas Perkins.

Rocky shook hands with Thomas and thanked him for all his help and for hollering at him when he was walking by. Having a horse would sure help him get to New Orleans a lot sooner.

Rocky went over to Miss Rose and took her hand and said, "Thank you, ma'am, and I hope you and Thomas and his mother continued success in the horse business."

Rose replied, "Thank you, and I hope you have a safe trip to New Orleans."

Rocky mounted Spring Rain and started to go back down the road toward New Orleans when he saw Nick running as fast as he could to him.

Spring Rain jumped forward a step or two before Rocky could stop him.

Rocky got off his horse and took hold of Nick and asked him, "What are you doing here, Nick? You're a long ways from home."

Nick turned back the way he had just come, and when Rocky didn't follow him, he stopped and came back.

Rocky said, "Go home, Nick!"

Nick just looked at him and started going back home, but again when Rocky didn't follow him, he stopped and came back to Rocky.

Rocky said, "Nick, I don't have time to play with you. Go on back home."

Again Nick started back toward home, and when Rocky didn't come with him, he stopped and started back toward Rocky.

Rocky said, "Okay, Nick, is the old lady in trouble?"

Nick wagged his tail and started toward home again. This time Rocky got back on Spring Rain and began following Nick.

Nick never slowed down, and Rocky and Spring Rain stayed right with him until they reached the little old lady's house.

Nick raced inside the house with Rocky following right behind him.

When Rocky got inside the house, he saw the old lady lying on the floor. He reached down to take hold of her to pick her up to put her on her bed and found she was already cold. She was dead.

Rocky took some quilts and wrapped her up in them as Nick stood by watching his every move but never showed any threat to Rocky.

Rocky found a shovel and pick and went out behind the small house to find a nice place for a grave for the old woman.

It took Rocky almost two hours to dig a grave for the old woman, all the while Nick stayed next to him. When Rocky had the grave dug, Nick followed him inside the house, and Rocky picked up the old woman and placed her in the grave.

When Rocky had placed her in the grave, Nick got in the grave and gave a small crying-like sound, but when Rocky told him he would have to get out of the grave, Nick came out and stayed by Rocky as he closed her grave.

Rocky found some papers in the little house that had the old lady's name on them. Her name was Letty Johnson.

Rocky fashioned a cross and wrote her name on the cross.

He took the cross and placed it at the head of the grave.

Rocky prayed, "Father, we ask you to take the departed soul of Letty Johnson into your heavenly kingdom to be reunited with her husband, and thank you for the many blessings you have bestowed on us. We ask this in the name of our savior, Jesus Christ. Amen."

Rocky went back inside the house and checked around and found his forty dollars on the kitchen table. He could see there was not much else left of any value in the place.

Outside the old lady had a few chickens and a couple of hogs, plus some things growing in her garden.

Rocky climbed up on Spring Rain and told Nick he'd better come with them.

Nick looked back at the house, went around to the old lady's grave, and then caught up with Rocky and Spring Rain. The three of them rode back to the plantation.

When Rocky reached the plantation, he saw Thomas working on a fence near the road, and Rocky told him about what had happened to the old lady.

Then he suggested to Thomas that he should go down to the little house and bring the chickens and the hogs back to the plantation to take care of them and use them.

Then Rocky, Spring Rain, and Nick continued on the small road, and as they traveled further, the road suddenly got bigger, and they began to see some other houses and people.

Before it was completely dark, they came to a small town with an inn, and Rocky asked if they had a bed for the night and something to eat.

They were in luck; they had a room with a bed, a stable, and Nick could stay in Rocky's room.

The next morning they found they were about forty miles away from New Orleans.

CHAPTER SIX

Arriving in New Orleans

Rocky arrived in New Orleans two days later with his two new traveling buddies, Nick and Spring Rain. He was able to find a livery stable for Spring Rain near his regular hotel, the Crescent.

When Rocky went to check in at the hotel with Nick standing right beside him, the desk clerk asked, "Is that you, Mr. Stone?"

It was obvious the desk clerk had never seen him in western dress and carrying a gun before.

Rocky replied, "Yes, it's me all right. I've had a lot of trouble since I left here a few days ago."

"Sorry, sir, do you want your regular suite, Mr. Stone?"

"No, I just need a small room on the ground floor since I have my dog with me, so it will be easier for me to take him outside."

"Yes, sir, I'll give you room number one."

"Thank you, John. It is John, isn't it?"

"Yes, sir, I'm John. Your lovely wife is not with you on this trip?"

"No, she's the reason I'm back in New Orleans. She disappeared off the riverboat, and I believe she was kidnapped before we left New Orleans. I'm back to find her and see that the people who took her pay for their sins."

As John was handing the room key to Rocky, he said, "I'm so sorry to hear about Mrs. Stone. She's such a fine lady. I certainly hope you can find her soon, sir."

"I'll find her, and God help the people who have her because I don't intend to bless them."

Rocky and Nick went into room number one. It was a nice enough room but certainly not the suite he and Latesha normally had in the Crescent Hotel.

After taking Nick outside to take care of his business, Rocky was soon in bed and asleep. It had been some very long days with very little rest.

The next morning when he woke up, he found Nick standing beside his bed looking at him, like, "Hey, it's almost seven o'clock in the morning. It's time to get going."

Rocky thought, *Yeah. It is time to get going, but I think I could learn to hate a smart-aleck dog.*

Nick continued to stare at him, so Rocky got out of bed, and Nick laid back down waiting for Rocky to get dressed and take him outside.

Rocky hurried and dressed and took Nick out; after Nick was finished with his chores, Rocky asked him if he wanted something to eat.

Nick barked once, like he knew exactly what Rocky asked him.

The two of them went back inside the hotel and went into the coffee shop. Rocky ordered his breakfast and a steak for Nick.

The waiter brought out Rocky's breakfast and a steak for Nick, along with a bowl of water for Nick.

The water went first, and then the steak was gone before Rocky finished three bites of his breakfast.

Rocky was pleased that after Nick finished his steak, he lay down at Rocky's feet waiting for Rocky to finish his breakfast.

When Rocky finished his meal, he charged it to his room and got up to leave, with Nick right by his side walking next to him step by step.

Rocky had never owned a dog before, and having Nick with him made him wonder why he didn't. He already loved this dog.

Rocky's first stop was at the telegraph office to send a telegram to his publisher, Bobby Longstreet, to cancel the meeting they were scheduled to have in St. Louis.

He told Bobby he could reach him at the Crescent Hotel in New Orleans.

The next telegram Rocky sent was to his father-in-law, Henry Hudson IV, telling him Latesha had been kidnapped.

God, Rocky hated to send such a telegram to his father-in-law telling him his only child had been kidnapped. Latesha meant everything to him. She was the only family Henry had.

Latesha's mother died giving birth to a son who was stillborn when Latesha was only three years old.

Henry wasn't happy about Latesha marrying Rocky, who took her west away from New York City and Newport, where Henry maintained homes.

Henry actually liked Rocky okay and was pleased his daughter was happy being married to him. It was just that he hated she didn't continue to live near him.

Henry's houses were certainly large enough for them to live with him and still have plenty of privacy.

Henry was certainly going to push for them to live with him when they got Latesha back because Henry had security personnel to look after them and keep them safe.

After Rocky sent his telegrams, his next stop was at the local police department.

The desk sergeant on duty asked Rocky what he wanted, and Rocky told him he wanted to report his wife had been kidnapped.

The desk clerk called one of the detectives to come up to the front desk.

A man came up to the desk and asked the desk clerk what he needed, and the desk clerk told him, "This man says his wife has been kidnapped."

The first thing the detective said, "Do you think he would like to have another one?"

Rocky didn't find it funny and said, "Detective, I don't find anything funny about that remark."

The detective quickly replied, "I'm sorry I said that. I hope you will forgive me. My name is Doc Knox. Please come with me as I'll need to make a report on your wife's kidnapping."

The detective asked him to follow him back to his office and led him and Nick back to a small room where the detective closed the office door.

Detective Knox asked Rocky to sit down as he pushed a chair over to him.

Rocky sat down across the desk from Detective Knox, and Nick lay down at Rocky's feet.

Detective Knox said, "I want to apologize again for my crude remark. I'm sorry I said what I did."

"I've had a lot worse things said to me. It just hurts right now, but I got it."

Detective Knox took out a report form and asked, "What's your name?"

"Rocky Stone."

"Like the guy who writes those dime novels?"

"Exactly like it, because I'm the guy who writes those dime novels."

"Well, I'll be damned."

"We probably all are."

"Rocky, what's your wife's name?"

"Her name is Latesha Kay Stone."

"Latesha, how do you spell it?

"It's spelled L-a-t-e-s-h-a."

"That's sure an unusual name, but it's pretty."

"What's your home address?"

"General Delivery, Boonville, Missouri."

"Where were you when your wife was kidnapped?"

"To the best of my knowledge, she was kidnapped off of *The Pride of St. Louis* steamboat while it was docked at the port of New Orleans."

"Why did you say 'to the best of your knowledge'?"

"Because I didn't know she was missing until after we had left the dock for probably a couple of hours, and by the time they searched the boat, we had been away from the dock for three or four hours."

"Where were you when she went missing?"

"Captain Jones asked me to have a drink with him in the bar while the boat was getting ready to leave the port. Captain Jones and I are old friends, and he had asked my wife and me to have dinner with him later that evening. Latesha wanted to straighten up our cabin a little bit and told me to go along with Captain Jones and have a little drink. So I did.

"When I came back to the cabin, Latesha was gone. At first, I thought she must have gone out for something she wanted to get. We've been doing so much traveling and have been gone from home for several weeks now, and I felt really tired, so I decided to lie down until she came back to the cabin. Of course, I fell asleep right away and slept for about an hour. When I woke up she hadn't returned to the cabin, so I went to find Captain Jones and ask him to help me find her."

"How much did you have to drink with the captain?"

"One drink of port wine."

"Did you find the captain right away?"

"Yes, he was in the dining room waiting for Latesha and me to have dinner with him. He had asked a fellow who is going to be taking over as captain of *The Pride of St. Louis* to have dinner with us. His name is Dan White.

"It seems Captain Jones has been promoted to director of operations for the St. Louis & New Orleans Shipping Lines. Dan White organized a search party, and the crew searched every inch of the boat and didn't find Latesha or anything to give us a clue as to what happened to her."

"What makes you think she was kidnapped? Maybe just got off the boat on her own accord."

"Well, we know she didn't just go down the gangplank and get off because no one saw her do that before they pulled up the gangplank."

"If she was kidnapped, how do you think they took her off the boat?"

"I really hate to tell you what I think they did to get her off the boat without anyone seeing them."

"Why is that, Mr. Stone?"

"Because I think they used something I wrote about in one of my dime novels. The book was called *Kidnapped off the Mississippi Queen*."

"So in your novel how did they do it, kidnapping someone off of a steamboat?"

"When a steamboat is getting underway, all the crew and the people onboard are watching what's going on the port side of the boat.

"The kidnapper takes the victim and puts her over on the river side of the boat onto a waiting little rowboat that's tied up to the steamboat. Then the kidnappers climb down to the rowboat, and they take the rowboat downriver, away from the direction that the riverboat will be traveling. Then they take her to an old warehouse and hold her there until the ransom is paid. In my book they let the victim go, but I'm not so sure that's what these people have in mind."

"Damned if it doesn't seem like that could work."

"Detective Knox, we checked on all of the passengers who were booked for the trip and found out three of the deck passengers were missing. That's another reason I'm sure she was kidnapped."

"How many days ago did this happen?"

"Four days ago."

"Have you had anyone contact you yet to pay a ransom?"

"No, but I haven't been anywhere where they could contact me."

"Let me ask you a question, do you make a lot of money writing those dime novels? Is that why they think you could pay a ransom for your wife?"

"Yes, I've made a lot of money on my novels, so I could pay the ransom."

"That's good, so how many of these dime novels have you written?"

"Eleven, not counting my latest book."

"How many books have you sold?"

"Oh, I don't know for sure anymore, but I know the last six books I wrote sold over six hundred thousand copies."

"You sold six hundred thousand books?"

"No, I meant that each one of the six books sold over six hundred thousand, which is roughly three million six hundred thousand books."

"Wow, that's a lot of books."

"Well, that's not counting what I sold in the first five books."

Another detective came in the office and said, "Captain. Knox, I understand you are taking a report on this man's missing wife, is that right?"

Detective Knox replied, "That's right, Detective Smith. This man's wife has been missing for about four days now. Why do you ask?"

Smith replied, "About four days ago they pulled a young woman's body out of the Mississippi not far from the pier where most of the steamboats dock."

"Where is her body now?"

"They have been holding it over at the ice plant to see if we can find out who she is."

Rocky asked, "What's an ice plant?"

Smith replied, "It's a building designed to keep ice from melting after it is shipped down from the north to help our breweries make beer."

Knox said, "We better take Mr. Stone over there right now to see if it's Mrs. Stone because you know they're not going to want to keep that body there much longer."

The three of them and Nick walked the few blocks over to this ice house thing they had told Rocky about.

Rocky was very upset thinking his Latesha could be dead.

Although he had seen enough dead bodies in his lifetime to suit him, he hated the thought of seeing this one since it could be his wife.

When they arrived at the ice house, the guard working there told Rocky that Nick couldn't go inside the building due to concerns he might touch something that could cause the ice not to be able to be used for their beer production.

Rocky wasn't sure if he could get Nick to stay outside and wait for him, but he had to try.

Rocky pointed to the ground by the front door of the ice plant where he hoped Nick would stay when he said, "Nick, stay here."

Rocky was pleased Nick lay down where he had pointed. When Nick was lying down, he looked up at Rocky and made a slight whimper.

Rocky said, "It will be all right. I'll be back in a few minutes."

Nick wagged his tail as the three men went inside the ice plant.

The first thing Rocky felt was it was really cold in here, and his anxiety was making him feel so much colder, to the point that he was now shaking.

One of the workers in the plant guided them into a small room where Rocky could see a woman's body lying on a block of ice. This made him shake even more thinking about it, as if he were lying on a huge block of ice.

Rocky slowly walked up to the woman's body. He could hardly make himself look at the body lying on the block of ice.

He finally made himself look at the body, and he shouted, "It's not Latesha."

The three of them left the ice house, and Rocky found Nick waiting for him exactly where he had told him to.

Rocky said, "Good dog."

Nick wagged his tail and got closer to Rocky's right leg.

CHAPTER SEVEN

The Ransom Note

Rocky and Nick left the police station and walked directly back to the Crescent Hotel, and when they approached the front desk, the desk clerk said, "Mr. Stone, I have a letter for you."

Rocky took the letter and went over to a couch in the front lobby, sat down, opened the envelope, took out the letter, and unfolded it.

Although the note inside the envelope was very hard to read, Rocky had no trouble making out what it said.

> We have your wife, and if you want her back, you have to pay $100,000 in gold to us before the end of next week.
>
> If you don't care that much for her, you can have her back the week after that for free like the woman the police fished out of the river four days ago.
>
> We wanted to be sure you knew how serious we are, so we dropped one dead woman in the river as an example of what we mean.
>
> We will contact you as to where you are to leave the money next week.
>
> Sincerely, one of your biggest fans because you write the best stories with the best ideas! Thanks.

If Rocky was cold a while ago, he was hot now, really hot. He only wished he could get his hands on his biggest fan right now!

He would show them how good of an idea he had for them.

Rocky sat there for several minutes trying to calm down and to regain his composure before saying or doing anything.

The one thing he knew for sure was the people holding Latesha were vicious killers, capable of doing anything, and he knew they planned to kill Latesha even if he paid the ransom.

By reading the way the ransom note was written, he was sure they never planned to let her live.

He had to find them before they could act, but how?

Just sitting here, Rocky thought, wasn't going to find Latesha. He had to do something.

Again the same question, what could he do?

Rocky knew he could pay the kidnappers, but would that bring Latesha back to him? They had already demonstrated their willingness to kill to prove the point of how serious they were.

The question was still, "Where's my wife?"

Rocky got up from the couch and walked back over to the front desk and asked the desk clerk, "Do you know who left this letter for me?"

"No, it was some little boy. I would say about ten years old. He looked like he was one of the poor kids who lives over in the Quarter."

"John, would you know him if you saw him again?"

"I'm pretty sure I would. Why, is it important?"

"The letter you gave me was from the people who are holding my wife."

"Mr. Stone, if you can find the boy, I'm sure I would recognize him."

"Thank you, John."

Rocky and Nick left the hotel and began walking back to the police station to let Detective Knox know he received a ransom note.

When Rocky and Nick arrived back at the police station, the desk sergeant recognized him and told him he could go directly back to Detective Knox's office.

The door to Detective Knox's office was open, and he was sitting at his desk reading a report.

When he saw Rocky, he said, "Come on in, Rocky. I was just reading a new report telling me the woman in the ice house has been identified as Dotty Ferguson. She was a dancer in one of the saloons on Bourbon Street.

"Her roommate ID'd her a few minutes after we left the ice house. Her roommate just came in to the station this morning after Dotty hadn't come home for several days. Apparently, for Dotty not to be home for a night or two wasn't anything new because she made a lot more money selling herself than she did dancing at the saloon. I understand from the report Dotty was an orphan and had been working the streets since she was about twelve."

Rocky replied, "I'm sorry to hear about Dotty. It sounds like the girl never got a break in this life."

"Yeah, we have a lot of people working on Bourbon Street that never got much of a break in their lives.

"What brings you back so soon?"

"When I got back to my hotel, there was a letter waiting there for me at the front desk. It was a ransom note telling me that they had my wife and wanted $100,000 in gold in order for me to get her back alive."

When Rocky finished telling Detective Knox this, he handed the ransom note to him.

Knox read over the ransom note and said, "I guess we know what happened to Dotty now. She was just a sample as to what they may do to your wife if you don't meet their demands."

"I don't think they plan to give me back my wife alive even if I pay the ransom."

"Why do you think that?"

"Simple, they already proved they could kill, and if they get the money, why should they take a chance by giving Latesha back when she could ID them? No, we've got to find her before we pay them the ransom. Otherwise, Latesha will be dead. I had a case like this once when I was the chief investigator for the Texas Rangers. The rancher paid the ransom, and he got his wife back in a pickle barrel."

53

"Rocky, you never told me you were a Texas Ranger or an investigator. I'm guessing that meant you were a detective, right?"

"Yes, that's what it means. When I left the Texas Rangers, I was in charge of all criminal investigations."

"Rocky, I thought you were just a writer of dime novels and your name Rocky Stone was made up to use on your novels."

"Well, my name was made up all right, but it was made up by my father who thought it would be pretty funny calling me Rocky when our last name was Stone."

"Well, your papa was right. It is pretty funny when you think about it."

"Thanks."

"Do you have anything else you know besides having the ransom letter?"

"Yes, the desk clerk said a boy about ten years old brought the letter in to the desk. He said he thought he would recognize the boy if he saw him again and thought the boy looked like one of the poor kids who hang around on Bourbon Street."

"Let's take a little walk down Bourbon Street to see if we can find this kid."

"Exactly what I had planned to do, Detective Knox."

"Rocky. Since we are going to be working together on this case, would you please call me by my first name?"

"Is your first name really Doc?"

"No, it's Donald, but I've been Doc since I was a little boy. My family and friends said they called me that because I always wanted to fix everything and everybody."

"Okay, Doc it is from now on."

"Rocky, I think the first thing we need to do now is to go over to Bourbon Street and see if we can find this kid."

"I agree. Doc, the chances of him knowing much is pretty slim, but at least it's a start."

Doc got up from behind his desk, and Rocky and Nick began following him out of the police station and over to Bourbon Street.

When they arrived on Bourbon Street, they saw several young boys hanging around in front of one of the big saloons. They wondered what the attraction was that had the boys looking under the swinging doors.

When they got closer to the saloon doors, they had no trouble seeing what the boys were watching. There on stage was a young girl dancing and singing, wearing very few clothes.

When Rocky took a good look at the girl, he saw she probably wasn't more than four or five years older than the boys outside watching her, only they were too young to go into the saloon.

New Orleans didn't have many laws they enforced, but keeping young boys out of the saloons was one they did.

Basically, it was enforced because the owners of the saloons didn't want them in there because they didn't have any money to spend and they might run into their fathers being someplace they weren't supposed to be.

Rocky soon found out that anything you ever wanted to buy or anything you might desire could be bought on Bourbon Street.

All you had to do was to have the money.

Bourbon Street never closed; it operated twenty-four hours a day, seven days a week.

Doc said to the young boys, "How come you young fellows aren't in school?"

One of the young men replied, "What the hell you bothering us for, copper?"

"Copper." Rocky had never heard that term used before and wondered what it meant.

Doc replied, "I think you boys may be in big trouble because one of you delivered a letter to a hotel today for some wanted criminals."

The same young boy said, "None of us did. We've been here all day watching this new girl, isn't that right, guys?"

The other four boys quickly replied, "Yeah, we've been here all day."

"Well, I guess I'll have to take all of you in to the station for more questioning."

The kid who had been doing the talking said, "Wait a minute, copper. None of us took a letter to no hotel, but I know who did.

"It was Bobby Delacroix. He did it. He was bragging to us about making two dollars for just going over to the Crescent Hotel and giving a letter to the desk clerk."

"Okay, where can we find Bobby Delacroix?"

The same kid replied, "He generally sleeps over behind the Green Gable Restaurant. He's got some cook who gives him food there and lets him sleep in a big crate back behind the restaurant. He ain't got no family."

Doc replied, "Thanks, fellows, we'll go check that out. Guys, I know she's really a good-looking girl, but stay out of the saloon. Okay?"

The same boy replied, "No problem, copper, we just want to look."

During all this, Rocky and Nick stood by listening, and Rocky wondered what kind of a place this New Orleans was.

All the times Rocky had been in New Orleans, he had never spent any time in the Quarter; it was a different world from the rest of New Orleans.

Doc said, "Let's go see if we can find Bobby Delacroix."

They walked a couple of blocks down Bourbon Street until they came to the Green Gable Restaurant and went inside.

A waiter came up to meet them and asked, "Two of you for lunch?"

Doc took his badge out of his pocket, showed it to the waiter, and asked, "Is Bobby Delacroix here?"

"I don't know. He stays out back of the restaurant. Come with me, and I'll show you where he stays."

The waiter motioned to them to follow him as they walked to rear of the restaurant and through the kitchen.

When they started going through the kitchen, the cook asked, "What's the matter?"

The waiter replied, "These policemen are looking for Bobby?"

The man shouted, "What did Bobby do?"

Doc stopped and asked the cook's name.

The cook answered, "My name is Charles Lake, and I look after Bobby. What has he done?"

Doc said, "I don't know that he has done anything against the law, but his name came up in an investigation."

Charles said, "Bobby don't cause anybody any trouble. He's a good boy,"

Doc replied, "I'm sure he is. We just need to talk to him."

Doc, Rocky, and Nick went out the back door of the restaurant with Charles Lake following right behind them.

Doc saw Bobby lying down in the crate and said, "Bobby, my name is Detective Doc Knox, and we need to talk with you for a few minutes."

Bobby got up and stood next to Charles Lake and asked, "Why do you need to talk with me?"

Doc asked, "Did you take a letter over to the Crescent Hotel this morning for someone?"

"Yeah, I did and got paid two silver dollars for taking it there. No law about that is there?" Bobby reached into his pants pocket and pulled out the two silver dollars.

"Bobby, who did you take the letter for?"

"One of the girls who works at the Red Dog Saloon."

"What's the name of the girl?"

"I don't know for sure, but I think it's Lucy Love or something like that."

"Bobby, I want you to come with us over to the Red Dog Saloon and show us the girl that gave you the letter."

"Okay."

Charles Lake asked, "Then Bobby's not in trouble?"

Doc replied, "No, he's not if he can point out the girl who gave him the letter."

Now there were four of them walking to the Red Dog Saloon: Rocky, Doc, Bobby, and Nick.

Arriving at the Red Dog Saloon, Doc pushed open the swinging doors of the saloon, and the four of them walked in. A bouncer at the door said, "Mister, you can't bring that kid into the saloon, or a dog."

Doc answered him as he showed the bouncer his badge, "Yes, I can. I'm here investigating a murder."

Doc then said to the bouncer, "We need to talk to Lucy Love right now."

The bouncer replied, "She ain't working here right now. She don't come to work until ten o'clock tonight."

"Where does she live? We need to talk to her right now."

"I don't know. You would have to talk to the boss. Maybe he knows where she lives."

"Okay, get the boss for us, and we'll sit down right over here and wait for him."

"Yes, sir."

The bouncer left them to go somewhere back in the saloon, and Doc, Rocky, and Bobby sat down at a table at the back of the saloon with Nick lying at Rocky's feet.

They waited for several minutes before the bouncer returned and told them his boss would be with them in just a minute.

Doc told Rocky as they sat waiting for the boss, a man by the name of Ruby Red Cato, "This guy is involved in every kind of crime we have in the city, but we've never been able to prove anything on him."

Ruby Red Cato came strutting out from the back of the saloon, walking directly toward where they were seated at the table.

Seeing Ruby Red Cato, Rocky understood where he got his name or nickname.

Ruby Red was a big man, about six foot four or five, weighing at least three hundred and fifty pounds, with bright red hair and mustache, piercing blue eyes, dressed in a black suit with a white fluffy shirt with ruby studs for buttons and a black string tie.

On his left hand he had a big, heavy gold ring on his ring finger with the biggest ruby Rocky had ever seen. It looked the size of a five-dollar gold piece.

Ruby arrived at their table and said, "Hello, Detective Knox, I didn't know they let you out of the station much these days. I understand you want to talk to Lucy Love. I'm sorry, but these girls move around so much I don't know where she lives. She's scheduled to come to work at ten tonight. She usually comes to work a few minutes before ten. Do you want me to tell her to come and see you in your office tomorrow morning?"

"That would be fine. I'd appreciate it if you would ask her to come to see me at the station in the morning."

Doc, Rocky, and Bobby got up from the table and walked out the doors of the saloon with Nick right by Rocky's side.

When they got out of the saloon, Doc told Bobby he could go back to the restaurant, and if they needed to talk to him, he would come back to the restaurant to see him.

After Bobby left them, Rocky said, "Aren't we going to come back to see Lucy Love tonight when she comes to work?"

"Sure we are, but I didn't want Ruby Red to know we wanted to see her that bad."

"Okay, I think Nick and I will go back to the hotel, and I'll meet you outside the Red Dog Saloon about nine thirty, if that's okay."

"Sounds good, see you about nine thirty."

Rocky and Nick returned to the hotel and planned to rest until it was time to meet Doc that evening.

About two and half hours later, Rocky heard a knock on his door.

Rocky went to answer the door and was surprised to find Doc standing at the door.

Doc said, "I came to tell you we don't have to meet tonight. Somebody shot and killed Lucy Love on Bourbon Street three blocks from the Red Dog Saloon an hour ago. I'm sorry to tell you, Rocky, but there goes our only lead."

"Damn, Doc, what are we going to do now?"

"I have no idea what we can do without any kind of a lead."

"Doc, give me some time to think. I'll see you tomorrow after I have time to think about what we can do to find Latesha, since we don't have a clue about where she is."

CHAPTER EIGHT

I Know What to Do

After spending a sleepless night, Rocky knew what he had to do to find Latesha. He would offer a reward for information leading to Latesha's safe return—not only a reward but a big reward of fifty thousand dollars for Latesha's safe return and another fifty thousand dollars if the kidnappers were captured and sent to prison or killed during the rescue of Latesha.

Rocky went to a small printing company located a short way from his hotel with a photo of Latesha and talked to the owner of the shop. He asked whether he could make five hundred posters for him quickly.

The printer said, "I don't think I could do it for you until sometime next week."

Rocky replied, "What if I paid you a bonus for doing them quickly?"

"How much bonus are you talking about?"

"I don't know, how much would you charge for five hundred posters?"

"Well, printing them on poster board, which I have it in stock for another job, I would normally charge two hundred fifty dollars for five hundred posters."

Rocky replied, "I'll tell you what I will do. I'll pay you five hundred dollars if you can have them ready by tomorrow."

"You've got a deal. I'll have them ready for you tomorrow morning if that's okay."

"That will be great, thank you."

"What do you want on the posters?"

"I have a picture of my wife I would like to have on them if you can do that."

"Let me see the picture."

Rocky showed the printer the picture, and he said, "I can do it, but it won't look as good on the posters."

"I hope it will look good enough for people to have an idea of what Latesha looks like."

"Oh, I'm sure they would be able to tell what she looks like by seeing her picture on the posters. I wouldn't worry about that."

"Good, I'll give you two hundred dollars as down payment for the printing and pay you the other three hundred dollars tomorrow when I pick up the posters."

"Thank you, that will be great."

Rocky paid the printer two hundred dollars and told him he would see him in the morning.

Rocky left the print shop and headed to the Red Dog Saloon. He wanted to have a talk with Ruby Red Cato.

Detective Knox told him Ruby Red was involved in every kind of crime in the city, so if he wasn't involved in the kidnapping of Latesha, maybe he knew who was, and for a price, maybe he would be willing to sell them out.

When Rocky arrived at the Red Dog Saloon, the bouncer recognized him from being with Detective Knox yesterday and figured he was a cop, so he told Rocky he would get Mr. Cato for him.

It didn't take long for Ruby Red Cato to come out of his office to talk with Rocky.

Cato said, "What can I do for you, Officer?"

Rocky replied, "First, I want you to know I'm not with the New Orleans Police Department. My name is Rocky Stone, and I'm not with any law enforcement organization.

"My wife has been kidnapped off of *The Pride of St. Louis* riverboat, and I'm wondering if you can help me find her and set her free."

Ruby said, "I thought you were a cop when you were here with Knox yesterday. What makes you think I know anything about your missing wife?"

"Detective Knox told me you knew a lot about what goes on in New Orleans."

"You can't believe everything that cop tells you about me. According to him if somebody stole an apple from an apple cart, I had something to do with it."

"I sorry to bother you, but I'm willing to pay a lot of money to get my wife back."

"Well, Mr. Stone, what do you think a lot of money is?"

"I'm willing to pay up to a hundred thousand dollars."

"That's a lot of money. Let's go back to my office and talk about it."

Ruby started walking back to his office with Rocky, Nick following right behind him.

When they got to Ruby's office, he told Rocky to have a seat and talk this over.

Rocky began, "I love my wife, and I want her back alive. I have a ransom note that tells me the kidnappers want a hundred thousand dollars for her return."

"So why don't you just pay them the money?"

"Because they have already killed a girl by the name of Dotty Ferguson and probably killed your gal, Lucy Love too, which means, I think, they not going to give back my wife alive if I pay them the money."

"So you think the people who killed Dotty and Lucy are the ones who kidnapped your wife?"

"I know for sure they killed Dotty Ferguson. They told me so in the ransom note. They killed her to let me know they were serious about killing my wife if I didn't pay the ransom. I'm pretty sure they killed Lucy Love to keep her from telling who paid her to hire the kid. Detective Knox and I were in yesterday with the kid who told us Lucy Love paid him two dollars to deliver the ransom note to my hotel."

"Okay, so what do you think I can do?"

"I don't know, but I understand you know a lot about what goes on in New Orleans, and maybe you could use some of your contacts to get information about where they're holding my wife."

"First, I would have to talk with my woman to see what she thinks about me getting involved."

"Do you think you would be in danger if you helped me?"

"Maybe, but I don't do anything without talking it over with my woman."

"Okay. How long would it be before you could let me know if you're willing to help me?"

"Not long. In fact you can come with me when I talk to her."

"Fair enough, I'd be glad to go with you."

Ruby said, "Okay, let's go."

Ruby got up from behind his desk and began walking toward the back of his office and pushed aside a curtain and opened a door located behind it.

Rocky and Nick followed him through the door.

When Rocky and Nick were outside the door, Ruby closed the door, and from outside the building, there didn't appear to be a door in the wall at all.

Rocky said, "That's quite a magic door you have there because from out here, it only looks like the rest of the wall of the building."

"Yeah, I planned it that way. It's my secret way to escape from the building if I had to."

Ruby began walking down the alley located behind the saloon, and he continued walking behind all the buildings on this side of Bourbon Street until he got to a very creepy-looking building.

Ruby found a chain and pulled it down, and when he did, a door opened to let them into that creepy-looking building.

Ruby, Rocky, and Nick went inside the building and found a woman who was doing some kind of voodoo.

Rocky wasn't sure what she was doing, and he didn't really want to know. He was afraid she might be doing some kind of spell on him or Ruby.

When the woman saw Ruby, she said, "Why are you here, Ruby? I didn't think I would see you until tonight."

Ruby replied, "Honey, this is Rocky Stone, and his wife has been kidnapped, and he wants me to help him find her. I want to know what you think. Should I try to help him or not?"

Rocky took a hard look at Ruby's Creole woman. She looked like she was maybe about forty years old and could have been a very nice-looking woman except she had her long black hair pulled straight back and held with combs of some kind. They looked like they were made of some kind of bones, and her face was painted with three different colors.

The area around her eyes was painted a bright blue color, around her nose it was dark green, and around her mouth and chin was orange.

While Rocky was looking over Ruby's woman, she was busy assessing him at the same time.

Finally, the woman spoke, she said, "My name is Cleo, the voodoo priestess. I'm married to Ruby."

Rocky answered, "I'm glad to meet you. I hope you and your husband will help me find my wife."

Cleo said, "Let's consult the spirits to see if they think we can help you."

Then she picked up a big bowl, and inside it, she put what looked to Rocky like a big bunch of chicken bones.

She then sat down on the floor and drew a big circle on the floor with chalk. Next, she took both hands and raised the bowl up high over her head and threw the bones up in the air and watched them fall to the floor.

Then she carefully studied the position of each of the bones that landed inside the circle and then the ones that landed out the circle.

Again, she took a long time before she spoke, and when she did, she said, "The sprits tell me you're a good man and you really want to find your wife, but they tell me it's dangerous for all who try."

Rocky said, "I'm sure it's dangerous because we already know the kidnappers have killed two women."

Ruby added, "The two women who were killed worked for me in the saloon. They were two of my most popular dancers, so I'm very interested in finding these people who killed my people."

Cleo said, "My husband, you must take extra caution because whoever is behind this may be also wishing harm to you."

Cleo replied, "Ruby, I want you to help Rocky Stone find these people before they destroy you, and when you do, you will find his wife."

Ruby said, "Okay, Rocky, my woman says I'm to help you find your wife. So I'm willing to do everything possible to help you."

"Thank you, Ruby and Cleo."

"Cleo, I want you to know I will do everything I can to keep your husband from being harmed."

Cleo replied, "Rocky, I feel you will do this, but I don't know if it will be enough. My sprits tell me there's more to this than the kidnapping of your wife. Strong movements are indicated to me by the sprits who tell me powerful men are behind this, and part of their plan is to kill my husband and take over his empire."

"Cleo, I will do everything I can to take care of Ruby for you, and I have some means of causing powerful men to be careful of my friends, and now Ruby is one of my friends."

"Thank you, Rocky."

With that Rocky, Ruby, and Nick left Cleo's creepy building and started walking back to Ruby's saloon.

On the walk back, Rocky told Ruby he was having five hundred posters printed asking for information for help finding Latesha.

Ruby said, "It might help, but I wouldn't count on it very much."

"You never know unless you try. You realize you never told me that both of the women that were killed worked for you."

"I didn't have any idea the reason they were killed had anything to do with your missing wife. I thought they were killed by my competition. You're a stranger in New Orleans, and you have no idea of what goes on here. The policeman you came to see me with yesterday, he works for my major competitor, Mayor Henri Rousseau."

"Ruby, you mean because he's the mayor in charge of the police department?"

"Hell no, he owns half of the saloons and gambling houses in the city. His name may not be on the deeds, but he owns them. He's the mayor because he can buy more votes than any of the good citizens of New Orleans could come up. It wouldn't matter who might run for mayor. They couldn't possibly muster enough honest votes to beat him. Henri is mayor for the payoffs he can get, and he can make sure the police don't shut his joints down."

"Ruby, do you think his people could be involved in some way with the kidnapping of my wife?"

"Don't sound like something he would want to be involved with. A one-time hundred-thousand-dollar payout is not big enough for him to bother with, unless he could find some other angle to make her kidnapping much more profitable.

"I'd say if he can find out something to help you find your wife, he probably would do it, so he could look like a hero, since you're a famous dude because you write novels. I'd say you should keep working with Detective Knox and let him help you as much as he can, but keep our arrangement to yourself.

"You don't have to worry about me. I'll be working to help you find your wife, and I'll have my people working to find out anything we can. I've got a lot of ears out there on the street. You're staying at the Crescent Hotel, aren't you? If I find out anything I'll have one of my people come to fetch you."

"How did you know I was staying at the Crescent Hotel?"

"It's the best hotel in New Orleans, so I would expect you to be staying there."

"Okay, Ruby, you got me. I like staying at the best hotel in the city or my wife does."

"Rocky, how are you going to get five hundred posters put up all over New Orleans?"

"I don't know. Do you have any idea on how I can get them put up?"

"I would suggest you hire the kids that hang around outside my saloon all the time and use that kid that came with you when you came to see me with that cop."

"Good idea, Ruby, maybe getting these kids some work might help them and their families out."

"I know it would help out most of their families if the kids earned a little money, and it might keep them from getting into trouble."

Rocky agreed.

Rocky went back to the hotel to think about what he could do next to find Latesha.

When he lay down on the bed to think, all he could think about was Latesha.

He thought about when they first met, he was in New York City to meet with his publisher, Bobby Longstreet.

Rocky could remember every little detail about that day.

During their meeting Bobby said he wanted Rocky to meet and have dinner with his wife, Lilly, and her best friend, Latesha Hudson.

He remembered telling Bobby it would be a pleasure to meet with Bobby's wife and her best friend, Latesha, for dinner.

Bobby said, "We'll meet you at your hotel and have a drink. Then we will go to dinner at Casey's Seafood Restaurant. It's just across the street from your hotel."

"Sounds like a good plan. What time do you want to meet?"

"Seven o'clock, we'll just meet you in the lobby."

"Fine, I'll see you and the ladies at seven."

Rocky remembered waiting in the lobby a little before seven and sitting there wondering what Bobby's wife and her friend would look like.

He didn't have to wait long because only a few minutes passed before Bobby, his wife, and Latesha arrived at the hotel.

Bobby said, "Rocky, this is my wife, Lilly, and her friend, Latesha Hudson. Ladies, this handsome fellow is my client and good friend, Rocky Stone."

Rocky replied, "I don't know about handsome, but I am Rocky Stone."

The two women laughed, and Lilly said, "Well, you look pretty good to me."

Latesha said, "I'm glad to meet you, Rocky. Bobby talks about you all the time, but I'm sure you could never live up to all of the stories he's told us about you."

Rocky replied, "I'm sure they're all lies. He's just trying to sell more of my books."

They had a quick drink at the hotel bar and went across the street to Casey's Seafood Restaurant.

It didn't take long before Rocky and Latesha were talking non-stop like they were the only two people at the dinner table.

Latesha told him about growing up in New York City, where her father carried on the family's business, something called the Hudson Bay Company. Her father, Henry Hudson IV, was the managing director for the US part of the company.

She was sent to a girl's finishing school in Newport, Rhode Island, where she met Lilly.

Rocky wasn't too sure what a girl's finishing school was, but he decided if Latesha was one of the finished products of the school, it must be a pretty good place for girls to get finished.

Rocky studied Latesha over with his trained Texas Ranger eyes and decided she was about five foot three or four inches tall, with dark brown eyes, light brown hair, and a face like a work of art of one of those French painters.

He loved the way she kind of tilted her head when she spoke, and her laugh was a beautiful melody playing in his ears.

Rocky realized he was in love with her before they had dessert.

Suddenly, Rocky's thoughts came back to reality; his wife was missing. Where was Latesha? He had to find her. She was everything to him.

CHAPTER NINE

The Search Goes On

Rocky got up and took Nick out to take care of his business and then went to dinner. The waiter asked him if his dog wanted his regular dinner.

Rocky told the waiter "yes," that Nick wanted the biggest steak they had in the kitchen along with a bowl of water. Rocky wanted the dinner special, which was black bean soup, crayfish, and corn bread.

Nick got his dinner first, and it took him about three minutes to finish off the steak, and then he needed another bowl of water.

After dinner, Rocky took Nick out one more time before going to bed.

The night moved slowly as Rocky kept looking at his watch; he felt sure he saw every hour throughout the entire night.

Finally, at 5:00 a.m. Rocky got up and dressed and got ready for the day. He still had his old Texas Ranger's badge in case someone asked him about carrying his Colt .44 in New Orleans.

Nick would get up every time Rocky got up to see what time it was, so when Rocky was getting dressed, Nick lay down with his eyes closed.

Rocky thought to himself, *I've kept my poor dog awake all night just because I couldn't sleep.* He actually felt sorry for his dog.

After Rocky finished dressing and was ready to leave the room, he asked, "Nick, are you ready to go?"

Nick opened his eyes, lifted his head, wagged his tail, and got up and was soon by Rocky's side.

Out the door they went and took a walk toward Canal Street. They walked south on Canal Street by several large homes, and Rocky could see the people who lived in these homes were beginning to stir around and get up.

After Rocky and Nick had been walking for some time, Rocky said, "That's enough walking. Let's go back to the hotel and have some breakfast."

Nick looked up at Rocky, and Rocky thought for sure Nick was going to tell him something, but instead Nick wagged his tail and turned around with Rocky.

After they returned to the hotel and both had something to eat, Rocky said, "Come on, Nick, we have to go to the print shop and pick up the posters."

Nick got up and waited for Rocky to get out of his chair before moving anywhere.

Rocky got up and said, "Nick, you're one smart dog."

Rocky and Nick made their way to the print shop and found the posters were ready just as the printer told Rocky they would be.

Rocky thanked the print shop owner for doing them so quickly and paid him the three hundred dollars he promised him for the quick service.

The print shop owner said, "We had to work all night, but we are glad we could help you, Mr. Stone, and we hope the posters will help you find your wife."

Rocky thanked him again and said, "I really appreciate your help, and the posters look very good."

Rocky took the five hundred posters, and he and Nick started walking toward the Red Dog Saloon to see if he could find the young boys who hung around outside.

Arriving at the saloon, Rocky could see the boys were still hanging out in front.

Rocky took a quick study of the six boys there and sized them up quickly. He knew the biggest one of the boys was the boss because he was the one who did all the talking yesterday when Detective Knox asked which one of them delivered a note to the Crescent Hotel.

Rocky knew the type well. He had seen them all his life so he asked, "Who's the boss of this gang?"

The same kid said, "I'm the boss around here, so what do you want, copper?"

Rocky walked straight up to the boy, took hold of his arm, held it firmly, and said, "Talking to a lawman that way will get you nothing but trouble. I'm going to tell you what I want. I'm offering all of you a job. The pay is ten dollars a day, and I think it will take you a couple of days to do the job, so are you interested or not?"

Rocky let go of the boy's arm and waited for his reply.

"Damn right we're interested in making twenty dollars for working two days."

Rocky said, "Okay, first things first, what's your name, Mister Boss Man?"

"Timmy Westerberg."

"Okay, Timmy, here's what I want you and your men to do. I want you to put up these posters, and I want them in every business in the Quarter."

Rocky took out one of the posters, and the six kids gathered around him and saw what the posters said.

Timmy said, "Gee, mister, we didn't know somebody kidnapped your wife."

The other five boys said things like, "I'm sorry," "That's awful," and "I can't believe it."

Rocky said, "I want all of you to keep your ears open and your mouths shut to see if any one of you could pick up any information that might help me find my wife. Do you all understand what I'm asking? The other thing that's important is when you go into the businesses in the Quarter, you ask the people who run the business if they would let you put a poster in their business.

"If they tell you no, then you thank them and go on to the next place of business. Remember, I want you on your best behavior when you're dealing with these people. Okay, does everyone understand what the job is and how you are to do it?"

All of them told him yes, they understood.

"One more thing, I don't work for the New Orleans Police Department, I write stories for dime novels."

Timmy asked, "Are you that Rocky Stone?"

"Guilty, I'm that Rocky Stone."

"Man, we love your stories."

"Then I'm sure you guys are going to do a great job helping me find my wife, and if I write a story about this, you will all be in it."

Timmy said, "Man, that would be great."

Then Timmy said, "Okay, guys, let's get going and get these posters up."

Timmy began directing each of the boys as to what streets they should go to and handing out a number of posters to each one of them.

After all the boys had gone, Timmy asked, "Mr. Stone, where will you be if we need some more posters?"

"I'm staying at the Crescent Hotel, but right now I'm going to see Mr. Cato. He's the one who told me I should hire you fellows to put up the posters."

Timmy replied, "He's not a bad guy, but you need to watch out for that copper—sorry, that officer you were with yesterday. He's bad news."

"Thanks, Timmy, I'll do that."

Timmy turned around with his arm full of posters and started walking down Bourbon Street to distribute his posters.

Rocky and Nick went into the saloon and asked if Ruby was in, and the bouncer told him to go on back to his office because he was there.

When Rocky got to the office, he knocked on the door and heard Ruby say, "Come on in."

Rocky opened the door and saw Ruby sitting behind his desk.

Ruby was busy reading a newspaper, but when he saw Rocky, he got up and said, "Good morning, Rocky, how are you?"

"I'd be a lot better if I could find Latesha."

"I understand that. I'd don't know what I would do if somebody kidnapped my woman."

Rocky and Ruby shook hands, and Ruby motioned for Rocky to have a seat.

After both of them were seated, Ruby said, "Rocky, I've been thinking, and I think you should go to the newspaper and give them the story about your wife being kidnapped off of *The Pride of St. Louis*."

"Why do you think that, Ruby?"

"Because it will put pressure on the New Orleans Police and on Mayor Henri Rousseau to do something, and if one of the mayor's gangs had any involvement, he would put a stop to it, and their body would be found floating in the Mississippi River. He couldn't take having stories in the newspaper that somehow he might be involved.

"Besides everything else, the owner of the newspaper hates the mayor and everything he stands for, and if he thought he could do anything to bring him and his regime down, he would do it in a minute."

"Okay, Ruby, I'll go talk to the newspaper to see what they can do to help us find Latesha."

Rocky and Nick left the saloon and headed to the office of the *Picayune* newspaper.

When they arrived at the newspaper office, Rocky told a clerk he wanted to talk with someone about his wife being kidnapped.

The clerk asked him to wait while he got a reporter for him, and soon the clerk returned with a newspaper reporter by the name of Buddy Larson.

Mr. Larson introduced himself to Rocky, and Rocky told him his name was Rocky Stone.

Larson said, "I understand you told the clerk your wife had been kidnapped, is that right?"

Rocky replied, "That's correct. My wife was kidnapped off of *The Pride of St. Louis*."

Larson asked, "When did this happen?"

"It was five days ago?"

"How come you didn't come to the newspaper to report it before now?"

"I didn't know she had been kidnapped until we had been gone from New Orleans for almost four hours, and it's taken me a few days to get back to New Orleans."

"Have you reported it to the New Orleans Police?"

"I did."

"When did you report it?"

"Yesterday."

"Wonder why we haven't heard about it from them?"

"I wouldn't have any idea."

"What did you say your name was?"

"Rocky Stone, and my dog's name is Nick."

"You're not the guy who writes those dime novels, are you? What a piece of trash those things are."

"It's always good to be paid a compliment by a fellow writer."

"I'm sorry, Mr. Stone, I had no idea you were the same person who did those books."

"No problem. I get the same thing from a lot of my underpaid writer friends."

"Mr. Stone, I think we better meet with the managing editor of the paper if your wife has been kidnapped. Please come with me."

Rocky and Nick began following Mr. Larson, and he took them back to very large office where an older man with white hair was busy going through stacks of stories.

Mr. Larson knocked on the door frame of the man's office since the door was standing open, and the older man said in a grumpy voice, "Come in, Larson."

Mr. Larson said, "Mr. Zwald, I want to introduce you to Mr. Rocky Stone and his dog, Nick."

In the same grumpy voice Mr. Zwald said, "Stone, the name sounds familiar. Why is it?"

"It's because I write those trashy dime novels."

Mr. Zwald replied, "Well, I've read a couple of your stories, and they're a lot less trashy than most. What can I do for you?"

"Mr. Zwald, my wife was kidnapped about five days ago off *The Pride of St. Louis* steamboat before we left the port of New Orleans. At least that's the best we can figure out. Yesterday, while staying at the Crescent Hotel, I received a ransom note asking for a hundred thousand dollars for her safe return.

"However, I don't think they will give her back to me alive because the note said they killed a woman by the name of Dotty Ferguson to let me know how serious they were as to what would happen to my wife if I didn't pay the ransom.

"The police found her body in the Mississippi River downstream from the dock our ship was leaving from. In addition to that they found out the woman, Lucy Love, who hired a kid to bring me the ransom note was shot and killed on Bourbon Street not long after the ransom note was delivered to me."

Mr. Zwald said, "Whoa, just a minute here, how come we haven't heard anything about this until now? None of my reporters have said anything about this alleged kidnapped and the murder of two women."

Rocky replied, "I don't have any idea. Maybe the police didn't want to say anything because they were trying to pick up a clue or something."

Zwald asked, "Mr. Stone, how do you know your wife didn't just decide to leave you for some other man and hatched up this plan to get a lot of money from you?"

"I have to tell you we are a very happily married couple, and she didn't just get off the steamboat.

"Very few people would know it, but my wife would inherit a lot more money from her father and grandfather than I would ever have."

"Okay, Stone, how do you know she just didn't get off the ship before it left port?"

"Because the crew was busy getting the last things on board before we left and all of the crew knew who she was. If she left on her own, she would have left the ship by the gangplank, and it was already up before the last time I was with her."

"Well, if someone kidnapped her, how could they get her off the ship, assuming the ship was searched for her before you came to the conclusion that she was kidnapped?"

At this point Buddy Larson jumped into the conversation and said, "The kidnappers had a rowboat waiting on the river side of the ship with one man in it, and two other men came on the ship as deck passengers. These two men kidnapped her, and while everyone was busy watching the preparations of getting the ship underway from the port, they lowered her down into the rowboat, along with themselves and rowed the rowboat down river away from the direction the steamboat was leaving."

Zwald said, "I'm surprised, Larson, you have that much imagination. That sounds like it could work."

Larson replied, "Actually, I don't, that's the way the kidnappers kidnapped the wife in Mr. Stone's book *Kidnapped off the Mississippi Queen*."

Zwald said, "You mean they kidnapped your wife the same way you wrote about it in one of your novels?"

"It certainly looks like it."

Zwald replied, "They got a lot of nerve using your own kidnapping scheme to kidnap your wife. A lot of guts."

"I feel pretty silly thinking that I wrote a story that someone actually used to commit a crime, but I do think they used my plan to kidnap my own wife."

Zwald asked, "So how did the hero in your book find the kidnappers and what happened to them when he did?"

"One of the kidnappers got cold feet and found my hero and told him where they were holding his wife. My hero broke into their hiding place and killed all of them."

Zwald said, "I guess I should have read that one. So what do you want us to do?"

"The first thing is I want you to do is run the story about the kidnapping of my wife and the killing of the two women, Dotty Ferguson and Lucy Love. Then I want to run a full-page ad in your newspaper offering a reward of fifty thousand dollars for information leading to the finding and rescuing Latesha Stone, alive, and an additional fifty thousand dollars reward for the arrest of the kidnappers or their deaths during the act of capturing them."

Zwald said, "You know, Mr. Stone, a full-page ad is going to cost you five hundred dollars."

"Okay, I also have posters being put in all of the businesses in the Quarter offering the same reward."

Zwald replied, "Mr. Stone, I'd say you're putting the posters up in the right part of town to find out anything about your missing wife because if there's any kind of crime committed in New Orleans, it's probably organized in the Quarter."

"That's what Detective Knox told me."

Zwald replied, "Well, if there's anybody who knows about crimes in New Orleans, it would be Detective Knox."

Just the way Mr. Zwald said that caused Rocky to ask, "Why do you say that? Is he a very good detective, or do you mean something else?"

Zwald responded, "You know, Mr. Stone, he could be one of the best detectives in the country, but in this town he can only do so much because of his boss, Mayor Henri Rousseau."

"Can you explain that a little more for an outsider?"

Zwald answered, "You see, Mr. Stone, our wonderful mayor is the biggest crook in this town, but getting him out of office or sending him to prison or hanging him like he should be ain't happening. Anybody that could do anything to him can't because he has too much dirt on them or they wind up dead. One or the other.

"Beating him in an election can't be done either because he can buy more voters than there are honest people in New Orleans who could vote against him. He's got his hands in everything that can make money. Hell, I wouldn't be surprised if he didn't have his hands in the kidnapping of your wife. Probably not directly, but some of his cutthroats pals may have had something to do with it."

"Tell me, Mr. Zwald, what do you think would happen if I went to the mayor and asked him to help me find my wife?"

"You know, son, that's a very interesting question. I think because you're famous and he probably doesn't have any idea who your wife is, it might get you some very quick results in finding your wife. By the way, who is your wife's father? I would like to use that in the story about your wife's kidnapping if it's all right."

"Latesha's father is Henry Hudson IV, the managing director of the Hudson Bay Company, US Operations, and one of the grandsons of the founder of the Hudson Bay Company."

"Mr. Stone, with your fame and your wife's pedigree, you should impress the hell out of the mayor. I'd suggest when you leave my office, you go directly over to city hall and act like you owned the place and tell his hirelings you want to see the mayor."

CHAPTER TEN

Visiting the Mayor

Rocky followed Mr. Zwald's advice; he went directly from the newspaper office to city hall, and when he arrived, he announced to the clerk he wanted to see Mayor Henri Rousseau.

The clerk said, "I'm sorry, no one can see the mayor without an appointment. I would be happy to see if I could work you in sometime later next week."

Rocky said, "Do you know who I am?"

"No, I don't, but it doesn't make any difference who you are, because no one can see the mayor without an appointment."

Rocky replied, "I'm Rocky Stone, the writer. You go tell the mayor I want to see him right now because my wife's been kidnapped in New Orleans."

The clerk said, "Yes, sir, Mr. Stone, I'm sure the mayor will make an exception for you."

The clerk returned in just a few minutes with Mayor Henri Rousseau in tow right behind him.

The clerk said, "Mr. Mayor, this is Rocky Stone, the writer."

Mayor Rousseau said, "How do you do? Won't you come into my office and please tell me about your wife being kidnapped in New Orleans? I haven't heard anything about it before now."

On their way into Mayor Rousseau's office, Rocky sized him up pretty quickly. He was a very short man with a round face and a stomach to match; he had only a few strands of white hair and very fat hands.

When Rocky and Nick entered the mayor's office, Rocky saw several tough-looking men seated at a long conference table.

The mayor asked Rocky to please have a seat at the end of the table while the mayor went around to the other end of the table and sat down.

The mayor said, "Gentlemen, I want to introduce you to Mr. Rocky Stone, the famous writer."

All the men around the table nodded their head without anyone saying a word.

The mayor continued, "Apparently, Mr. Stone's wife has been kidnapped here in New Orleans, and this is the first I have heard about it. Mr. Stone, would you please tell us about how and where your wife was when she was kidnapped?"

Rocky proceeded to tell the mayor and the six men sitting at the table all the details about Latesha's kidnapping, including the fact the kidnappers used his plan to kidnap his wife.

The men at the table couldn't help themselves from smiling when they heard that.

If Latesha hadn't have been kidnapped, he would have thought it was pretty funny himself.

Rocky explained to the mayor and his men about his concern that if he paid the ransom, he was sure they planned to kill Latesha since the kidnappers had already killed two women.

He told the men he had filed a police report with Detective Knox and was having posters put into businesses in the Quarter and running a full-page ad in the New Orleans *Picayune* newspaper offering a hundred-thousand-dollar reward for information that would free Latesha, alive, and for the capture or killing the kidnappers.

The mayor and his men were impressed with the size of the reward he was offering.

One of the men said, "You must love your wife a lot and really want her back offering that kind of money."

When the mayor heard the man say that, he gave the fellow a very mean look and said, "Gentleman, I'm quite sure Mr. Stone loves his wife very much and wants her back alive."

None of the other men at the table said one more word.

Rocky said, "Mr. Mayor, I really need your help to get my wife back alive, and I know her family, the Hudsons, would be very grateful as well. I hope I can count of you to do everything possible to help me find her and bring her home safely."

The mayor asked, "Her family's name is Hudson?"

Rocky replied, "Yes, the Hudsons who own Hudson Bay Company. It was her great-grandfather who started the company."

The mayor said, "Oh, that Hudson."

Then the mayor said, "Mr. Stone, I want you to know that the New Orleans Police and my office will do everything possible to help you find your wife and bring her home safely to you. I want you to know how much I appreciate you bringing this to my attention, and you can be assured my office will do everything possible to help you get your wife back alive. If there anything else I can do to help you with while you're here in New Orleans, just let me know."

Rocky got up from his chair, and Nick rose from the floor where he had been waiting next to Rocky's feet. The mayor came around the table and shook hands with him and said, "You certainly have a well-trained dog. I wish my kids were that well behaved."

Rocky replied, "I want to thank you again for seeing me, and Nick is certainly a very special dog."

Rocky reached down and gave Nick a pat on the head. Nick rubbed up against Rocky's right leg.

Rocky walked out of the mayor's office thinking, *This guy is really smooth. No wonder he keeps getting reelected.*

Rocky thought the mayor would certainly get a lot of votes without paying people to vote for him.

As soon as Rocky was out of the mayor's office, the mayor went back to his chair at the head of the conference table and said, "I want you men to turn over every stone in this parish and find out who was stupid enough to kidnap Rocky Stone's wife. Whoever is involved must be a really dumb son of a bitch, and I won't stand for such a crime in my town. It will bring nothing but trouble to everybody doing business in town. This kind of thing could put all of our rackets in jeopardy. Hell, it could even bring that damn Yankee federal government looking into crime in our city.

"I figure we can handle anything from the state, but whoever did this doesn't have any idea of what kidnapping the wife of a famous, powerful writer and the daughter of a family like the Hudsons could do to this town. We could all wind up in prison even if we didn't have anything to do with kidnapping this woman. We don't want people looking around at our enterprises. I want each one of you and your men out on the streets shaking down everybody who might have even thought about pulling off such a kidnapping. I wanted them squeezed until somebody talks. Got it? Get out of my office and get busy!"

As soon as the six men left his office, he yelled at his clerk to come into his office. The clerk ran into the office as quickly as he could and said, "Yes, sir, Mr. Mayor, what can I do for you?"

"Duncan, send a messenger over to the police department and tell Detective Knox to come over to my office."

Duncan replied, "Yes, sir, right away."

Duncan closed the mayor's office door and sat down at his desk and called one of the young boys over who were working in a file room and asked him to run over to the police headquarters and tell Detective Knox the mayor wanted to see him right away.

Duncan repeated what he had just told the boy to make sure he understood.

The boy nodded his head yes, and began running through city hall and out the doors of city hall. He didn't slow down until he was at the police station.

The young man asked for Detective Knox because he had a message from the mayor for him, and the desk clerk took the kid into Detective Knox's office.

Knox was talking with two detectives about the kidnapping and the murder of two women that appeared to be tied to the kidnapping when the messenger arrived in his office.

The young man delivered the message he was given by Mr. Duncan. Knox thanked him and told the young man he would be on his way to see the mayor as soon as he finished briefing his detectives on the case.

Knox said, "I guess you both know now about as much as I do about Mrs. Stone's kidnapping. If I don't get over to the mayor's office, the old man might fire me because I didn't walk fast enough getting over to see him."

The two detectives nodded their heads like they understood exactly what Knox meant.

As Detective Doc Knox was walking over to the mayor's office, he thought back to when he first joined the department as a beat cop working in the Quarter.

He and his wife, Sarah, had only been married for a year, and he had always want to be a policeman because his father was a policeman; he knew he got the job because of his father.

Doc's father had been a detective with the New Orleans Police Department when Doc was a little boy and had been killed during a gun battle with four men who were trying to rob the Bank of New Orleans.

His father was a true hero, as he single-handedly killed all four of the bank robbers before they could get away with the money.

His father was on his way into the bank just to change a twenty-dollar gold piece to give Doc's mother some money to buy grocery, but instead of getting his money changed, he had walked into the bank as the bank robbers were leaving with the money.

His dad saw what was happening and ordered the four men to drop the money and throw down their guns.

One of the robbers shot him in the chest, and his dad fell to the floor.

Lying on the floor, mortally wounded, his father fired six shots and killed all four of the bank robbers before they could get out of the bank. His dad had been shot four more times.

The Bank of New Orleans gave Doc's mother a reward of two thousand dollars for his father's actions saving their money.

The New Orleans Police Department provided them with nothing for his dad giving his life in the line of duty.

The money from the bank allowed his mother to be able to take care of their rent and food for almost four years before she had to find a job to provide for their basic living expenses.

His mother got a job as a maid and a cook for one of the rich families living in one of those big mansions on South Canal Street. His mother worked for them until she died at age thirty-four. Doc was fourteen years old when she died.

His mother's sister and her husband took him in until he was eighteen.

At eighteen, Doc knew he had to make it on his own because his aunt and uncle were doing everything they could to feed their own six kids.

After Doc's mother died, she had left him an envelope that said not to open it until he had his eighteenth birthday.

When he opened the envelope, he found a letter addressed to him from his mother as well as a note from his dad, written when he was born.

His mother's letter told him how much she loved him and how she hoped he could find a wonderful wife and asked him to have as many children as he could.

When he read her letter, tears ran down his face; he was so glad he hadn't opened the letter until he was alone.

He missed his mother so much and felt she was cheated out of so much happiness in her life because his father was killed when she was so young. She wanted a lot more children, but Doc was her only child.

His father's note was very short. It said,

> My dear son, Michael William Knox Jr., you are reading this letter, written on the night you were born, because being a police officer is not the safest job you can have, so you have this letter in case I am not here on earth with you on your eighteenth birthday.
>
> Although I may not be with you, I wanted you to know that because you are your mother's and my son, you will always be loved as much as any child born on this earth will ever be.
>
> I pray when you grow up, you want to follow in my footsteps and be a police officer. In

this job I charge you to always do your duty in an honest way and to the best of your ability and always remember you are a servant of the people. They are to be treated with respect even if they are the scum of the earth. If you want respect, you have to show respect. Love always, Michael William Knox Sr.

Doc also found the twenty-dollar gold piece his father had been carrying the day he was killed and a note from his mother asking him to "always carry this coin and it will protect you."

Doc always carried the coin in his pocket, but he often wondered when his mother needed money so badly, why she didn't use the twenty-dollar coin, but she never did; she had always kept it.

He now understood it was sacred to her.

Doc walked into the mayor's office, and the mayor asked him to sit down and then asked him, "How come you didn't tell me Rocky Stone's wife was kidnapped?"

"Sir, I didn't know you were interested in all the cases we're investigating. I'm sorry, but I can begin sending you a daily report on all our cases if you want me to."

"Don't be stupid. I don't care about every little case you people are looking into. I had to find out Rocky Stone's wife was kidnapped here when he came storming into my office this morning asking for my help finding his wife."

"What did you tell him, sir?"

"I told him the New Orleans Police Department would do everything possible to help him get his wife back alive, and I would, too."

"Mr. Mayor, we are doing everything we can. The kidnappers have already killed two women, and so far we don't have any clues as to where she is or who's holding her. We've got everybody out trying to find out something. If it's somebody local that's responsible, they have really covered their tracks well since none of our informers knows anything about it."

"Captain Knox, do you have any idea who Rocky Stone's wife is?"

"No, sir, only that she's Mr. Stone's wife."

"My god, man, it's not bad enough for New Orleans that someone kidnapped the wife of a famous writer, she's one of the Hudsons—you know, the family who owns the Hudson Bay Company."

"No, sir, I didn't know that. Rocky never said anything about her being one of the Hudsons."

"Well, he told me who she was, and, Captain, you better use all of your men and spend all of your time working on finding her, even if you have to work twenty-four hours a day. Captain, I'd suggest you tell your wife and kids you won't see them for a while because we can't have her killed by these kidnappers. You have no idea how bad that would be for New Orleans. You do like being a captain, don't you, Knox? Because if she's killed, you can look forward to pounding a beat again as a patrolman."

"Thank you for reminding me of the city's appreciation for what the employees do for the city, especially those of us who work for the police and fire departments."

"Are you getting smart with me, Knox? If you think you are being smart, you're dead wrong. I won't put up with back talk from you or anyone else who works for me."

"No, sir, I'm sorry, I didn't mean to be disrespectful to you, sir."

Doc didn't say any more. He just turned around and did what the mayor told him to. He got out the mayor's office as quickly as he could.

He was muttering under his breath to himself as he left the office, "One day, Mr. Mayor, my men and I will have enough solid proof to nail you for all the crooked things you and your men are doing. Then we will have a chance to clean up this city once and for all. One day, Mr. Mayor."

Doc didn't go back to his office. He went directly home to tell his wife what was going on and the threat the mayor made about demoting him if Rocky Stone's wife was killed before they were able to find and free her from the kidnappers.

He said, "As a result, I don't know when I will be coming home to do more than change my clothes and get cleaned up. I love you, and tell the kids I love them, too."

Sarah replied, "I love you, too, and don't worry about the kids. They know you love them. I don't know why you don't tell the mayor to go to hell and find some other line of work. I'm sure you could make a lot more money doing something else."

"Sarah, you know how much I love my job. I was born to be a cop."

"I know that, Doc, I wish you had somebody better to work for besides this mayor."

"You know I've trying to nail this lousy crook for all of his crooked deals for years, but it's really hard to get enough solid evidence to be sure we can convict him and his men."

"Okay, love. I only hope you can do it soon. Life's too short to always have to live the way you do with the pressure he puts on you."

"You understand, Sarah, he never wanted to promote me to captain, but because of some of the cases I was able to solve and the headlines I was getting in the newspaper, he had to find somehow to get into the act. Promoting me to captain was one way he could grab some of the headlines."

Doc kissed Sarah goodbye and headed back to his office to try to find some way to find and save Latesha Stone.

CHAPTER ELEVEN

The Kidnappers' Problem

Charlie Christian wasn't happy as he read one of the posters offering a hundred-thousand-dollar reward for information leading to the finding and freeing Rocky Stone's wife and for the capture of the people who had kidnapped her. The same information was on the front page of the New Orleans *Picayune* newspaper.

Charlie never expected Rocky Stone to make such an offer.

Before seeing these two papers, he was certain Rocky would pay the ransom without making much of a fuss.

Then Charlie could send his darling wife, Latesha, back to him in a nice box, and he would even put some nice flowers in the box with her.

Charlie knew now he had a problem. How was he going to be able to control his men if one of them decided to sell him out and collect the reward for himself?

If they did, they could have all the money for themselves, not just a small part of it.

Charlie decided that he had to do something, but what? He decided he needed to ask for more money from Rocky.

If they were getting more money, it would make it less attractive for one of his men to sell him out, and besides, his men were afraid of him and for good reason.

He also had picked men for his gang who were not as smart as he was. If they turned out to be too smart, he got rid of them one way or the other.

He still had to wonder if getting more money would be enough to keep them loyal. He certainly hoped so.

Charlie had waited a long time to pay Rocky Stone back for the years he cost him in prison.

Charlie escaped being hung once only because one of his men was holding a jury member's wife with the threat of killing her if he didn't keep Charlie from being hung.

Rocky had sent him to prison once before for robbing a stagecoach and had hounded him as soon as he got out of prison.

It seemed to Charlie that Rocky or one of his men watched him everywhere he went in Texas, and it was a very big state.

After Rocky left the Texas Rangers, Charlie found he was writing those dime novels, and he became a big fan trying to learn how Rocky thought.

When he read the story in the New Orleans newspaper about Rocky and his wife being in New Orleans, he remembered Rocky's book *Kidnapped off the Mississippi Queen*, and he knew exactly what he was going to do to get even with him.

He would kidnap his wife using Rocky's own plan, collect the ransom, and then kill his wife.

Let Rocky suffer the way he did. Charlie went years without having a woman, let's see how Rocky liked it.

It probably would have been easier for Charlie to just have killed Rocky, but that would be letting Rocky off too easy.

He wanted him to feel real pain and wanted Rocky to hurt and keep hurting, like he did in prison over those long years.

Christian may have been Charlie's last name, but he was no Christian. He was a killer by the time he was twelve years old. He killed his own father because he wouldn't give him his horse.

When he returned home by himself, he told his mother his father was killed by Indians and he escaped death only because he was able to get mounted on his father's fast horse.

The next morning he stole what little money his mother had in an old crock jar, took his father's rifle and his Colt .44, saddled his father's horse, and left his mother to make it on her own.

From then on he had only one rule: take what you want, no matter to whom it belongs, and if they don't want to give it to you, kill them.

He started out robbing small farmers and small merchants; his next move was to rob banks, so he took on a partner.

After they did the first couple of banks and Charlie saw how much money he was giving his partner, he decided to dissolve their partnership with one bullet.

A bullet cost less than a partner.

This system worked well until he had a partner who was just as fast on the draw as he was, so he decided to keep him until he could figure out a way to end their partnership.

The next bank job took care of that problem for him, because as they were riding out of the town, the local sheriff got off a lucky shot at his partner and hit him in the left side.

The sheriff and some local cowboys who had stopped in the local saloon for a drink before going back to their ranch started chasing after them.

His partner's wound was worse than they thought, and before they had ridden less than five miles out of town, his partner fell off his horse.

Charlie turned around as he saw the posse coming up quickly behind them. He rode back to where his partner had fallen and caught his horse on the way.

When his partner saw Charlie coming back for him with his horse, he made it to his feet and began walking toward him.

Suddenly, Charlie fired one shot into his partner's chest; his partner fell to the ground.

Charlie quickly wheeled his horse around and hightailed it away as fast as the two horses could run.

Charlie had no choice but to go back and get his partner's horse since it had the money on it, and he certainly wasn't going to leave the money behind.

The posse stopped where his partner lay dying, and by the time they picked up the pursuit of Charlie again, he was long gone.

After killing his last partner, Charlie always had his own gang of several men, which he ruled like he was God. They each got a smaller part of the money they stole, and if one of them complained or got out of line, he killed them in front of the other men in his gang.

Charlie ruled his gang by fear and by being ruthless when it came to the jobs they pulled.

However, most of the men in his gang had more money than they ever had in their whole lives by working for Charlie, so they were all pretty happy.

Charlie was the best planner of jobs than any of them had ever been with before, and they had far more success pulling off big jobs than anyone else.

Charlie had been caught only two times in his life, and that was when he got involved with a woman.

The type of women Charlie liked were saloon girls who had plenty of experience with men and were hard talking and liked things rough.

The two times he was caught by Rocky Stone were due to him bragging about the jobs he pulled to the woman he had spent a few days with.

After Rocky Stone got him this way the first time, if some big job had been pulled off in Texas, Rocky would send his rangers to all the saloons in the area looking for the type of women Charlie liked and warning them about Charlie.

Why would they listen to the rangers? Because after the first woman got Charlie caught, he began killing each one of them when he was through with them.

Since these women liked living, they paid attention to the rangers' warnings about Charlie.

The second time Charlie was caught by Rocky, it was because the woman he was with had been warned about him by the Texas Rangers, so after she had been to bed with him, she got him so drunk he fell asleep.

Then she got hold of the rangers, and they took him away while he was sleeping it off.

When Charlie woke up in jail, who do you think was the first person he saw? Of course it was Rocky Stone.

Charlie swore right then and there to get even with Rocky Stone if it was the last thing he ever did.

He was getting very close to getting even with him now. Only a couple of more days to go and he would have paid him back in spades.

Charlie decided he would write another ransom note to Rocky and raise the ransom up to two hundred and fifty thousand dollars because Rocky had gone to the police department, printed posters offering a reward for help him find his wife, and gone to the newspaper offering a reward to people who would help find Latesha.

After Charlie finished writing the new ransom note, he put it into an envelope, sealed it up, and gave it to Sandy Barr. He told him to take it to the Crescent Hotel and leave it with the desk clerk.

Sandy went directly to the Crescent Hotel and found the desk clerk who was busy checking people into the hotel, so he left the envelope lying on the counter and walked out of the hotel without anyone paying any attention to him.

When the desk clerk finished checking in the new guests, he saw the envelope on the counter and saw it was for Rocky Stone, so he put the envelope in the mail slot for Rocky's room number.

A few minutes later Rocky and Nick came into the hotel, and the desk clerk handed the envelope to him.

Rocky took the envelope to his room and opened it up and read the new ransom note.

> Rocky Stone, you have been a bad boy going to the cops, putting up posters, talking to the newspaper about your missing wife, and offering a reward to people who help you find her.
>
> Therefore it's going to cost you more money to get your wife back. We want $250,000 and you have to pay us in three days. If not, your Latesha will be killed.

We will tell you where you are to leave the money in two days.

You better play it straight if you ever want to get your wife back alive.

After Rocky read this new ransom note, he knew he had to do two things right away.

First, he had to send a telegram to Bobby Longstreet asking him to make arrangements to have $250,000 transferred from the Bank of New York to the Bank of New Orleans in order for Rocky to have the money available to pay the ransom.

Second, he had to take the new ransom note over to the police department to meet with Doc Knox so he could see what the kidnappers had to say after seeing the posters and the newspaper article.

Rocky had managed to get a reaction to the posters and the newspaper article, just not the kind he was looking for.

Charlie told Sandy's brother, Tom, to go check on Latesha to be sure she was all right.

Tom got up from the poker game the boys were playing and went into the room where Latesha was been held.

When Tom got there, he lit a candle. Since it was so dark in this little room, he couldn't see Latesha. The room where she was being held didn't have any windows and only the one door in.

Latesha was lying on the bed. That and a dresser were the only furniture in the room.

Tom said, "Are you all right, lady?"

Latesha struggled to speak because her throat was so dry from lack of water and finally uttered, "No."

Tom asked, "What's wrong with you?"

"Water, I need water."

Tom took the candle closer to the bed to get a better look at her.

Arriving next to the bed, he could see a different woman than the one they brought here.

She looked so much older now. Her cheeks were drawn in, her eyes had dark circles under them, and she looked like she was really old and sick.

She could hardly raise her head off the bed. Tom could see there was no way she could get up off her bed; she didn't have the strength to do anything.

Tom said, "I'll see if I can bring you some water."

He turned around, taking the candle with him and leaving Latesha totally in the dark again, and went back to ask Charlie if he could give the woman some water.

Charlie told him he could give the woman a small cup of water, no more.

Tom said, "Boss, the lady looks to me like she dying."

Charlie replied, "Good, that will save me from having to kill her."

"All right, boss. I'll give her a little bit of water."

"Okay, but no more than a little and no food, got it?"

"Yes, sir."

Tom got a lamp and lit it and got a little bigger cup of water than Charlie wanted him to give Latesha, but Tom managed to walk by Charlie without him seeing how much water he had in the cup.

When Tom got back next to Latesha's bed, he sat the lamp on the floor and helped Latesha to sit up on the side of the bed.

He held the cup up to her lips with one hand, as he was holding her up on her bed with the other arm.

Latesha took one small sip and began coughing. After she quit coughing, she took another sip, and this time the water went down. Then she couldn't get the rest of the water down quickly enough.

Soon the water was all gone from the cup, and she asked for more.

Tom said, "I don't think you should have any more right now, and I don't think my boss would let me give you any more."

In a very low voice, Latesha whispered, "Please, mister, please."

Tom slowly lowered Latesha back down on her cot and said, "I'll see what I can do. Right now, you better get some rest."

Tom looked at this poor woman lying on the bed. She had nothing to eat since they kidnapped her and almost no water either. He felt really sorry for her, but what could he do?

He knew better than to cross Charlie. Those who did died a violent death.

Tom took the lamp and left Latesha alone in the dark like she had been since they brought her to this warehouse.

As Latesha lay there on her bed, she wondered what she had ever done in her life to deserve to be treated this way. She decided she had never done anything to anybody for her to be suffering the way she was. So why was she?

What did these people want, and how did she get here in the first place?

The last thing she remembered was that she was in her stateroom on *The Pride of St. Louis* starting to put her some of her clothes in the closet when she heard a knock on the cabin door.

She remembered opening the cabin door and remembered seeing three men standing there.

The next thing she remembered was one of them striking her on the head with something, and she began falling to the floor.

The next time she remembered anything was when the men laid her down on this bed in this very dark room.

Latesha had no idea where she was or why she was here.

She tried to open the door once or twice, but the door out of the room was bolted or locked someway, and she knew she couldn't get out of this awful dark room.

She remembered wondering what these men did with Rocky. Where was he?

She couldn't think anymore; she fell back, either asleep or in a state of unconsciousness again.

She began dreaming about being home in Boonville. She was so happy, and she was walking hand in hand with Rocky out to their favorite place by her flower garden behind their home.

From here they could look down on the Missouri River and watch all the activities going on down there.

It never made any difference to them if it was a steamboat passing by or if they were just watching the birds that lived around the river. Something was always happening on their river. They loved it there.

She felt so happy to be home again and being with Rocky. It was always good to be anywhere as long as she was with Rocky. It was always wonderful, but being home watching their river was extra special to her.

Then her dreams took her back to her childhood in New York City and wondering what wonderful presents her father would be getting her for Christmas. Christmas was her favorite time of the year. She loved it.

Some of her dreams were of the first meeting she had with Rocky and how handsome and tall he was and how he talked so differently than anyone she had ever met.

She loved his stories of growing up in Texas and becoming a Texas Ranger and how he started writing those dime novels that made him so much money.

Maybe he didn't have as much money as her father, but he earned his money all by himself; he didn't have it handed down from his father and grandfather like her father did.

She was dreaming of him making love with her, and suddenly she woke up thinking, *Rocky has to find me and take me home!*

She hated the dark, and she began crying again, lying alone in this awful place.

Latesha kept thinking, *Why are these people doing this to me?*

Then she was out again.

CHAPTER TWELVE

We've Got to Find Latesha Now

Rocky and Nick rushed to the police department to talk with Detective Knox as quickly as they could. Rocky asked for him at the desk sergeant's office.

Rocky was told Detective Knox wasn't in right now, but Rocky could go back to his office and wait for him there because the sergeant was sure he would be back in a few minutes.

Rocky and Nick made their way back to Detective's Knox's office, and one of his men, a Detective Scott, told Rocky he was sure Doc would be back shortly since he went to the mayor's office sometime ago.

Rocky thanked Detective Scott and sat down in a chair in Doc's office, with Nick lying on the floor next to Rocky's feet.

The desk sergeant and Detective Scott were right because Rocky had only been waiting for about ten minutes when Doc Knox came into his office.

Doc asked, "What brings you here, Rocky?"

"I have another ransom note, increasing the amount of the ransom to $250,000 because of the posters and the newspaper article offering a reward to help free Latesha and capturing her kidnappers."

"Rocky, let me see the note. How was the note delivered?"

Rocky replied, "It was left at the front desk."

Rocky handed the ransom note over to Doc, and he read it and said, "Well, it looks like you have spooked the kidnappers, which is a good thing and a bad thing."

Rocky asked, "Why do you think it's good and bad thing?"

Doc said, "The worse thing, of course, would be if they killed Latesha and leave without even trying to get the ransom, fearing we are about to catch them."

"Okay, Doc, that would be a really bad thing, so what's the good thing?"

"Because they may be beginning to feel we are getting closer to finding them, and they may make a big mistake and lead us right to them and let us find and free Latesha."

"Well, Doc, that would be great. I hope it happens."

"Rocky, I have to know something. Why didn't you tell me your wife was one of the Hudsons?"

"I didn't think it was important for you to know that. I never thought it would help you in any way to find my wife."

"Well, Rocky, when you told the mayor she was a Hudson, it certainly made an impression on him. As a result, he has certainly put the pressure of me and the police department to find her."

"Doc, I'm sorry to be causing you and the department problems, but I was told the mayor might have ways of knowing something about the kidnapping."

"I have no idea who told you such a thing, but it seems to me the mayor does know a lot about certain things that go on in this city that's not exactly legal."

"Doc, that's kind of what I was told. The mayor did say he would try to find out who was behind her kidnapping."

"You know, Rocky, between the two of us, he may be willing to really help you find your wife because I'm sure he doesn't want too many people looking into everything that goes on around New Orleans."

"Doc, you're trying to say you think the mayor is involved in some illegal activities here in New Orleans?"

"Rocky, let's just say I know he is, but I can't prove it, and the chief is one of the mayor's people who make sure I can't. You remember I took you to meet Ruby Red Cato? He's small time compared to all the things the mayor's got his fingers in.

"He never loses an election because he pays off more people to vote for him than any of the good people of the city could ever get to vote, and besides he controls the ballot boxes. So you see, we can't get a break. The mayor's got us one way or the other. I'm very sure the mayor wouldn't like to have a bunch of law folks looking around too much in New Orleans. They might uncover something illegal he has his fingers in."

"Doc, how do you work in such a city and police department when you know all of this is going on?"

"It gets harder every year. I keep hoping the mayor makes a big enough mistake that I can nail him red-handed and get him out of New Orleans once and for all."

"You know, Doc, I wish I could help you do that. It's too bad America's let men like your mayor get away with this kind of crap. I know they know better, but too many times they don't have the guts to stick up for what's right. It's easier to just let it slide than to make waves, and sometimes the ones who do make waves wind up dead or in prison."

"I can tell you, Rocky, a lot of them in New Orleans who tried to do the right thing are found floating in the river. I've got a file full of those of people who were found in the river or shot down in their own homes. We also have a lot of people who finally just leave New Orleans because they don't think enough people of New Orleans care enough about cleaning this city up, which is really too bad."

"Sorry, Doc, to bring something like this up I know you are trying your best to find Latesha for me."

"Rocky, I wish I had something I could tell you that was positive, but I can't. We don't have any more news on Latesha—no leads, no nothing."

"Doc, I'm making arrangements to pay the $250,000, but my gut feeling is that even when I pay them their money, they're still going to kill Latesha. They're not leaving any witnesses so no one can identify them. That's based on what they done by killing Dotty Ferguson and Lucy Love. I would make a guess that whoever is behind Latesha's kidnapping doesn't plan to leave any of his men alive either so they couldn't testify against him."

CHAPTER THIRTEEN

Henry Hudson IV

Henry Hudson IV was obsessed while raising his daughter, Latesha. She was to have the best of everything since she was the only family he had left in America.

Latesha was the only link he had with his late wife, who he loved more than life itself.

Latesha had the best nannies, nurses, teachers, and security people to look after her ever since the day his wife died while trying to give birth to a stillborn son.

There was nothing he wouldn't do for her.

Henry inherited more money than anyone could spend in a lifetime from his father and grandfather, and he doubled it into even more money and more value than either of them ever thought of having.

The big difference between him and his father and grandfather was he never cared if he was the richest person in the world. Yes, it was great having enough money to do anything he wanted to, but he would have traded all the money to have his wife back.

Henry had a knack of knowing when and where to invest his money so as to not only make more money for him and Latesha but create jobs for thousands of other people.

He had invested in railroads, steel, electrical systems, steamboats, shipping companies, telegraphs, and telephone companies. No one except Henry and Latesha actually knew all his investments.

His latest interest was in some people who were trying to make horseless carriages. He was certain that one day these devices would replace horses as the major form of transportation in the world.

Henry began to talk to Latesha about business and deciding what kinds of companies he should invest in when she was only about ten years old. He was amazed at her grasp of such things at such a young age.

Latesha was always interested in learning about different businesses if they would make life easier for people and would provide work for people. She liked to think her father's investments would help poor people find work that would give them a better life.

She understood her father and she were rich beyond belief and could buy anything and everything they would ever want in life, but she knew most people couldn't do this, and she wanted to find ways to help improve their lives.

Since her father cared about what Latesha thought about, helping other people to live better, he always asked questions about how many people would be employed with his investment in this company, unlike the robber barons of his generation who were only interested in how much money they could make with their investments.

One company Henry invested in was the Pullman Company, and he had a private railcar built for his and Latesha's personal use.

When Henry received the telegram from Rocky about Latesha being kidnapped, he contacted the local rail company and asked them to make up a special train for his personal car, along with enough Pullman cars to take up to forty people, as well as a dining car equipped with enough staff to feed everyone.

They asked him where the train was going, and he told them it was going to New Orleans because his daughter had been kidnapped there.

He asked to have the train ready as soon as possible. They told him it would take about three days to get everything ready.

Next, he contacted the governor of New York and asked him to provide either military personnel or marshals to help him recover his daughter from kidnappers.

When the governor said he didn't have people he could sent to New Orleans to help him, the governor suggested he contact the president of the United States and ask him for help in providing the men.

Henry thanked him and called the White House and asked to speak with the president. He was told by a secretary that she would give the president the message and have him return the call.

Ten minutes later the president returned his call and asked Henry, "What can I do for you?"

Henry explained to the president that his daughter had been kidnapped in New Orleans and he wanted to get some men to help find and free her.

The president explained that the United States didn't have federal agents that could help in that kind of a crime, but he could supply a combination of US marshals and a small army unit, but Henry would have to pay all their expenses and their salaries for the time they were with him.

Henry agreed to pay their salaries and their expenses and then asked, "How soon can you get these people to New York City?"

The president said he was sure they could be in New York by the next afternoon.

Henry thanked him and told the president he certainly appreciated his help.

Henry sent a telegram to Rocky to let him know he was coming to New Orleans and was bringing some people to help find Latesha.

Next, Henry told his chief of security, Chuck Carson, he wanted him and as many of his men that they could spare away from the estate to go with him to New Orleans to help search for Latesha.

Henry had hired Chuck Carson as his chief of security after Chuck retired from the army.

Chuck was a colonel at the time of his retirement and was due to be promoted to general, but he would have been assigned to a post somewhere out west. His wife, Sarah, was so tired of moving from post to post, or worse, being left alone after she had been alone for so much of her married life.

After thinking about it for a short time, Chuck decided to take retirement, and when Henry heard about Chuck retiring, and since Henry had met Chuck and knew of his excellent military record, he offered him the job as his chief of security.

Chuck was a graduate of West Point almost at the end of the Civil War, but he soon found his way into several of the battles, first as a platoon leader and then as a company commander.

He and his company were highly decorated by the end of the war. Then he was assigned to several tours of duty out west and finally came back to West Point as an instructor of military tactics.

Chuck told Henry he would need to leave about six of his men at the estate to be sure everything there would be properly protected. That was fine with Henry. As far as Henry was concerned, the only one he really wanted to go with him was Chuck so he would be able to work with the local police in New Orleans, plus the federal agents and troops coming from Washington.

The following day the federal marshals, along with a platoon of soldiers, arrived just as the president had told Henry they would.

Henry had accommodations for these men at a hotel near the train station where they would be leaving the following morning.

Chuck met with the chief marshal, Captain Robert Lawrence, and the commander of the army unit, Captain Leon Cooper, and explained who he was and what his position was working for Henry Hudson.

Captain Lawrence knew Chuck because he was a platoon leader in one of his companies, and Captain Cooper knew him as well from serving with him in Virginia as a first sergeant when Chuck Carson was the post commander.

Both men liked and respected Chuck and were pleased to be working with him trying to find Latesha.

They were very surprised and so impressed and pleased to meet Henry Hudson IV the next day.

They both knew he was one of the richest and most powerful men in the country and found he was also one of the nicest, most considerate men they had ever met in their lives.

Henry was concerned if their hotel rooms were okay and if they had been well fed and if there was anything they needed before the train left New York.

They both explained their rooms were very nice, that they had plenty to eat and drink, and that even their men were happy with the food.

Henry seemed to be pleased to hear they had been well taken care of by the hotel, and he promised he would do his best to see to it that they and their men were well looked after on the long train ride to New Orleans.

Because they were on a special train, using several different railroad companies' tracks, it took them four days to arrive in New Orleans since they had to sit on side tracks and watch as the regular trains went by several times during the trip.

When they arrived in New Orleans, Captains Cooper and Lawrence assembled their men in formation and marched them from the train station to the hotel near where Henry's special train would remain parked for as long as they were in New Orleans.

Henry had made arrangements to take over the closest hotel to his train, the New Orleans River Hotel, for the men he brought with him to help look for Latesha.

As the men marched along from the train to the hotel, several of the local men who saw them marching made some very unkind remarks about the "damn Yankee soldiers" and called for them to go home!

Henry decided the hotel was not in the best part of the city, but he was told by Captains Cooper and Lawrence that the rooms in the hotel were fine.

While the men were getting settled into the hotel, Henry, Chuck, and the two captains went to the Crescent Hotel to meet with Rocky.

Rocky was really happy to see his father-in-law and told Henry how bad he felt about Latesha being kidnapped but was so pleased he had come to help him find Latesha.

Where's My Wife?

Henry introduced Rocky to the men he brought with him to help in the search for Latesha and explained to the men that Rocky was his son-in-law.

All the men knew Rocky Stone from the dime novels he wrote and were pleased to meet him.

Rocky said, "I want to thank each one of you for coming to help me search for my wife. It means so much to me. I'll never forget it."

All the while they were talking, Nick lay at Rocky's feet.

Henry said, "Rocky, when did you and Latesha get a dog?"

"It's a long story, Henry, but we didn't get a dog. After Latesha was kidnapped, Nick here kind of adopted me. Nick is the dog's name, and I can't go anywhere without him. He watches over me like a hawk over a rabbit."

Henry replied, "Well, Rocky, it looks like you have made a new friend for life, and maybe Nick is watching out for you."

Then Rocky said, "I want to take you gentlemen to meet Detective Knox. He's in charge of the investigation and is a very good man. He's trying very hard but, I'm sorry to say, without much success."

Henry replied, "I think that's a good first step, so everyone knows what kind of effort the police department has been making up to this point."

Everyone agreed, and the group left the Crescent Hotel with Nick right by Rocky's side and proceeded to the police station to meet with Detective Knox.

When they arrived at the station, the smart-talking police desk sergeant said, "Well, Rocky, it looks like you brought a lot of reinforcements with you today."

"That's right, Sergeant, is Detective Knox in his office?"

"He is, Rocky. You go right on back. I know you know the way."

Rocky led the group of men back to Detective Knox's office, and when they arrived, Knox said, "Good morning, Rocky, I didn't know you were bringing guests. Let's go over to the conference room so your guests can have somewhere to sit down."

Detective Knox led the group to the conference room and asked the men to sit down.

When they were all seated at the conference table, Rocky said, "Gentlemen, this is Detective Captain Doc Knox."

Each of the men acknowledged Captain Knox, and then Rocky said, "Doc, I want to introduce you to Latesha's father, Henry Hudson. Next to Henry is Chuck Carson, who's in charge of security for my father-in-law. Next to Chuck is Captain Robert Lawrence, head of a military platoon, here to assist us in finding Latesha, and last is Captain Leon Cooper, commander of the US Marshal Unit sent to help us."

Doc Knox was overwhelmed being introduced to these men and said, "Gentlemen, first I want to say thank you for coming to New Orleans to help us look for Latesha Hudson Stone. I can tell you it is greatly appreciated. Also since we have so many captains, I would like to propose we resort to only using our first names. I'm Doc."

Henry replied, "Well, I'm not a captain, and Chuck is a colonel, but first names works for me."

All the rest of the men at the conference table nodded their heads in agreement.

Doc stuttered a little as he began to speak, "Thank you, Henry. I would like to bring all of you up to date on the investigation of Latesha's kidnapping. I'm sorry to say we have nothing except the two ransom notes. We have combed this city for clues and talked with every informer we have, and we have no other clues whatsoever.

"It's unbelievable when no one in the underworld in this city knows anything about the kidnapping. As I said, no one seems to know anything about the kidnapping, and because of this we have to think the kidnapping was done by people who are not from New Orleans."

Henry asked, "Did you think some of these people would talk if you offered them enough money?"

Doc replied, "Considering the $150,000 reward Rocky has already offered and how no one has come forward yet, I would have to say no. We just don't believe anyone from New Orleans knows anything about the kidnapping. I can tell you most of the people in our underworld would sell out their own mother for a couple of thousand dollars, much less have a chance of getting $150,000."

Henry said, "I just had to ask, because if more money would do it, we would get it in a minute. We certainly would be willing to pay them more money, a lot more money, if it would help us get Latesha back to us."

Chuck asked, "Doc, what else have you done trying to find Latesha?"

"Chuck, we have tried to check out some of the old warehouses along the riverfront, but we have a limited number of men who can search them, and there are a lot of warehouses in the area. So far, we have found nothing, but we are still trying."

Henry asked, "Would more men help you in the search?"

"It certainly would, Henry."

Henry replied, "Well, how about forty-five more men? That's what we brought with us."

"Wow! That would be great, Henry."

Henry said, "Doc, you work with Chuck, and Leon and Robert will organize the search of the warehouses for you, if that would help?"

"It would certainly help. I would greatly appreciate all the help we can get."

Rocky said, "Henry, I think we should let these men work out the details of the search and we should go back to the hotel."

Henry was a little puzzled by Rocky's statement but replied, "Okay, Rocky, if you think that's best."

As Rocky and Henry and Nick were leaving, Doc had given out maps of the city, which were now spread out on the conference table to show where they had searched.

The three men Henry brought from New York were busy dividing up the other areas of the city so each of them knew which area of the city they would be searching for Latesha.

After Rocky and Henry were out of the police station, Rocky said, "I want to take you to someone else who has close contact with the underworld of New Orleans. His name is Ruby Red Cato. He runs the Red Dog Saloon. I want to talk to him to see if he was able to find out anything about Latesha. I think he has better connections on what going on in the crime world in New Orleans than Doc Knox and his people have."

"Okay, Rocky, I was wondering why you wanted to get away from the police station so fast. I understand now."

CHAPTER FOURTEEN

The Visit with Ruby Red

Rocky, Henry, and Nick made their way to the Red Dog Saloon to meet with Ruby Red Cato.

As Rocky, Henry, and Nick made their way past the saloon's bouncer, Rocky said, "Boris, we're going back to Ruby Red's office."

The bouncer replied, "Okay, Mr. Stone."

After they were some distance away from the bouncer, Henry said, "That fellow is a real brute of a man. I certainly wouldn't want to tangle with him."

"Neither would I. I think the guy was an ex-fighter or an ex-bodyguard for somebody who everyone hated. So the guy had to have the meanest and toughest bodyguard there was, so they had Boris."

In spite of the circumstances, Henry still had to laugh at what Rocky said about the bouncer being an ex-bodyguard to someone who everyone hated.

By this time they had reached Ruby Red's office, and Rocky knocked quietly on the office door. Rocky heard Ruby say, "Come on in."

Rocky and Nick entered the door first, with Henry following right behind them.

When Ruby saw Rocky, he said, "Rocky, I was just thinking about you. Come on in and have a seat."

Rocky and Nick approached Ruby's desk and said, "Ruby, I want to introduce you to my father-in-law, Henry Hudson." He turned. "Henry, I want you to meet Ruby Red Cato."

Ruby replied, "How do you do, Mr. Hudson? I'm pleased to meet you. I'm very sorry about your daughter being kidnapped."

"Thank you, Ruby, please call me Henry."

Then the two men shook hands, and Ruby said, "Please have a seat, Mr. Hudson—I mean, Henry."

The three men sat down with Ruby seated behind his desk and Rocky and Henry seated across the desk from Ruby, with Nick lying at Rocky's feet.

Ruby said, "Rocky, I wish I could give you better news about what I've found out about your wife's kidnapping. After shaking down all my sources, I found no one who knows anything about it. I've come to the conclusion that whoever kidnapped your wife is not associated with any of the local New Orleans' gangs."

Rocky asked, "Ruby, do you think whoever kidnapped Latesha was from out of town?"

"That's my best guess. I've called in a lot of favors and offered a lot of money to people, and the only answer I ever got was the same: no one knows anything about any kidnapping in New Orleans or the killing of the two women. I'm telling you, Rocky, nobody knows nothing."

"Ruby, you came up with the same thing the New Orleans Police Department did. They believe whoever took Latesha is from out of town. So right now, they, along with people Henry brought from back east, are getting ready to search every warehouse in New Orleans to see if they can find Latesha."

"Rocky, that sounds like a good plan to me. I only hope they have some luck searching the warehouses and finding Latesha for you. Because I sure didn't have any luck getting you any answers on who took your wife or where she was been held. I believe maybe that's the only hope you have of finding her."

"Ruby, you don't understand. I will find her, and I'll make the men pay for taking her."

Ruby replied, "You know, Rocky, somehow I believe you will, and I hope I'm around to see it when you do. Rocky, just so you know. I plan to keep trying to find out anything that might help you rescue your wife from these men."

"Thank you, Ruby, I know both Henry and I appreciate whatever you can do to help us."

Henry had sat there without ever saying a word, but as they were leaving Ruby's office, he said, "Thank you for your time, Ruby. I will certainly appreciate it if you keep trying to help us find my daughter. She means the world to me, and I don't want to lose her."

"You can be sure my men and I will keep working to find her for you and Rocky."

"Thank you, Ruby."

By the time Rocky, Henry, and Nick returned to Henry's train car, they found that Buddy Larson from the *Picayune* newspaper was waiting outside Henry's private train car for them."

Rocky asked, "Mr. Larson, what are you doing here?"

"Well, it's not every day someone arrives in New Orleans with their own private train, so I had to find out who it was."

Rocky explained, "Mr. Larson, I want to introduce you to my father-in-law, Mr. Henry Hudson. This is his train, and he came from New York to help us find Latesha."

"Henry, this gentleman is Mr. Buddy Larson. He's with the *Picayune* newspaper of New Orleans."

Henry stuck out his hand to shake hands with Buddy Larson and said, "How do you do, Mr. Lawson? What can I do for you?"

Buddy asked, "Mr. Hudson, can you tell me what you are doing here in New Orleans?"

"Buddy, obviously, I'm here to help my son-in-law, Rocky Stone, find my daughter, his wife, and rescue her from her kidnappers."

"Mr. Hudson, how do you plan to do this?"

"Well, Mr. Larson, I didn't plan to do it by myself. I brought my chief of security, Chuck Carson, and some of his security force, as well as a company of US marshals and platoon of a US Army unit."

"I see, Mr. Hudson, so what are these men doing right now?"

"They are proceeding to make the effort to search for my daughter in all of the warehouses along the Mississippi River here in New Orleans."

"Do you believe she's being held in a warehouse here in New Orleans?"

"We don't know for sure that's where she's being held, but we have reason to believe it."

"Mr. Hudson, how long do you and your men plan to stay here in New Orleans?"

"As long as it takes to get my daughter back."

Larson continued to write notes from his interview with Henry Hudson as they talked.

Lawson asked a few more questions about the train and when they left New York City and where the men came from to help search for Latesha.

When Henry told Mr. Lawson the president of the United States offered the marshals and the soldiers to help him find his daughter, he was very impressed.

Henry explained to Larson the only condition the president had for the men's help was that Henry was to pay their salaries and their expenses for as long as Henry needed them.

Larson had his headline for tomorrow's newspaper: *President of the United States Sends US Marshals and US Army Troops to New Orleans to Help Find Latesha Hudson Stone.*

CHAPTER FIFTEEN

Reactions to Today's Newspaper Story

The mayor's secretary said, "Mr. Mayor, have you seen today's *Picayune* paper?"

"No, Charles, what's in it?"

Charles held up the paper so the mayor could see the front page, and the mayor screamed, "Good god, why do I have find out about this by reading it in the damn newspaper? I'm the damn mayor of this city, and nobody tells me anything!"

The mayor grabbed the newspaper out of Charles's hands and stormed into his office and slammed the door behind him.

Twenty minutes later, the mayor came out of his office and said, "Charles, send somebody over to Mr. Hudson's private railroad car with a note from me inviting him to visit me in my office so I can ask him what I can do to help him find his daughter.

"Then get all of my key men in here for a meeting as soon as they can all be located. Make sure they know I mean for them to be in my office posthaste. Got it, Charles?"

"Yes, sir, Mr. Mayor, I'll have a note sent to Mr. Hudson right away and get our runners looking for your key men for a meeting posthaste."

"Good, Charles."

Then the mayor returned to his office to reread the story in the newspaper again.

After the mayor read the story for a third time, he slammed the paper down on his desk and exclaimed, "That damn newspaper editor has always hated my guts, that no good son of a bitch. I'll bet he's happy this morning, laughing his head off because I didn't know a damn thing about the president sending troops and marshals here to look for Latesha Stone right here in my city. Damn his soul anyway."

At about the same time, in one of the old warehouses on the riverfront, Sandy Barr handed today's copy of the *Picayune* newspaper to his boss, Charlie Christian, and when Charlie opened up the newspaper and saw the headlines, he yelled at Sandy, Tom, and the rest of his men to come quick.

When all his men were gathered around him, Charlie said, "Do you have any idea what's in the newspaper today?"

The men all shook their heads and said, "No, boss, what's in it?"

"It says the father of the girl we kidnapped, whose name is Henry Hudson IV, got the president of the United States to send US marshals and Yankee soldiers to New Orleans to help him find his daughter."

Tom Barr said, "That don't sound good to me, boss."

Charlie replied, "It ain't good, that's for sure, and we've got to move fast, because it also says in the paper that the soldiers, marshals and police are searching all of the warehouses along the waterfront for her. Tom, you and Sandy go quickly and rent a team with a wagon. Then stop at an undertaker, buy a coffin, and get back here as soon as you can, got it?"

Tom responded, "We've got it, boss."

Tom and Sandy left the warehouse, where they had been staying after they kidnapped Latesha, to rent a team and a wagon as their boss told them to do.

After they left Charlie said, "I want you guys to clean this place up and be ready to leave here as soon as Tom and Sandy get back. While you men are cleaning things up around here, I'm going to see if I can find someplace to rent where we can stay for the next few days until we get rid of the woman."

Then his men started working at getting everything cleaned up in the building.

Charlie left to find somewhere they could hole up for a few more days before they got the ransom money and returned the woman to her husband and father.

Charlie thought it would be a good idea if they moved either across the river into Algiers or somewhere farther away from the river, like maybe in the Quarter.

The one thing he didn't like about being in the Quarter was there was always too much going on there, night and day. Charlie decided the Quarter was too risky for them.

He decided to take the Canal Street/Algiers Ferry across to Algiers and see what he could find there to rent for a few days.

When he got to Algiers, he began walking along the riverbank until he saw a sign for a small business building that was for rent on Alix Street.

He turned down Alix Street and found the building that was for rent. It was right on the corner of Bounty and Alix Streets.

It looked like it could use a lot of work as it had large windows that had been painted over.

He couldn't see anything through the windows about the condition inside the building, which made Charlie think the building would be perfect for them.

On the building was an address for the owner of the building, a real estate company named Jones Realty.

Charlie remembered seeing a sign for that company as he was getting off the ferryboat; in fact, it was located just across the street from the ferryboat office.

Charlie walked back to the ferryboat office and saw the Jones Realty office was just where he remembered.

Charlie went into the Jones Realty office and told the man working at a desk that he was interested in the business building they had for rent over on Alix Street.

The man said, "I'm Bob Jones, and we still do have that building for rent right now, although I have someone who's thinking about renting the building, though he hasn't made up his mind yet. What kind of business are you thinking about starting?"

"Does it make any difference what kind of business I'm thinking about starting?"

"No, but I think I can tell you if you're likely to have any success in that location since I've been in this business for a long time so I have a good idea what type of businesses could make it in that location."

Charlie thought for a minute and said, "A funeral parlor, you know our clients are just dying to get into our place—sorry, a little undertaker's humor."

"Well, mister, what did you say your name was?"

"I didn't, but it's Charlie Bassett."

"Mr. Bassett, I think your business could do very well in that location."

"How much is the rent per month?"

"Fifty dollars a month."

"Fifty dollars. Well, that's a little more than I planned to spend, but I guess I can do it."

"Okay, Mr. Bassett, I'll be happy to show you the property right now."

"You know, Mr. Jones, that won't be necessary because we'll have to fix the property up anyway to be able to use it for our business. So I'll go ahead and take it right now, if you will give me the key.

"I can pay you, and we can begin working on getting the place set up for our business."

"Okay, Mr. Bassett, I'll just draw up the rental agreement for one year, with the rent payable today for the first and last month's rent."

"All right, Mr. Jones, go ahead and fill out the papers so I can get going."

Jones filled out the papers, and Charlie paid him a hundred dollars and then got the next ferry back to Canal Street.

By the time Charlie returned to the warehouse, Tom and Sandy were back with a team and wagon, and they had already brought the coffin inside the warehouse.

Charlie told the gang to gather up all their things and put them in the wagon, but to leave room for the coffin on one side of the wagon, and then start walking down to the ferry boat office.

Charlie told Tom and Sandy to bring the coffin into Latesha's room, where they placed her inside the coffin.

Latesha wasn't dead, but she looked like she could be. She never made a move or a sound when they picked her up and put her in the coffin.

Next, they loaded the coffin onto the wagon.

Tom had made sure he left the lid up a little so Latesha had some air to breathe.

After they loaded the coffin into the wagon, Charlie covered the coffin with a large black cloth, but just as they were getting ready to pull away from the warehouse, a Yankee soldier came up to them and asked, "You men just bring that coffin out of that warehouse?"

Charlie said, "Yes, sir, captain, we had to pick up this woman's body from this warehouse. The owner found her body there this morning and asked us to pick it up and bury her. The owner's a real nice guy. He even paid us extra money to bury her. He said he guessed she broke into the warehouse and had been living there for some time because he said that the warehouse had been empty for a long time."

The soldier said, "I'm not a captain, but I'm going to have to look at that body before you leave because we're looking for a woman who's been kidnapped."

Charlie said, "No problem, but don't get too close to the body because we think she might have died from typhoid fever. You can't be too careful."

Tom climbed up into the wagon, with the soldier following right behind him.

Tom pulled the black cloth back from the coffin and opened the coffin.

The soldier took one look at Latesha and said, "That's sure not the woman we're looking for, and she's sure dead. Okay, you men can go on your way to bury this poor lady."

Charlie said, "Thank you, captain."

The soldier smiled to be mistaken for a captain. The other men in his unit were going to be surprised to hear about his day, when somebody thought a private was a captain.

As the wagon was moving down the street, a whole lot of soldiers came walking down the street toward them and stopped and watched as they drove past them. Some of the soldiers even took off their caps when they saw the coffin in the back of the wagon.

Tom drove the wagon to the Algiers-Canal Street Ferry port and waited for the ferry to return from Algiers. While they sat waiting for the ferry, several more Yankee soldiers came walking down Canal Street.

After they and their wagon were safely on the ferry and the ferry was moving across the Mississippi River toward Algiers, Charlie said, "We need to send a thank-you letter to the *Picayune* newspaper for running that story this morning about the warehouses being searched. It certainly saved us. You know, Tom, it's better to be lucky than good. You know, that Yankee boy who peeked at the woman in the coffin wouldn't know a dead person if he saw one, which was really good for us.

"He stupidly saved his life and saved me from spending a bullet."

Tom said, "You know, Charlie, you're a hard-hearted son of a gun."

Charlie replied, "That's why I'm still alive. In our business if you ever become softhearted, that's when you get killed."

Tom retorted, "You're going to live to be an old bastard then, because you never have had a kind thought in your head, and I'm not sure you even have a heart."

Charlie agreed, "You are absolutely right, Tom. I am going to live to a ripe old age with money to spend while you will be pushing up daisies."

They arrived at the port in Algiers, and Tom drove the wagon off the ferry and found the rest of their men waiting there for them.

Charlie directed them to their new hideout.

Charlie told Tom to drive down Bounty Street until he got to Alix Street and then turn right. Their building was on the corner of Bounty and Alix Streets.

As Tom drove the team down Bounty Street, the rest of the men followed along beside the wagon.

Arriving at the corner of Bounty and Alix Streets, Tom pulled the wagon up next to the building. The men who had been walking along with them took the coffin with Latesha in it off the wagon.

Charlie unlocked the door, and the men brought the coffin inside the building.

Charlie told them to take the coffin to the back room, then he had them set the coffin on the floor.

He told his men, "We need to go back to the used furniture store I saw as we were coming down Bounty Street and buy a bed for Latesha and a table and some chairs for us while we still have the wagon to bring the things back here."

Charlie and Tom took the wagon and made their way back to the used furniture store. Charlie bought a bed for Latesha, along with a table and several chairs, plus another small table and chair for Latesha.

They hauled the furniture back to the newly rented building, where Charlie got the rest of his men to unload the furniture and place it where he wanted it in their new hideout.

While the men were doing this, Sandy got some water and had it ready for Latesha when they got her out of the coffin and onto her bed.

As soon as they had her bed set up, Sandy and Tom lifted Latesha out of the coffin and put her carefully on the bed.

After Latesha was lying on her new bed for a few moments, Sandy took a wet cloth and rubbed it on her face and lips.

When Latesha felt the water on her lips, she began trying to get the wet washcloth into her mouth.

Sandy and Tom sat her up in her bed, and as Tom held her up, Sandy gave her a drink of water. He only let her have a small sip of water to start with. Then he let her hold the cup, and she drank the water down as quickly as she could and asked for more water.

Sandy looked at Tom, and Tom said, "Give her some more water."

Sandy refilled the cup, and Latesha drank the second cup down almost as quickly as she did the first cup.

Latesha said, "May I please have another cup of water? I'm so dry, please."

Tom took the empty cup from her hand and went to the bucket of water Sandy had brought in. He refilled the cup and brought it back to her and said, "Drink a little bit of it at a time so it doesn't make you sick, okay?"

Latesha replied, "Okay, just a little at a time."

This time Latesha took her time, taking only small sips of water at a time, and this cup of water lasted at least fifteen minutes.

Then Latesha said, "I think I have to lie back…"

Latesha couldn't quite finish her statement, so Tom did it for her, "Down."

Sandy caught her head and gently lay her head back down on her pillow and covered her up with small blanket.

Tom said quietly to Sandy, "We've got to get this girl something to eat. She's going to die if we don't."

Sandy whispered, "We can't, Tom. Charlie would kill us if we did."

"I don't know how we're going to get her something, but I'll be damned if I'm going to let her starve to death."

"Don't do it, Tommie. Charlie's just looking for an excuse to kill you. You know he doesn't like you anyway."

"Sandy, he doesn't like any of us, and if he gets his hands on that ransom money, I can tell you he doesn't plan to split any of the money with us. He plans to kill us all off, one at a time."

"What makes you say that?"

"Because he's a no-good, greedy bastard. He's never seen that much money at any one time in his life, so this is his big score, and he doesn't plan to share it. He told me today he plans to live to be an old man."

"Tom, do you think we should talk to the other men about your thoughts, about him keeping all of the money after he gets the ransom?"

"Sandy, I think we'd better plan to look out for ourselves because if we said anything to any of the others, they might tell Charlie, and our goose would be cooked. No, Sandy, we need to be sure we're always together, and we better do our best to keep him from killing this woman, or we will all hang for it if we're caught. I don't know about you, but I'd really like to live a lot more years."

"Me too, Tommie, and Ma and Pa won't be happy if we got ourselves hung."

"No, Sandy, they would die of shame."

It took a long time for all the mayor's so-called key men to be rounded up for a meeting with the mayor, and by the time they arrived at his office, the mayor had already had a meeting with Mr. Henry Hudson and his son-in-law, Rocky Stone.

The mayor was gracious to a fault, expressing his concerns about Latesha not being found after so many days and telling Mr. Hudson how much he appreciated him bringing the US marshals and the federal troops to help the New Orleans Police Department in the search for his daughter.

Henry Hudson was just as gracious, telling the mayor he knew how hard it was these days to have enough money to hire enough police officers to take care of the daily routine of everyday crimes in cities the size of New Orleans, much less the kidnapping of his daughter.

Henry also expressed his appreciation for the work his police department was doing and especially the efforts of Captain Doc Knox, who was working around the clock trying to find his daughter.

The short meeting ended with the mayor telling Mr. Hudson to let him know if there was anything he could personally do, in any way, to help in the recovery of his daughter.

Henry thanked him and said if he found anything the mayor could do for him, he would let him know right away, and the meeting ended.

After Henry and Rocky left the mayor's office, the mayor met with his six key men and asked them what they had been able to find out about the kidnapping of Latesha Stone, and to a man, they said they had found out nothing from any of the gangs operating in New Orleans.

Their conclusion was that whoever kidnapped her had to be from out of town since nobody had any idea of who was holding her.

The mayor said, "Gentlemen, we've got a big problem if these US marshals start doing too much investigating in New Orleans. This could bring down all of our businesses we have spent so many years building.

"All of you need to get back out on the street and keep pushing people to try to help find this damn girl before our empire crumbles. Don't leave any stone unturned, Keep talking to people see if anyone knows anything about renting a warehouse to a stranger in the last month or so.

"The police, marshals, and the Yankee soldiers are searching all of the warehouses right now, but that doesn't mean these people are still there. They may have got wind of the searching and have cleared out. If they did, it's probably because they read about the searching of warehouses in the damn *Picayune* newspaper. That damn editor would do anything to get rid of me."

One of the mayor's men said, "I told you we should have knocked him off a long time ago."

"Maybe you're right, but we sure can't do it right now."

CHAPTER SIXTEEN

The Investigation Continues

Detective Knox called for a meeting with all the principals involved in the search for Latesha Stone: Captain Robert Lawrence, commander of the US Army unit; Captain Leon Cooper, commander of the US marshals; and Colonel Chuck Carson, chief of security for the Hudson Bay Company, along with Rocky Stone and Henry Hudson IV, to discuss the lack of results of searching of the warehouses along the New Orleans waterfront.

Detective Knox said, "First, on behalf of the New Orleans Police Department, I want to thank each of you and your men for the help of searching all of the warehouses. I know I'm disappointed as much as Rocky and Henry are that the search yielded no results in finding Latesha.

"I want to ask each of you to interview all of your men to see if there is any possibility that we could have missed searching one of the warehouses or if during the search your men saw anything unusual that happened, anything at all. If possible, I would like to meet all of you again around two o'clock this afternoon. I guess I should ask all of you, will this give you enough time to talk with all of your people?"

Everyone agreed that would be enough time.

Knox said, "Good, then I will see everyone back here at two o'clock."

After Captains Lawrence and Cooper and Chuck Carson left to talk with their men, Rocky and Henry waited to talk with Detective Knox.

Rocky said, "Doc, it doesn't look very good to me right now that we're going to find her in time to save her."

Henry said, "Doc, do you have any new ideas on how we can find Latesha?"

Doc answered, "Rocky, don't give up on us yet, and, Henry, I do have one idea that might help us to find Latesha, and that is for you to offer a $250,000 reward for information for finding and saving Latesha. Include in the offer immunity from prosecution if Latesha is returned alive and the kidnappers are captured or killed."

Rocky said, "Doc, do you think offering a reward for more money will help us find Latesha?"

"Rocky, I think offering the additional money and the immunity from prosecution will make one of those gang members think pretty hard about double-crossing the rest of the gang. For that kind of money and not be going to prison, yes, I do."

Henry said, "Then let's get it done today. Maybe we could have the *Picayune* newspaper put out a special edition of the paper to make the announcement of the increase in the reward and immunity from prosecution."

Doc said, "That's a great idea. We don't have much more time before Rocky has to pay the ransom. What do you have, a day or is it two days?"

Rocky replied, "One day. Okay, Henry, let's get to the newspaper office."

Rocky, Henry, and Nick left the police station and walked directly to the *Picayune* newspaper office, and Rocky asked to speak with the managing editor, Mr. Zwald.

The man he spoke to asked them to follow him, and he took them to Mr. Zwald's office.

When Mr. Zwald saw Rocky, he said, "Come in, Rocky, what can I do for you?"

"Mr. Zwald, I would like to introduce you to my father-in-law, Henry Hudson."

Mr. Zwald said, "How do you do, Mr. Hudson? I've heard a lot of good things about you, and it gives me great pleasure having the opportunity to meet you."

Henry stuck out his right hand and said, "Well, Mr. Zwald, I'm very happy to meet you and hope you don't believe everything people have said about me."

Zwald asked, "As I said to Rocky, and since you're here, I'll change that to 'what can I do for both of you'?"

Henry answered, "We're going to ask you to do what your newspaper may never have done before—we want you to put out a special edition to help us find Latesha Stone."

Zwald said, "You want us to put out a special edition of our newspaper? When would you want us to do it?"

Henry said, "Today, as soon as you could get it printed."

Zwald replied, "You want us to print a special edition of our newspaper today to help you find your daughter, is that right?"

Henry said, "That's exactly right. We need something on the street today. I guess the one thing I didn't say was, I will pay you for whatever it costs to get it printed and on the street, but it has to be today. Otherwise it might be too late to keep my daughter alive."

Rocky said, "Mr. Zwald, I have to pay the ransom tomorrow, and we believe that as soon as I pay the ransom, the kidnappers plan to kill Latesha. That's why the special edition has to be out today."

Zwald asked, "What all do you want in this special edition?"

Rocky responded, "In the biggest type you can print. We want a story offering $250,000 reward for the return of Latesha Stone alive and for the capture or killing of her kidnappers with full immunity from prosecution."

Zwald asked, "Will the police go along with the immunity from prosecution for an informer?"

Rocky replied, "It was Captain Knox's idea. He thinks this may be our only chance of saving Latesha."

Zwald said, "Knox may be right, so we will do your special edition. A newspaper doesn't usually get to be in the position of helping to save a life. Normally we only get to print about someone being killed."

Zwald opened his office door and shouted, "Get Buddy Larson in here right now."

Everyone in the office started yelling for Buddy Larson to go to Mr. Zwald's office.

A couple of minutes later, Buddy Larson came into Mr. Zwald's office and said, "Are you looking for me, Mr. Zwald?"

Zwald said, "Buddy, you already know Rocky and Mr. Hudson. They've got a job for us, and I need you to take the lead on it. We're putting out a special edition of the *Picayune* newspaper this afternoon to help find and save Latesha Stone, and you can use my office to interview Rocky and Mr. Hudson."

Buddy asked, "We're putting out a special edition of the newspaper this afternoon?"

Zwald answered, "That's what I just told you, so you'd better get busy and get the story."

"Yes, sir, I'm on it!"

Then Buddy asked, "Rocky, what do you want this special edition to be about?"

"My father-in-law and I want big headlines, as big as the paper can print, announcing a $250,000 reward for information leading to the rescue and capture or killing of her kidnappers. Further, the informer will be given immunity from prosecution if they were involved in the kidnapping. Do you understand what I'm saying?"

Buddy said, "I know what you are saying, but I don't understand it. Why would you make such an offer?"

Rocky answered, "Buddy, we don't have much time left before I have to pay the ransom, and we think as soon as the kidnappers have the money, they plan to kill Latesha."

"Okay, Rocky, I understand it now. I'll get the story written and have it ready for the press in an hour. Who should I say to contact with the information?"

Rocky said, "They can either contact Captain Knox of the New Orleans Police Department, or me at the Crescent Hotel, or Buddy Larson at the *Picayune* newspaper. How about that?"

Buddy asked, "Are you sure you would want to include me as one of the people to contact with the information?"

Rocky replied, "I'm sure. The person might feel safer talking to a newspaper reporter than to me or the police department. However, you're going to have to stay at the newspaper until tomorrow night to be sure you're available for them to contact you."

Buddy said, "Okay, I'll do it. I can tell you, though, I'll feel a lot better about it if they contact either you or Captain Knox. I'm not sure I could handle such a thing."

Rocky answered, "Of course you can, you're a newspaper reporter. You are used to getting people to talk."

Buddy said, "I'm glad you're sure, but I've got to get going on the story right now if we're going to have this special edition out this afternoon."

When Buddy finished saying this, he turned and left to go to his desk to write the story.

Three hours later the special edition was ready to hit the streets of New Orleans.

The special edition screamed these headlines:

> REWARD FOR INFORMATION LEADING TO THE SAFE RETURN OF LATESHA STONE WHO WAS KIDNAPPED
>
> REWARD HAS BEEN INCREASED TO $250,000, ALONG WITH THE OFFER OF COMPLETE IMMUNITY FROM PROSECUTION
>
> CONTACT CAPTAIN KNOX WITH THE NEW ORLEANS POLICE DEPT. OR ROCKY STONE AT ROOM ONE AT THE CRESCENT HOTEL OR REPORTER BUDDY LARSON AT THE PICAYUNE NEWSPAPER

Buddy handed copies of the newspapers to Rocky and Mr. Hudson and said, "What do you think? Will you get any takers on this deal?"

Rocky said, "I certainly hope so. If not, I'm afraid they're going to kill my wife."

Henry Hudson said, "Buddy, you did a great job. If anything can get Latesha some help, this newspaper should do it."

Buddy said, "Thank you, Mr. Hudson, I certainly hope it works."

Rocky said, "Buddy, we're going to go over to the Crescent Hotel to be sure I'm available if someone comes there with information about Latesha. One last thing, if you hear anything from someone, contact Captain Knox as quickly as you can, okay?"

Buddy replied, "Don't worry, I'll get in touch with him if I'm contacted by anyone.

"These papers are being distributed in New Orleans and throughout all of the surrounding areas of New Orleans."

When Captain Lawrence talked with his men who had been involved in searching the warehouses in the area assigned to them, everyone was sure they had been in every warehouse and they had checked off each of the warehouses on their maps.

When Captain Lawrence asked if anything unusual happened during the search of the warehouses, no one answered that they had seen anything until one of his men in the back of the room said, "Sir, I did have one thing which I would say was unusual. I stopped a wagon with a coffin on it and asked where they were going, and the men said they were on the way to bury a woman."

All the other men started to laugh at hearing these men were on their way to bury a coffin because they thought, *What else were they going to do with a coffin?*

The solider said, "I asked the men where they picked the body up, and they told me from inside the warehouse the wagon was in front of.

"They said the man who owned the building found the body that morning, and he asked them to pick up the woman's body and bury her. They said he told them she must have broken into the building because it wasn't open, and it looked like she had been staying there for some time. There was a sign in front of the building saying the warehouse was for rent. I had them open the coffin, and there was a dead woman in the coffin all right, but it certainly wasn't Latesha Stone. This woman looked much older than the picture of Mrs. Stone."

Captain Lawrence said, "Solider, show me on the map where this warehouse is located."

The solider came up to Captain Lawrence, looked at the map, and placed his finger on the location on the warehouse.

Captain Lawrence asked the sergeant who had been in charge of searching the warehouses on that street if they actually went in and searched that warehouse, and the sergeant said, "No, sir, the warehouse was locked up, and no one was around."

Captain Lawrence thanked the men for the information and said he would talk with Detective Knox about that warehouse that afternoon.

Captain Cooper talked with his men, and no one observed anything unusual during the search of their warehouses.

Same story for Chuck Carson's men, nothing unusual observed during their search.

The three men went back to the police station to meet with Detective Knox, and when Captain Lawrence told him about the wagon and a coffin, Detective Knox yelled at Detective Clyde Johnson to come into the room where they were meeting.

Detective Johnson asked Doc, "Yes, sir, do you have something we need to check out?"

"I want you and Detective Seth Black to go check out this warehouse. It didn't get searched because it was empty and had a For Rent sign in front of it. We need to check it out anyway."

"We're on it, Captain Knox."

Detective Johnson told Detective Black they had an assignment to check out another warehouse.

When Detectives Johnson and Black arrived at the warehouse, they saw who the rental agent was and went directly to their office and told them they needed to check out the warehouse they had for rent.

They were told that actually, the warehouse they were talking about was rented for a month right now and there should be somebody there.

Detective Johnson said, "We just came from the warehouse, and it's all locked up, and we have to search it because we're looking for a woman who's been kidnapped. We have reason to believe she is being held in a warehouse."

The manager of the rental agency, Leo Banks, overheard the conversation in his office and came out to where the detectives and his clerk where talking and said, "I'll take you down to the see the warehouse since I'm the one who rented it."

Detective Black asked, "What's your name?"

"My name is Leo Banks. I'm the manager of the rental agency."

"Mr. Banks, I'm Detective Black, and this is Detective Johnson. We would appreciate it if you would show us through the warehouse."

"No problem, just let me get a key for the building."

Mr. Banks took a key out of a key cabinet and started out the office door with Detectives Johnson and Black following right behind him.

As they were walking over to the warehouse, Mr. Banks said, "We don't normally rent out a building for just one month, but an old friend of mine, Dotty Ferguson, asked me to do it, so I told her I'd do it for her."

Johnson said, "Did you say your friend's name was Dotty Ferguson?"

"Yes, that's right. She came into my office a few days ago and said one of her friends had a small shipment coming in, and they needed a place to keep the small shipment for a few days until they could move it on."

Black asked, "Did you know Dotty Ferguson was murdered a few days ago?"

"No, I haven't heard anything about it. I quit taking the newspaper a few weeks ago because I was tired of reading nothing but bad news."

Johnson said, "I guess you don't know anything about the kidnapping of a woman by the name of Latesha Stone. She's the woman we're searching for. We have a feeling the people who kidnapped Mrs. Stone were the ones who rented your warehouse."

"Oh no, I hope not."

Black said, "We know Dotty Ferguson was killed by the people who kidnapped Mrs. Stone. In the ransom note they sent to Rocky

Stone, they said they killed her. They said they wanted to show him how serious they were. If he failed to pay the ransom, they would kill Mrs. Stone just like they did Dotty Ferguson."

When the three men got close to the warehouse, Detective Johnson said, "Seth, I don't know if we should go into the warehouse by ourselves without have some backup since we have no idea how many of the kidnappers there are."

Black said, "I don't think we should wait for help. These people may be getting ready to kill Mrs. Stone if they haven't done it already."

Johnson replied, "Okay, I agree, let's get our guns out and be ready to shoot. Mr. Banks, as soon as you unlock the door, get away from the door and stay outside until we give you the okay to come in."

Banks unlocked the door and jumped back away from the door as Johnson and Black ran into the building and hit the floor, pointing their weapons at anything that might be waiting for them inside the building.

When they didn't see anyone or hear anything, they got to their feet and went into the next room with their weapons at the ready; again, there was no one in sight or no noise except their hard breathing.

They continued to check the building room by room and found no one in the building.

After making their way through the entire building except for one room where the door was closed, they came back to the room with the closed door.

Johnson motioned to Black to open the door and then get back away from it. When he did, Johnson rushed into the room and again fell hard onto the floor, waving his weapon all around, ready to shoot anyone in sight.

Same story, there was no one in the room. Johnson said, "Seth, go back and tell Mr. Banks he can come in. The building is all clear."

While Seth was making his way back to the front door of the warehouse, Clyde looked around and found a lamp and lit it so he could see what was in this room.

After the lamp was lit, he saw that the room had been used for a bedroom since it had a bed and a dresser in it.

Clyde looked the room over carefully and could see the room had been recently been cleaned up. He continued to look all around on the floor and saw something shining on the floor next to the head of the bed. Whatever the object was, it was wedged between the bed and the wall.

Clyde got down on the floor and managed to get the object free, and when he was able to get up from the floor and closer to the lamplight, Clyde saw it was a very fancy button.

Clyde was sure it was a button from a woman's fancy dress, probably not from some warehouse worker's wife's clothes.

When Seth and Mr. Banks made their way back to the bedroom, Clyde showed the button to both of them.

Bank said, "I don't think Dotty Ferguson's dresses would have had fancy buttons on them like this."

Clyde asked, "When you rented the warehouse to Dotty for a month, did you have any paperwork she filled out?"

Banks replied, "Yes, she filled out a standard rental agreement form."

Clyde asked, "Can we see the rental form?"

"Certainly, the one thing I remember is the name of the company she listed as the renter of the building because it was the darnedest name I ever heard of for a company."

Clyde asked, "What was the name of the company?"

"It was called *The Rocky Payback Company*, darnedest name I ever heard."

Clyde said, "Mr. Banks, we're going to need that rental agreement."

"No problem, are you finished checking out the building?"

"No, we need to carefully go through the building. It may takes us another hour or so to completely check the building out. If you want to go back to your office and find the rental agreement for us, you leave us the key. We'll lock the building up and bring you back your key."

"Thank you, Detective Johnson, I'll find the rental agreement for you and have it ready for you to pick up when you're finished going through the building and dropping my key off."

"Thank you, Mr. Banks, we'll do that."

Banks left to go back to his office, and Clyde and Seth went back to the front of the building and took their time, carefully checking over every room in the warehouse.

The button off a lady's fancy dress was the only thing they found that didn't appear to belong in the warehouse.

Clyde and Seth stopped by Mr. Banks's office and dropped off the key for the building and picked up the rental agreement and returned to the police station.

When they got back to the police station, they went directly to Captain Knox's office and found he was there talking with Rocky Stone and Henry Hudson IV.

Knox asked, "What did you finding out about the warehouse we missed when we were searching all the warehouses along the waterfront?"

Johnson replied, "We found that it had been rented by Dotty Ferguson for a company called *the Rocky Payback Company*, and the only thing we found in the warehouse that we thought was important is this lady's button."

Doc said, "Rocky, take a look at this button and see if you can recognize it as belonging to Latesha."

Detective Johnson handed the button to Rocky, and he said, "Yes, it's a button from the dress she was wearing when we boarded the steamboat.

"It was one of the new dresses she bought here in New Orleans."

Doc asked, "Rocky, what do you think the name of the company means?"

Rocky answered, "I think it means exactly what you think it means. The people kidnapped Latesha to get even with me for something I did to them. I don't have a clue of who wants to get even with me. I wish I did because maybe that would help us find them. I know one thing we need to do is to find out where that coffin came from that the solider saw the woman's body in by that warehouse."

Doc said, "Clyde, you and Seth check out all of the undertakers that are located near our warehouse and get some men to check on the livery stables to find out who rented a team and wagon yesterday."

Clyde replied, "No problem. Seth, why don't you take some men and check out the livery stables, and I'll take some to check on the undertakers."

Seth said, "Sounds good to me. I'm on my way."

Henry asked, "Rocky, you don't have any idea who it is that wants to get even with you?"

"I'm sorry, Henry, I don't know if it is somebody who doesn't like my books or if it's someone I sent to prison when I was a Texas Ranger. I have no idea. It's been a long time since I was a Texas Ranger, and all of my work was in Texas. It's kind of hard to believe it was someone I sent to prison, but who knows?"

CHAPTER SEVENTEEN

Interesting Development

Charlie told Tom and Sandy to go out and try to find some place to buy food for all the men and bring it back to their new hideout.

Tom and Sandy left the hideout in Algiers walking on Bounty Street back toward the ferryboat port and were able to find a restaurant that could make dinner for them and all the men.

While they were waiting for everything to be prepared, Tom found a copy of the *Picayune Extra* newspaper lying on the counter, telling about the offer of $250,000 and the offer of immunity from prosecution for information leading to the freeing of Latesha Stone and the arrest or killing of the kidnappers.

Tom said, "Sandy, read this article."

"Okay, what's it all about?"

"Read it and you'll know how big a mess Charlie has gotten us into."

Sandy took the copy of the newspaper and read the story and said quietly, "Tom, we've got to get out of here before this all blows up and we get hung. Our ma and pa aren't ever going to get over it. We just can't do that to them."

Tom replied, "No, we can't just get out. We need a plan to be sure Latesha Stone gets back to her family safely. You know we're not like the rest of Charlie's gang. They're all killers and rustlers. The only reason we ever got mixed up with Charlie and his gang to start with was because we got them some horses when a posse was chasing them.

"We sold them some of Pa's horses, and Charlie told us we could come with him and his friends. The only good part was Charlie at least paid us for the horses, and we left the money for the horses for Pa. It sounded so exciting to go on the road robbing banks and seeing new places. I was eighteen, and you were seventeen, and we'd never even been off the ranch except to go to town sometimes with Pa.

"Actually we were never directly involved in the bank robberies. The only thing we did was to wait outside of town to make sure they had fresh horses in case they had another posse chasing them. Then we could give them fresh mounts to make their getaway. Thank goodness they never had a posse chasing them while we were with them."

Sandy said, "Well, we were certainly involved in kidnapping Latesha Stone. We were waiting with the rowboat to get Latesha Stone and the men away from the steamboat."

"True, Sandy, but the newspaper said if we helped recover Latesha Stone and catch the kidnappers, we would be given immunity from prosecution."

"That may be true, Tom, but if something went wrong, we could wind up getting killed by Charlie and his men."

"Sandy, think about this. What if another member of the gang decided to contact the law, and then we get caught with the rest of the gang, and then we get hung?"

"I want you think about this. What if we turned them in and Charlie escaped? He would head right to Ma and Pa's ranch and kill them and our two brothers and three little sisters."

"Sandy, you're right about that. Even if they got Charlie and Billy Jack got away, he would do it for Charlie. The only other one we know who always wants to kill people, besides Charlie, is Billy Jack.

"On the other hand, what if we were able to save Latesha Stone and all of them got caught and we would be free with lots of money? Think what we could do with $250,000. We could pay off Pa's bank loan and maybe add some land to the ranch and build Ma a nicer home and still have plenty left. Plus, we could go back home and help Pa run the ranch and be with our family, and, Sandy, you might be able to marry that Crockett girl, what was her name?"

"Julie Crockett, you're making it sound like maybe we could do it."

"You know, Sandy, I think we can. One thing we must do is to never let Charlie or anyone of the gang see a copy of this paper."

"Okay, Tom, I agree we should try to get in contact with the New Orleans Police or maybe the newspaper reporter, but how can we do it?"

The man who had been fixing their food said, "Okay, we've got everything ready for you."

Tom turned around to pay for the food and started getting money out of his pocket when the cook said, "I'm going to have to charge you for the plates and silverware, but if you bring them back, I can refund the money."

Tom said, "What if I bring them back when we ordered more food? Can we just exchange the dishes?"

The cook said, "Sure, you bring back all of these things, and I'll either exchange them or give you your money back. Is that fair enough?"

Tom replied, "Sounds fair enough to me."

Tom paid for the dishes and the food, and he and Sandy started back to the hideout.

As they walked along Tom said, "Sandy, we've got to find a way to get away from Charlie and the gang and have some time to get back over to Canal Street and talk to that reporter, but I don't know how we're going to do it."

When Tom and Sandy arrived back at their hideout, everyone was glad to see them coming back with food.

Tom and Sandy served the food to Charlie and the gang, and when everyone finished eating, Charlie said, "Tom, I'm going to write a note to Rocky Stone telling him where to put the ransom, and I want you and Sandy to take it over to Rocky's hotel and leave it with the desk clerk like you did with the second ransom note."

Tom replied, "Okay, Charlie, whatever you say, but I don't need to take Sandy with me."

Sandy couldn't believe Tom was saying that he didn't need to take him with him.

Tom had just told him on the way back to the hideout with the food that they had to find a way to get away from Charlie and his gang, and here was the perfect chance, with Charlie telling Tom to take him with him.

Charlie never liked to be challenged anytime by anyone when he gave an order.

Charlie said, "Tom, I told you I wanted you to take Sandy with you to be sure you don't have any trouble getting the note to Rocky Stone. I don't want any slipups because this is where we get our money and I get to kill Latesha and make Rocky suffer like I did in prison."

Tom said, "Sorry, boss, I just thought there was no need for two of us going to drop off a note."

Charlie angrily replied, "I'll do the thinking around here. You just follow my orders. You understand that, don't you, Tom?"

"Yes, sir, I'll follow your orders."

The rest of the gang certainly understood what Charlie just said. Charlie was about to dispatch Tom in a very permanent manner.

They knew Charlie meant to kill Tom as soon as it was convenient.

Tom did too much thinking to suit Charlie; people who thought too much and didn't jump when he gave an order were soon gone.

The gang had seen it lots of time before.

Charlie began to write the note telling Rocky where he wanted the money left for Latesha's release.

> Rocky Stone, tomorrow you need to place the $250,000 in a wooden box and take it to Jackson Square and leave the wooden box on the river side of the square at 2:00 p.m.
>
> We will be watching to be sure no one else takes the box. When we have our money, we will tell you where you can find Latesha.

Charlie put the note in an envelope and handed it to Tom and said, "Now take your brother with you and get this note over to the hotel like I told you."

Tom replied, "Yes, sir, we're on our way."

Tom took the ransom note and said, "Come on, Sandy, let's get going like the boss told us to."

Sandy got up from his chair and started for the door, with Tom leading the way.

As soon as they were a little way from the house, Sandy asked, "What the hell was that about telling Charlie I didn't need to go with you?"

"It was because I wanted to make sure you were with me. I didn't want Charlie to change his mind about you going with me, and I knew if I told him you didn't need to go, he would make me take you with me."

"How did you know that?"

"Because I know Charlie. He hates to have anyone question his authority."

Tom and Sandy made their way back to the ferry station to go back to over to Canal Street.

Arriving at the station, they found the ferry had just left so they had to wait for about thirty minutes for the next one.

As they sat waiting for the ferry, Tom said, "Sandy, we have to be careful and make sure none of Charlie's gang is following us. I'm glad they would have to go by ferry to get back across the river."

About that time the ferry arrived, and after all the passengers got off, they were allowed to get aboard.

Sandy kept looking back to see if any of the gang got on board after they were on the ferry. He didn't see any of them get on.

The ferry soon had them across the river and docked at the Canal Street Station.

Tom and Sandy made their way off the ferry and started walking in the direction of the Crescent Hotel, where Rocky was staying.

Arriving at the hotel, Tom told Sandy to stay outside the hotel to make sure none of Charlie's gang had followed them.

Tom went into the hotel and asked for the room number of Rocky Stone and was told it was number one and it was the first room down the hall right off of the lobby.

Tom went directly down the hall and knocked on the door of room number one and waited to see if somebody would answer the door.

A few minutes passed, and Rocky opened the door and saw a young man standing there.

Rocky asked, "Can I help you?"

Tom replied, "Are you Rocky Stone?"

"I'm Rocky Stone."

"Mr. Stone, my name is Tom Barr, and I'm one of the men who kidnapped your wife, Latesha. I read the article in the paper offering a $250,000 reward for helping to save your wife and not prosecuting the person who helped you get your wife back."

Rocky said, "Come in and talk to me."

Tom entered Rocky's room, and when he did, he saw Rocky had two other men in the room with him and a big dog standing next to Rocky's right leg.

Rocky said, "Tell me your name."

"My name is Tom Barr, and me and my brother, Sandy, were sent to deliver you a new ransom letter tonight."

"So where is your brother? Sandy, was it?"

"He's waiting outside the hotel to make sure none of the other gang members have followed us."

Rocky said, "Doc, why don't you go bring Sandy in here to be with us?"

Doc Knox got up from the couch and walked out of the room to bring Sandy inside to be with his brother.

Rocky said, "Tom, why don't you sit down on the couch over there, and we'll wait to talk until your brother is here."

Only a few minutes passed before Doc came back to the room with Sandy. Doc told Sandy to sit down on the couch with his brother.

After both of the young men were sitting down on the couch, Rocky said, "Tell me about your involvement in the kidnapping of my wife."

Tom said, "Since Sandy and I were the only ones in the gang who knew how to operate a rowboat, we were the ones waiting in it for the men to lower your wife down from the ship. After your wife was aboard the rowboat and the other men who got her were on the boat, we brought her to a warehouse, and the other men took her into the warehouse while we got rid of the rowboat."

Rocky asked, "How is Latesha? Is she still alive?"

Tom answered, "Yes, she's alive but not in very good condition."

Rocky said, "Why is she not in good condition?"

"Because they've kept her doped up and won't let her have anything to eat and drink."

"You mean she's gone this long without any food or water?"

Sandy answered, "Well, Tom and I have been giving her water but not enough because our boss threatens to kill anybody who gives her much water."

Rocky asked, "Who is your boss?"

Tom replied, "Charlie Christian. He hates you for sending him to prison twice, and he plans to kill your wife as soon as he gets the ransom money."

Rocky said loudly, "Charlie Christian, that no-good son of a bitch! He should have been hung a long time ago for killing several women in Texas. Tom, let me see this ransom note."

Tom took the envelope out of his pocket and handed it to Rocky.

Rocky opened the ransom note, read it over, and handed the note to Doc Knox.

After Doc read the note, he said, "Well, it looks like the same handwriting as the other two notes. I'd say the same man wrote all three notes."

Rocky said, "I never knew Charlie Christian could even write his name, much less be able to write anything this well."

Rocky asked, "Where's my wife? Is she still in the warehouse where you took her?"

Tom replied, "No, when you began searching warehouses, Charlie had us move to a new building across the river in Algiers. She was there an hour and a half ago, along with the rest of the gang. You need to move pretty fast, though, because Charlie keeps saying he's going to kill her as soon as he gets the money. He really hates you."

Rocky said, "My feeling for Charlie is beginning to develop into a real hate for him, too.

"Doc, how soon do you think you and the other men could be ready to move to save Latesha and capture these kidnappers?"

Doc said, "We need to get in touch with Colonel Carson, Captain Lawrence, and Captain Cooper to have their men ready to move right now."

The third man who had been in the room with Rocky and Doc spoke up and said, "I'll have my man who's waiting in the lobby go to them and have them assemble their men at the ferryboat terminal."

Doc said, "That will be good, and we'll go there to meet them."

The third man who'd been in Rocky's room went out to the lobby and talked to his man waiting there, and after he spoke to the man, he returned.

Rocky said, "Tom, Sandy, this is my father-in-law, Mr. Henry Hudson, Latesha's father, who's come all the way from New York City to help find his daughter and even had the president of the United States send federal marshals and an army company to help with her recovery."

Tom and Sandy just stared at Mr. Hudson, and finally Tom said, "Mr. Hudson, you have no idea how badly we feel about being part of the kidnapping of your daughter."

Henry replied, "Young men, if we are able to save my daughter, you will be forgiven by me and receive a big reward for your help. I can't speak for Rocky, but if we're successful in getting Latesha home alive, I'm pretty sure he will forgive you as well."

The Barr brothers both answered, "Thank you, sir."

Doc went to the front desk and telephoned police headquarters and talked to the desk sergeant. He told him to have a squad of police officers meet him at the ferryboat terminal.

Then Doc called Buddy Larson at the *Picayune* newspaper and told him to meet him at the ferryboat terminal as soon as he could, so he could be there when they tried to rescue Latesha Hudson Stone.

Buddy Larson would certainly be there.

CHAPTER EIGHTEEN

The Rescue of Latesha

A few minutes after Doc Knox, Rocky Stone, Henry Hudson, and Tom and Sandy Barr arrived at the Canal Street Ferryboat Terminal, five New Orleans police officers came to meet Captain Knox.

Doc Knox told one of the officers to place handcuffs on Tom and Sandy Barr and keep them with him at all times.

Tom started to wonder if he and Sandy had made a mistake trusting the newspaper ad saying they would not be charged for kidnapping if they gave information to help rescue Latesha Stone.

Tom told Sandy just to play along and let them put on the handcuffs.

Doc Knox met the officer on duty at the ferryboat company and told him his men would require the ferryboat until they completed their mission. They needed to take him and his people across to Algiers and wait until they returned.

He made the officer understand they could not allow any other passengers on board until their mission was completed.

The officer told Doc he understood and would take charge of the ferryboat and go with them to Algiers and wait for their return.

Soon after that, the rest of the men who had been searching for Latesha arrived at the ferryboat station: Colonel Chuck Carson with Mr. Hudson's security detail, Captain Robert Lawrence with his team of US marshals, and Captain Leon Cooper with his platoon of US Army soldiers.

All in all, there were around seventy-five men armed, trained, and ready for whatever they came up against.

When the ferryboat arrived at the Canal Street Terminal and as soon as the arriving passengers were off the ferryboat, the officer in charge loaded on all the rescue team and advised the regular ferryboat passengers that would not be allowed on the ferryboat.

On the Algiers side of the river, hidden in some bushes outside of the ferryboat terminal, Charlie Christian and Billy Jack Reynolds lay waiting with their rifles for Tom and Sandy Barr to return from delivering the latest ransom note.

As Charlie told Billy Jack after they left the building, he was really tired of Tom Barr thinking he was smarter than the rest of them, and they didn't need them anymore.

Charlie told Billy Jack, while they lay waiting, to kill Tom and Sandy as they got off the ferryboat. It would give the rest of the men more money.

Charlie saw the ferryboat getting into position to land at the Algiers Terminal, and suddenly he could see a lot of men.

As the ferryboat got closer, he saw several men wearing the uniforms of US soldiers, men wearing US marshal badges, and then he saw New Orleans police officers, and lastly he spotted Tom and Sandy Barr with their arms behind their backs, handcuffed.

Before the men could begin getting off the ferryboat Charlie said, "Billy Jack, we've to get out of here quick. They've captured Tom and Sandy."

Billy Jack asked, "Do we go back and get the other men?"

Charlie replied, "Do you think I'm crazy? We got to get as far away from here as fast as we can. We can't take on all these men."

Charlie and Billy Jack got up and began walking away from the ferryboat terminal as quickly as they could, in the opposite direction of the building where they had been holding Latesha.

As they walked down the street, they came upon a carriage with a team of horses, and Charlie said, "Get in, and let's get out of here."

Both of the men climbed into the carriage, and Charlie picked up the reins and told the horses to get up. The horse started down the street.

After they had gone a little way away from the ferryboat terminal, Charlie urged the team to go faster, and they did.

Soon the ferryboat terminal was no longer in sight.

Charlie had no idea where they were going, but any place would be better for them than where they had just left.

As Charlie Christian and Black Jack Reynolds were making their way away from the ferryboat terminal, the rescue team was leaving the ferryboat. First off were the New Orleans Police Department led by Captain Doc Knox, and Tom and Sandy Barr in handcuffs following directly behind the police officers.

Next came the US marshals led by Captain Robert Lawrence, then followed the US Army soldiers led by Captain Leon Cooper.

Finally, Henry Hudson's security men led by Colonel Chuck Carson; Rocky Stone and his dog, Nick; Henry Hudson and Buddy Larson left the ferryboat.

Tom had told Doc Knox that the building where they were holding Latesha was at the corner of Bounty and Alix Streets. Doc knew the area very well since at one time, he had a murder case in the same building.

The whole rescue team went down Bounty Street as quietly as possible, and just before they arrived at the building, Doc had a meeting with Captain Lawrence, Captain Cooper, Colonel Carson, and Rocky Stone.

Doc asked Rocky what he thought would be the best way to disperse the men.

Rocky said, "Based on my experience with this type of operation, I would say Captain Cooper should have his men seal off the perimeter of the area, then have Captain Lawrence's marshals on the outside of the building and have Colonel Carson's men fill in with the marshals.

"I would suggest we have Tom Barr go to the door, and when the men inside the building open the door, you and I and your police officers storm inside the building as quickly as possible. We need to be trying really hard not to get Tom or any of the rest of us killed when we go through that door. Gentlemen, do any of the rest of you have a better plan in mind? If so, please speak up."

No one said anything, so Doc Knox said, "All right then, let's get Captain Cooper's men in place, then Captain Lawrence and Colonel Carson's men in place, and I'll get my men ready to go."

"I'll get the handcuffs off Tom and tell him what he needs to do, and after the rest of you have your people in place, we'll go. Good luck, everybody."

Captain Cooper met with his men, and they began to set up positions on the perimeter of the property; next Captain Lawrence and Colonel Carson surrounded the entire building.

When Captain Doc Knox got the signal that all these men were in place, he took the handcuffs off Tom Barr and told him what he wanted him to do.

Captain Knox said, "Tom, I want you to knock on the door, and when they open the door, you go inside and get out of the doorway as quickly as possible because Rocky and I are coming in right behind you with the rest of my men. If you can, get down on the floor away from the door, got that? Can you do it all right or not, Tom?"

Tom replied, "Do I have a choice?"

Rocky answered, "No, not really, if you want to get out of the position you and your brother are in facing kidnapping charges."

"Okay, I'm as ready as I'm ever going to be."

Doc said, "Let's go!"

Tom, Doc, and Rocky, with Nick by his side, approached the door, and Tom knocked on the door, with Doc and Rocky standing off on the side so whoever opened the door couldn't see them.

James Newton opened the door and said, "Tom, glad to see you're back. Come in."

Tom went inside the door and moved over to the side as Doc and Rocky, with guns drawn, rushed through the door as the rest of the police officers poured through the door right behind them.

Doc shouted, "Get your hands in the air and don't move!"

Tony Caraway moved to pull his gun. Rocky saw him make a move for it and shot him in the chest, and Tony fell to floor screaming with pain and holding his chest.

One of the police officers took Tony's gun away from him.

James Newton, Ronnie Barnhill, and Jack Robinson were sitting around a table where they had been playing cards, and they didn't move except to put their hands up in the air.

Police officers took all their guns and began getting all the men up from the table and putting handcuffs on each of them.

Rocky said, "Tom, where's Latesha?"

"She's in the back room!"

Rocky picked up one of the lamps and took it with him as he and Tom went in to the back room.

Rocky held the light up, and when he did, he saw Latesha lying on a bed, still wearing the same clothes she had on when he last saw her.

Rocky went over to her, and he was having a hard time looking at her because she looked like she was just skin and bones. Her face was drawn, with dark circles under her eyes, and her face and skin looked like white ash.

Latesha's hair had dried mud in it and was so tangled in looked as it was tied in knots.

In spite of all the noise in the other room, Latesha hadn't moved or even tried to say a word.

Rocky thought she must be dead or in a coma. It was pretty hard to decide which one.

Rocky continued to stand looking at her and finally said, "Latesha, can you hear me?"

Although her eyes remained closed, she whispered one word, "Water."

Tom said, "I'll get her some water, Mr. Stone."

Tom left to get some water for Latesha as Rocky continued to try to get her to open her eyes.

Latesha just kept muttering one word, "water," over and over.

Tom returned with a glass of water and handed it to Rocky.

Rocky took the glass in his left hand and dipped his fingers in the water and rubbed his wet fingers on Latesha's lips.

Latesha didn't open her eyes, but she licked the moisture from Rocky's fingers.

Rocky said, "Sweetheart, would you like to have a glass of water?"

"No, they won't let me have a glass of water."

"Latesha, it's Rocky, honey, you can have all the water you want."

"Rocky, is that really you? How did you find me?"

"It's a long story. Your father is here with me. Would you like to open your eyes now?"

"Can I have a whole glass of water?"

"Open your eyes and you can have a whole glass of water, and I will even help you hold your glass."

Latesha slowly opened her eyes and saw Rocky standing next to her and said, "It's really you."

"Yes, it is, my love. Can you sit up to drink your water?"

Latesha tried to raise herself up, and Rocky saw she couldn't, so he reached under her back with his right arm and raised Latesha up and held the glass of water to her lips with his left hand.

Rocky put the water glass up to her lips and saw her try lift her right hand to take the glass, but she couldn't do it.

So Rocky began to slowly tilt the glass up against Latesha's lips; she opened her mouth a little bit, and he could slowly begin to give her a small amount of water.

As soon as she got a little too much water in her mouth, she started choking, so Rocky slowed the tilting of the glass to reduce the volume of water going into her mouth.

Still, water from her mouth was running down her face in almost the same volume as she was swallowing. Soon the glass was empty, and Latesha said, "More water, please."

Rocky turned to Tom and asked him to bring another glass of water.

Tom took the glass from Rocky and dutifully brought another glass of water to Rocky for Latesha.

This time, Rocky and Latesha both did much better getting most of this glass of water down her throat and much less down the side of her face.

Doc Knox came into the room and brought along Latesha's father, Henry Hudson, with him.

Henry said, "My precious daughter, you're still alive! Thank you, God."

Henry leaned over Latesha and took his hankie and wiped the water from her sweet face and gave her a kiss on the cheek.

Latesha muttered, "Father, you're here too."

"Of course, I am, I had to be here to help find you and make sure you are safe and all right."

"Thank you, Father."

Rocky said, "Latesha, this man is Captain Doc Knox. He's with the New Orleans Police Department, and he's been in charge of finding you."

Latesha didn't say anything she just looked at Doc Knox and closed her eyes again.

Rocky laid her back down on her bed and said, "Doc, we need to get Latesha to the hospital as soon as we can."

Doc replied, "I'll get some of the soldiers to help carry her to the ferryboat terminal, and I'll call and have a wagon waiting for us at the Canal Street Terminal."

Doc Knox left the room and a few minutes later returned with six soldiers, and they determined the best thing they could do was to take Latesha in her bed to the ferryboat terminal.

The six soldiers picked up the bed and took Latesha out of the room, and they were soon on their way to the ferryboat terminal.

The New Orleans Police Officers and the US marshals had all the gang members in handcuffs, other than Tony Caraway, who died from his gunshot wound. The rest of the soldiers were going back to the ferryboat terminal, followed by Doc, Tom and Sandy Barr, Rocky and Nick, and Henry.

Arriving at the ferryboat terminal, Doc telephoned the police department and told them to have a wagon at the ferryboat terminal to transport Latesha to the hospital.

Soon the entire party was loaded onto the ferryboat and underway to the Canal Street Terminal.

Arriving at the Canal Street Terminal, they were met by police officers with a wagon to transport Latesha to the hospital.

The six soldiers loaded the bed with Latesha into the bed of the wagon and then got inside the wagon to accompany her to the hospital.

Doc, Henry, Rocky, and Nick took a waiting hack and had it follow behind the wagon transporting Latesha to the hospital.

Arriving at the hospital, the soldiers unloaded Latesha and her bed from the wagon, and then hospital attendants transferred her out of that bed, placed her on a stretcher, and took her into an examination room.

Rocky asked to go with her into the examination room and was told "sorry," he would have to wait outside until the doctor had a chance to examine her.

Rocky and Nick, Doc and Henry were shown to a waiting room to wait to talk with the doctor after he had a chance to examine Latesha.

A hospital attendant tried to tell them the dog couldn't stay with them in the waiting room.

Doc showed the attendant his badge and said the dog was here on official police business.

Rocky, Henry, and Doc sat down, and Nick lay down on the floor next to Rocky.

After they had been waiting for about thirty minutes to talk with a doctor, Detective Smith, who worked for Doc, came from the police station to talk to him.

Doc got up from his chair and told the detective they would go outside to talk.

Doc and Detective Smith walked outside the hospital, and Rocky and Henry watched as Detective Smith was telling Doc something that appeared to anger Doc.

They talked for a few more minutes before Doc came back into the waiting area. When he did, Rocky asked, "Is everything all right, Doc? We saw you talking to Detective Smith, and you seemed to get very upset."

"Rocky, I am very upset. It appears your man, Charlie Christian, and another one of his gang, a Billy Jack Reynolds, escaped.

When Detective Smith was questioning Ronnie Barnhill, he told him he overheard Charlie tell Billy Jack they were going to the ferryboat terminal and wait for Tom and Sandy Barr to come back from delivering the ransom note and he planned to kill them.

Rocky said, "I'll be damned, that no-good son of a bitch got away."

CHAPTER NINETEEN

Latesha's Condition

The doctor came out from the examination room after examining Latesha and asked, "Are you Latesha Stone's family?"

Rocky replied, "Yes, I'm her husband, and this is Henry Hudson, Latesha's father, and you may know Detective Doc Knox."

"My name is Dr. Paul Johnson, and I can tell you, you have a very sick girl here. She's dehydrated, malnourished, in shock, going in and out of a coma, and who knows what other long-term problems she may have. Frankly, I'm not sure we are prepared to take care of all of her problems, but I will assure you we will do everything we can do to help her get stable and somewhat better."

Henry asked, "Dr. Johnson, can you tell me if it would be safe to move Latesha to another hospital?"

Dr. Johnson responded, "Exactly what do you mean 'safe to move her to another hospital'?"

"Doctor, I mean, would it cause her condition to get worse?"

"I don't think so, providing you had a nurse or someone with medical training to look after her during the trip, unless you're talking about taking her somewhere by wagon. She couldn't take bouncing around for a long period of time."

Henry asked, "Dr. Johnson, have you heard about a medical facility called St Mary's Hospital headed by Dr. William Mayo up in Rochester, Minnesota?"

"Yes, I heard of it, but don't know much about it."

Henry said, "I met Dr. Charles Mayo, the chief of staff of the hospital, and he told me about the research they are doing there, and I believed in what he and his sons are trying to do, so I have been a financial supporter of their hospital. I believe that's where my daughter should be.

"One other thing, Dr. Johnson, is it possible you could find a nurse to go with us to look after Latesha on the trip to Rochester? Of course, we would be willing to pay her salary and expenses while she was away from the hospital."

"Mr. Hudson, I can get someone to go with you, and I can arrange to put together all of the equipment and supplies needed to look after your daughter on the trip."

"Doctor, how much time do you need to make all of these arrangements?"

"We would need a couple of days, and your daughter needs to have time to get some care here, to see if we can improve her condition before we let her leave the hospital. Mr. Hudson, exactly how are you planning to take your daughter to this St. Mary's Hospital in Minnesota?"

"Dr. Johnson, I have my own personal railroad car here, and Latesha would be transported in it from here to Rochester, so once she was on the car, she wouldn't have to be moved until we arrived there. One other thing before we start all of this, I need to know if my son-in-law agrees with this plan or if he thinks Latesha should stay here and let you do the best that you can for her.

"You know, Doctor, when you're used to making decisions by yourself all the time, sometimes you can get carried away, especially when it comes to my daughter. Since her mother died when she was three and up to the time she was married, I probably made most of the decisions for her myself." Henry turned to his son-in-law.

"What are your thoughts, Rocky, and please forgive me for overstepping my place by trying to make decisions for your wife."

"Henry, there nothing to forgive. I know you want to do the best for Latesha, just like I do. Besides, Dr. Johnson told us he was afraid they couldn't do all of the things Latesha needed for her to totally recover. I want her back like she was before she was kidnapped. I love her as much as you do, probably even more. Henry, if you believe in what these fellows are trying to do in Minnesota, I believe in you, so there's no question we should get her there as soon as she's fit to make the trip."

Dr. Johnson said, "Okay, gentlemen, I'll get started making arrangements for a nurse and the necessary equipment and supplies to transport Mrs. Stone to Minnesota. I will let you know how she is doing and will let you know when you can see her."

Dr. Johnson left the three men standing in the hallway.

After he was gone, Rocky said, "Henry, there's one other thing I need to tell you right now, and that's you're going to have to be the one who goes and stays with Latesha. Because I'm the one who has to go after Charlie Christian. I know more about him than any other lawman. Besides, I intend to kill him for what he did to Latesha and the two other innocent women he killed in New Orleans while he was trying to get my attention. Henry, I know you and Latesha won't understand this, but if I let him live, he will be after us for the rest of our lives.

"Doc, I need to you to file charges against Charlie Christian and Black Jack Reynolds for kidnapping and murder and offer a reward to bring them in dead or alive. Then I can go after them as a bounty hunter so I can't get into any trouble for killing them, okay?"

Doc Knox had been standing listening to all the things the doctor had to say about Latesha's condition, Henry's plan to move Latesha to St. Mary's Hospital in Minnesota, and Rocky's plan to go after Charlie Christian and Black Jack Reynolds.

Hearing what Rocky had to say about going after these two killers by himself did surprise him, but he understood it.

So Doc replied to Rocky's request, "Rocky, it's not a problem filing kidnapping and murder charges against Christian and Reynolds and offering a reward for them, but are you sure you're up to going after these men by yourself? It's been a long time since you were a Texas Ranger."

"Doc, I don't know if I'm up to it or not, but it's what I have to do. I've caught Charlie Christian twice before, and I know what it takes to find him. He should have been hung the last time I got him for murdering a woman in Waco, but somehow he was only sent to prison. I don't plan to let him get away with any more murders, if you get what I mean."

Doc replied, "Rocky, I know exactly what you mean, and by the way, you handled yourself well during the raid in Algiers. I'm sure you saved my life by shooting that guy who was pulling his gun."

Henry piped up and said, "Detective Knox, if you need to attach a reward for the wanted poster, I'll put up a reward of one hundred thousand dollars for each one of these men."

"That will be great, Mr. Hudson. The reward posters will say there is a reward of one hundred thousand dollars for each man, dead or alive."

Rocky asked, "Doc, how soon do you think you could have some of the wanted posters made up?"

"I'm sure we can have them by tomorrow or the next day. Anyway, as soon as I can get a proof, I'll get a copy of it to you. Mr. Hudson, Rocky, I'm going to go back to police headquarters and see how the interrogations of the prisoners are going. I'll see you sometime tomorrow. I'm glad we got Latesha and hope she gets better very soon. Good night."

Not long after Doc left to go to police headquarters, Dr. Johnson came out and told Rocky and Henry they could see Latesha now.

Rocky, Henry, and Nick went into the examination room to see how Latesha was doing; arriving in the examination room, they found a nurse talking to her.

They heard the nurse say, "Latesha honey, your husband and father are here to see you. Can you open your eyes?"

There was no response from Latesha.

The nurse turned toward Rocky and Henry and said, "Sorry, she just goes in and out of her coma. Maybe if you try talking to her, she will respond better to one of you."

Rocky replied, "Thank you, nurse, she certainly looks better now that you've got her cleaned up and out of the clothes she been wearing since she was kidnapped. We appreciate your help, and, yes, we will try to talk to her to see if we can get any response from her. Thank you."

The nurse told them she would be back in a few minutes and left the room with all the clothes Latesha had been wearing.

Rocky put his hand on Latesha's right hand and gently said, "Latesha honey, can you hear me? I love you so much. Can you please open your eyes and talk to me? Your daddy is here with me. He would sure like you to say hello to him. He's come a long way to be here with you and to help you. Can you please tell him hello?"

Latesha just lay there and never opened those beautiful brown eyes.

Henry was on the other side of the bed, and he started talking to Latesha, "Latesha baby, it's your daddy. Can you open your eyes for me and tell me how you are doing? Can you just say something?"

Rocky and Henry took turns talking to Latesha, but no matter how much they begged her to open her eyes or say something, they got no response from her at all.

The nurse returned fifteen minutes later and said, "We have a room ready for Latesha now, and a couple of orderlies will be here in a few minutes to move her to her room."

The nurse hardly had time to finish her sentence when two orderlies came in to the examination room to move Latesha to her room. They told Rocky and Henry that Latesha would be in room 112 on the first floor of the hospital.

As the orderlies moved Latesha to her room, Rocky, Henry, and Nick followed along behind them.

They arrived at her new room and transferred into her bed, and after the orderlies straightened up her bed covers, they were gone.

A few minutes later, another nurse came in to check on Latesha and to look over her chart. She introduced herself and said, "My name is Susan Ray. I will be the nurse looking after Mrs. Stone for the rest of the night."

Rocky said, "I'm Latesha's husband, Rocky, and this is Latesha's father, Henry Hudson, and my dog, Nick."

Susan said, "I'm very glad to meet both of you and your dog, Nick. I know Latesha is in pretty bad condition after her ordeal. I'll do the best I can to help her get better while she's here. I understand

Where's My Wife?

you will be taking her to another hospital when she's in a little bit better condition."

Henry replied, "Yes, we will be taking her to a place called St. Mary's Hospital in Rochester, Minnesota. We believe they may be able to help her since Dr. Johnson said he thought she needed to go to another hospital with better capabilities."

Susan replied, "I think Dr. Johnson is telling you the truth. We don't have as much of the latest medical knowledge here as they have in the north."

Rocky said, "Well, we hope they do, and we really appreciated Dr. Johnson's advice."

Henry added, "Yes, we certainly do appreciate the doctor's thoughts on Latesha's need to go to another hospital for care."

Susan said, "Dr. Johnson is a fine doctor, and he tells it like it is. If he thought we could get your wife back to the way she was before her ordeal, he would never have suggested moving her from our hospital."

Susan began checking Latesha's vital signs, and when she finished, she told Rocky and Henry that Latesha's vital signs looked pretty good.

Susan then said, "You know, gentlemen, Latesha's is resting comfortably right now. I would suggest you both should try to get some rest because it won't do her any good if both of you get sick."

Henry said, "Rocky, I think Nurse Susan is right. We better see if we can get some rest. It's been a long day and night."

Rocky agreed and leaned down and kissed Latesha good night and said, "Okay, nurse, you win. She's in your care for the rest of the night."

Henry and Rocky looked Latesha over one more time and left her room.

CHAPTER TWENTY

Meeting between Rocky and Henry

Rocky had a hard time trying to go to sleep thinking about how bad Latesha's condition was, even though they had found and rescued her.

Rocky didn't know if she would ever be his Latesha again or even if she was going to live.

Besides worrying about getting Latesha's health back, he had to think about what he had to do to find Charlie Christian.

Rocky now believed that unless he found Charlie and killed him, he would come back again to try to kill Latesha or him.

Rocky was sure killing Charlie was the only way to prevent him from trying to kill Latesha again.

Rocky tossed and turned, and Nick got up from beside his bed to see if Rocky was getting up, and when he didn't get out of bed, Nick lay back down on the floor, gave a big yawn, and went back to sleep.

It had been a long day and night for him, too.

Finally, the need for sleep overtook Rocky, and he went to sleep without solving any of his problems.

Nick was happy Rocky had finally quit tossing and turning in his bed so he could get some sleep.

Rocky woke up at ten in the morning and sat up in his bed and saw Nick standing next to his bed, watching to see if he was really going to get up now.

Where's My Wife?

Rocky did, indeed, get out of bed. He took a quick shower, dressed as quickly as he could, and took Nick outside so he could take care of his business.

Then he went into the dining room to get something to eat, both for himself and Nick.

Nick got much quicker service, as the waiter brought his steak to him as soon as Rocky sat down at the table.

As Nick began eating his steak, Rocky ordered three eggs, a rasher of bacon, a slice of ham, fried potatoes, bread and butter, and a pot of black coffee.

After Rocky ordered all his food, he realized he hadn't had anything to eat since breakfast yesterday morning. No wonder he was so hungry.

Then Rocky remembered he hadn't fed Nick since yesterday morning either, so he had the waiter bring Rocky another steak, which Nick ate as quickly as he had the first one a few minutes ago.

Rocky said, "Sorry, Nick, we were so busy yesterday I forgot to get you anything else to eat for the day."

Nick looked up at Rocky with his big brown eyes and laid his head down on Rocky's leg, like, it's okay, we were just too busy yesterday saving Latesha.

Rocky patted Nick's head then rubbed behind his ears. Nick always seemed to like that.

The waiter brought Rocky's breakfast, and Rocky ate his breakfast almost as quickly as Nick ate his two big steaks. Rocky ate every bite of his breakfast and drank his whole pot of coffee in a matter of minutes.

Rocky surveyed his empty plates and told the waiter he guessed he was finished with his breakfast since there wasn't anything else left to eat except the empty plates.

The waiter smiled and said, "Mr. Stone, if you're still hungry, I'm sure we can make you something else."

Rocky replied, "No, I don't think I need anything else to eat right now, but thank you for the offer." Rocky thanked the waiter again and told Nick they needed to go.

Rocky got up from the table, and he and Nick left the dining room and went out of the hotel to walk directly to police headquarters.

Arriving at police headquarters, Rocky asked if Doc Knox was in his office and was told he was and to go on ahead to his office.

When Rocky and Nick got to Doc's office, they found him with his head down on his desk, asleep.

One of Doc's detectives told Rocky that Doc hadn't gone home; he had been working all night and had just put his head down on his desk not more than ten minutes ago.

Rocky sat down on a chair next to Doc's desk, and Nick lay down next to Rocky's right foot.

Only a few minutes passed when another of Doc's detectives came into Doc's office and saw he was sleeping with his head on his desk.

The detective said to Rocky, "You may not remember me, but Doc introduced me to you. I'm Detective Smith. I was one of the men who went into the building last night with you and Doc. I saw you shoot the guy who was pulling a gun. Thanks a lot. I'm not sure how many of us might have gotten hit if it weren't for you and your quick-action shooting the guy before he could get off a shot."

"Sure, I remember you, Detective Smith. I saw the guy pulling the gun when I came through the door and got off a lucky shot, that's all. I'm glad none of our people got hurt because you never know how one of those raids go down. We were just lucky."

"Mr. Stone, you can say it was just a lucky shot, but I know better. For you to see the guy pulling a gun and reacting that quickly isn't just luck. It's skill and experience. Anyway, thanks again. I know you saved us from getting shot and maybe one or more of us killed. I'll never forget it. I only thought you wrote those dime novels. I never realized that you could have actually lived through those stories you write."

"Thanks, Detective Smith. I did actually live to tell stories about my experiences as a Texas Ranger. However, some of my stories I just make up out of my head, like the one about my wife being kidnapped off a riverboat. You know, I'm really sorry I ever made that one up."

Where's My Wife?

A few minutes more passed, and a man from the printer came into Doc's office and had a proof of the reward poster for his approval.

Since Doc was still asleep, Rocky asked to see the poster and the fellow from the printer handed the proof to Rocky. Rocky looked the poster over and saw it had everything he needed on it and told the man it was approved.

The man from the printer said, "Somebody has to okay the proof, and then we will begin printing them."

Rocky asked, "Where do I need to sign to approve it so you can get started printing?"

The guy said, "Right here." He pointed to a blank space on the proof for a signature.

Rocky signed the proof and handed it back to the man. Before the man left, Rocky asked if he had another copy that he could have to show his boss. He did, and he took out another copy and handed it to Rocky.

Then the man was on his way back to the print shop so they could start running the job.

Rocky folded the poster, put in into his pocket, and told Detective Smith he was going to go to the hospital to see how his wife was doing. He would be back to see Detective Knox later today or tomorrow.

Rocky and Nick left the police station and made their way to the hospital and then to room 112 to see Latesha.

When Rocky opened the door to Latesha's room, he saw Dr. Johnson and a nurse working with Latesha. Rocky asked, "Do you want me to come back when you're finished?"

Dr. Johnson answered, "No, you can stay. We will be finished working with Latesha in a few minutes."

Rocky couldn't see what they were doing with Latesha, but he could hear her coughing softly.

A few minutes passed and Dr. Johnson came over to where Rocky was sitting, with Nick laying by his feet, and said, "We are trying to find a way to get Latesha some water when she's in her coma. We have come up with a way to slowly pour a small amount of water into her mouth without choking her. It's a slow process, but if we can make it work, we may be able to make some soup and get her some nourishment, which would be a big help in her recovery."

Rocky asked, "What have you come up with to try to do this?"

Dr. Johnson replied, "It's a hollowed-out reed like ones some American Indians used to breathe under water with when they were hiding in a river or lake. We've got a small funnel, and we the put the small end inside the reed and pour the liquid into the bowl of the funnel to try to get water down Latesha's throat.

"It's working pretty well, except we have to be very careful we don't get too much water into the bowl and make her choke. It takes lots of time to get such a small amount of water into her. But it's better than not getting any water in her. We'll work on it to see if we can do better, and if we can, we'll make her some chicken broth and try to get that down her."

"That sounds good. I hope it works. I know she needs food and know it would be so much easier if she could stay out of the coma."

"Rocky, I can tell you if we could keep her awake, we could really make a lot of progress getting her on the road to recovery. The one thing I know you and her father can do to help us is to keep talking to her and see if we can bring her back and keep her awake long enough to get enough water and food in her to do her some good."

Rocky replied, "I will talk with her all the time I'm here, and I'll talk with her father and tell him to do the same. Dr. Johnson, do you think it makes any difference what we say to her?"

"I don't think so. You can read her a book if you want to, anything that's letting her hear human voices talking to her. I think if it's a voice she knows, it may help wake her up, so keep trying. Rocky, I have to go see some other patients right now. I will see you later this evening."

Dr. Johnson turned and walked out of Latesha's room.

Rocky and Nick went over and stood by Latesha's bed. Rocky started talking to her about going home to Boonville, Missouri, and spending time watching the traffic on the Missouri River from their bluff high up above the river.

Where's My Wife?

Rocky knew Latesha loved to do that, and they could spend hours watching the river below their home.

A short time later, Henry Hudson came to Latesha's room and asked, "Rocky, has any progress been made in waking up Latesha?"

"No, there been no progress on that, but they have devised a way to get some water into Latesha using a hollow reed and a small funnel. They say it's a lot of work and really slow, but at least they're getting some water in her."

"That sounds good, Rocky."

"Henry, they tell me it's not getting her nearly enough water, but it's better than not getting any water in her at all. Dr. Johnson told me to keep talking to Latesha and to ask you to do the same. If we can't think of anything to say, we should just read her books since he thinks it might help to bring her back to us.

"The other thing, Henry, is that I'm going to have to leave here very soon and leave you with all the responsibility of looking after Latesha—that is, if I have any hope of catching up with Charlie Christian and Billy Jack Reynolds. I know it's not anything new for you to have all the responsibility of caring for Latesha, because you have been doing it all of her life. I'm really sorry to be going and leaving the two of you when I should be here for her, but I can't help it.

"When Latesha wakes up, I'm afraid she's going to think I've abandoned her. She's not going to understand me leaving her in her condition, but I hope you can explain it to her. You really have to make her understand that I wanted to stay with her, but I couldn't let Charlie Christian keep living to have another chance of coming after her again."

"Rocky, we come from two different worlds, but I do understand the need to protect your loved one, and if I could get this Charlie Christian fellow in front of a gun, I'd kill him myself for what he's done to Latesha. So you can count on me to do everything possible to get Latesha back and to make her understand why you had to go after that awful man.

"Just one thing, Rocky, you have to take care of yourself, because I would never be able to explain to Latesha why I let you go off by yourself to go after this man if something happened to you. Do you understand, Rocky? My girl loves you, and that makes me responsible for you, too. She always thinks I can take care of everything, but you know I can't."

"Henry, no one can take care of everything, but you do so much for so many people. Latesha has told me about how you have worked so hard to help provide jobs and better living conditions for not only the people who work for your companies but for the whole country by investing in the development of new and better products and even coming up with new inventions."

"You know, Rocky, it was Latesha who made me think about doing these things. I had gone through life always having money and never giving much thought about the people who earned that money for me.

"My life was like my father's and grandfather's—they were always blessed by having money due to the work done by their fathers and grandfathers before them. They just never gave much thought about who was really providing the money to them, but, of course, the money was being provided by the people who worked for them. They never really gave those people lot of thought or care.

"Latesha was the one who made me consider those people and to make me try to improve their lives, which I can say also improved my life as well. My girl is really something, and we're going to get her well because one day she will have to take over all of the responsibility for the people who work for us. "I'm sure she will do a better job of that than I did."

"Henry, please don't sell yourself short. What you have done for people and still are doing is wonderful, like you helping to fund this St. Mary's Hospital. They may turn out to be able to do things for people that no one else has ever done. Maybe they can even help Latesha come out of her coma."

"God, I certainly hope they can."

"Rocky, I wanted to tell you I have made arrangements to leave New Orleans day after tomorrow, and we will be traveling directly to Chicago, and then our private train car will be attached to another train and taken to Rochester, Minnesota. We should be in Rochester in five days from the time we leave New Orleans."

"Henry, that's sounds wonderful. Have you contacted St. Mary's Hospital to let them know you are bringing your daughter for treatment?"

"Yes, we sent a telegram to Dr. Charles Mayo, and he answered my telegram and said they would be expecting our arrival in the next five or six days."

"That's great, Henry, I glad you've heard from them and hope they can work a miracle for Latesha."

There was a knock on the door, and when Rocky opened the door to Latesha's hospital room, Doc Knox was standing there waiting to see Rocky.

Rocky thought Doc looked awful; he was unshaven, his hair uncombed, and his clothes looked like he had been wearing them for several days, which he had been. He looked just plain tired, which he was.

Doc said, "I'm sorry I was asleep when you came to see me at the office. I understand you saw and approved the 'wanted' poster for Charlie Christian and Billy Jack Reynolds for me."

"Sorry, Doc. I needed a copy of it so I could get started going after them as soon as I could. I hope you understand why I did it. Would you like to see a copy of the poster?"

Rocky reached in his pocket and took out the poster and handed it to Doc, who said, "Thanks, Rocky, I'm glad you let me see it before I have thousands of them."

Doc looked over the poster and said, "I agree, Rocky, it looks just like it should, and I approve of what you approved for me."

Rocky couldn't help himself. He started laughing, and his laughing made Henry and Doc laugh too.

Rocky looked over at Latesha as Henry and Doc were laughing and saw Latesha had a little smile on her face.

Rocky said, "Quick, look at Latesha. She has a little smile on her face."

Both men turned toward Latesha and saw she was actually smiling, not a big smile but a smile anyway, and then it was gone.

Rocky said, "I think that shows us Latesha is still there, hidden under that cloak of darkness."

Henry and Doc agreed.

Doc said, "Rocky, before you start chasing after Charlie and Billy Jack, I think you should know that Tom and Sandy Barr have offered to go with you to help you find them. I have no idea if they would be of any help to you or not, but I think the offer is genuine.

"The other thing I think is worrying them is they are afraid Charlie and Billy Jack may go to their folks' ranch and kill their folks and their brothers and sisters. They believe that because Charlie saw them with us, they were leading us to their hideout.

"We're pretty sure Charlie and Billy Jack would have seen them with us because Jack Robinson overheard Charlie telling Billy Jack to bring his rifle and come with him. They were going to wait for the Barr brothers to come back on the ferryboat from delivering the last ransom note, and they were going to kill them both as they got off the ferryboat. Nice guys, huh? It seems Charlie didn't like Tom Barr because he was too smart, so he planned to kill him and his brother, Sandy."

Rocky replied, "No, they are not nice guys, but I think it would be better for the Barr brothers to go home and try to help look after their folks. Besides he who goes alone travels the fastest, and I intend to be traveling pretty fast.

"Doc, please thank them for me, but tell them I will try to take care of Charlie and Billy Jack so they don't have to worry about them in the future."

Doc said, "That's what I thought you would say, but I wanted you to know they made the offer. Those kids had no idea what they were getting into when they went with Charlie Christian and his gang. Talking with the other gang members, they said the only thing the kids ever did was stay outside of towns with extra horses when the gang was robbing banks, just in case the gang was being chased by a posse.

"They did operate the rowboat when your wife was kidnapped because nobody else in the gang knew how to operate a rowboat. The men also told us Tom and Sandy took a lot of risks giving Latesha more water than Charlie wanted her to have. They said Charlie killed more gang members for a lot less than what Tom and Sandy were doing by giving Latesha water."

Rocky said, "Thank you, Doc, for all your help, and I do hope to see you again one day under better conditions. You know, Doc, you need to go home and get some rest. Thanks again for everything."

Doc shook hands with Rocky and Henry and left.

Rocky said, "Henry, Nick and I are going to go now, and I pray you and the doctors get my Latesha back. I love her so much."

Rocky shook hands with Henry and walked over to Latesha's bed. He leaned down and put his arms around her, held her up, and gave her one more long kiss, then he laid her back down, turned, and he and Nick went out the door.

CHAPTER TWENTY-ONE

The Hunt for Charlie and Billy Jack

Rocky went to the livery stable and picked up his horse, Spring Rain.

As someone long ago once said, the longest journey begins with the first step, and Rocky and Nick were beginning their journey without a specific destination.

They only had one goal in mind for their journey, and that was to find Charlie Christian and Billy Jack Reynolds and kill them.

Rocky was pretty sure Charlie wouldn't stay in Louisiana. He would make his way back to Texas, where he knew his way around and had a few friends.

Rocky always wondered how someone like Charlie could ever have any friends.

Before Rocky left New Orleans, he decided to check to see if there was still a ship that left New Orleans going to Galveston. Even if it did, Rocky knew he would be a long way from the areas of Texas where Charlie had always operated.

He decided to check anyway. If they did still have a ship going there, he would at least be in Texas, where he had a lot more friends than Charlie did.

He could get his friends with the Texas Rangers to help him look for Charlie and Billy Jack.

Rocky figured Charlie was going to have to pull a bank job soon because he certainly didn't leave New Orleans with the money he planned to.

Tom Barr told him the gang had been in New Orleans for some time, so Charlie had to be getting low on money by now.

He would have to get money somewhere, and Charlie was a creature of habit. If you needed money, you robbed a bank. Simple enough. Now all Rocky had to do was to find out where the bank job was pulled, and he would have an idea of where Charlie was.

Any bank robbery in Texas would be reported to the Texas Rangers, and Rocky could get the information from them on where and when a robbery occurred.

That would help him get to the area of Texas Charlie was in.

Texas was a big place; it was as big as some of the largest countries in Europe.

From there Rocky would start looking for saloons where the liquor flowed freely and the women were easy and available.

Charlie had to have his women; he loved to use them, abuse them, and he left far too many of them dead when he was through with them.

The more Rocky thought about Charlie, the more he became obsessed with finding and killing him. He had to get rid of this monster if it was the last thing he ever did on this earth.

Arriving at the docks, Rocky tied Spring Rain up, and he and Nick set out to ask about passage on a ship from New Orleans to Galveston. He was told yes, they still had the service, but it wouldn't be sailing for two weeks.

When Rocky told the agent he had to get to Texas before then, the agent asked him where in Texas he wanted to go. Rocky told him somewhere near Fort Worth.

The agent suggested he take a train to Shreveport, and from there he could get a train to Fort Worth. The agent said, "They have a train leaving here every day for Shreveport, but you'll need to check with the station agent to find out when it leaves."

Rocky thanked him and turned to go back to Spring Rain so he could ride him to the train station, and, of course, Nick followed Rocky and stayed right by Spring Rain's side.

When they got to the train station, Rocky found a place to tie up his horse, and then he and Nick made their way into the station and up to agent and asked about getting a train to Fort Worth.

The agent said, "You have to go to Shreveport then transfer to another train from there to Fort Worth."

Rocky asked, "What time does the train leave to go to Shreveport?"

The agent replied, "It leaves at noon today."

"Can I get a ticket for the train today?"

"No problem, we have plenty of room on today's train."

"How about transportation for my horse, is it available?"

"Yes, it's available for an extra charge."

"How about my dog, can I bring him along with me?"

"I don't see any problem if he's well-behaved. You can buy him a ticket."

"As you can see, he's very well-behaved and always stays right at my feet."

"Okay, I'll make out your tickets."

The agent made out their tickets, and Rocky paid for the tickets. Then they waited for the time when they could board the train.

After they had waited a couple of hours, a man came up to Rocky and said, "I understand you have a horse going with you on the train today, is that right?"

Rocky replied, "Yes, I do."

The man said, "Can you show me where he is so I can make arrangements to load him?"

"Certainly, he's tied up in front of the station. Come on, and I'll help you get him."

Rocky got up, and he and Nick led the man out to where Spring Rain was tied.

The man said, "Your horse is a beautiful animal. Is he well-trained?"

Rocky replied, "He's very well-trained, and he is beautiful, isn't he?"

"Yes, sir, I hope he's going to like riding on a train. Has he ever been on a train before?"

"No, he hasn't."

"Well, sir, we'll do our best to take good care of him on the trip."

"Thank you, I'd appreciate it, and I'm sure he will, too."

"We've got a nice stall waiting just for him and some oats and water too."

"It sounds like he may have a better deal than we do. I don't think anybody's going to feed Nick and me on the trip."

"No, sir, but they do make a stop on the way to Shreveport so they can service the train, and then you and your dog could get something to eat there."

Rocky and Nick followed along behind the man who was leading Spring Rain to the train car where he would be loaded onto the train.

The man had no trouble with walking Spring Rain up the loading ramp and into the train car.

Once there, the man placed him inside his stall, unsaddled him, and gave him some water and a bucket of oats.

The man came back out of the train car and said, "Yes, sir, Spring Rain is a real gentleman. He went on board the car without any trouble at all."

Rocky thanked the man, and then he and Nick went back inside the station to wait for their time to board the train.

It was soon time to get aboard. Rocky located the train car number they were to be on, and Rocky and Nick got onto the train and found their assigned seats.

Rocky took the seat next to the window, and Nick lay down on the floor next to him.

The trip to Shreveport was uneventful, and Rocky stayed in his seat until they made the stop to service the train.

At that stop he and Nick left the train so Nick could have the chance to take care of his business and to get something to eat for both of them.

In Shreveport, they had a six-hour layover to wait for the train bound for Fort Worth.

Rocky checked to be sure Spring Rain had been taken off the train and found he was waiting just like he and Nick were.

He was in a corral next to the station, and Rocky saw Spring Rain's saddle and tack lying on a small cart next to the corral.

Time passed by slowly, but it was now time to board the train bound for Fort Worth. Before Rocky got on the train, he checked to see if Spring Rain had been loaded on the train.

Rocky found both him and his saddle and tack had been loaded onto the train car.

Shortly after Rocky and Nick boarded the train, they entered into Texas.

Rocky had no idea how Charlie and Billy Jack were going to get back to Texas, but he was certain Charlie was going to get back there someway somehow.

When they arrived in Fort Worth and as soon as Rocky and Nick claimed Spring Rain from the railroad, Rocky saddled Spring Rain and rode directly to the Texas Rangers Headquarters in Fort Worth.

Arriving there, Rocky was met by several of his old friends, who instantly began giving him a hard time, asking if the famous writer had run out of stories and had to come back to work for the Rangers.

However, after Rocky explained about Latesha being kidnapped and the pitiful condition she was in now, the mood changed rapidly, and the men who had been giving him a hard time were now asking him what they could do to help.

Rocky showed his friends the wanted poster for Charlie Christian and Billy Jack Reynolds, and they said they would have a copy of the poster printed up and get them to all the Texas Rangers' offices.

They told him that Charlie's gang robbed several banks in East Texas a few weeks before Latesha was kidnapped in New Orleans and there hadn't had been another bank robbery anywhere in Texas since then.

Rocky explained why he was here since he was sure Charlie was on his way back to Texas and would soon be active again. He was also sure he was running out of money and would be back robbing banks again very soon.

He told the Rangers he wanted them to let him know if they heard anything about a bank robbery in Texas.

He said, "I plan to get to that area as quickly as possible because I know it's going to be Charlie and Billy Jack who rob the bank. The rest of Charlie's gang is in jail in New Orleans, and I had to kill one of them when we rescued Latesha. Charlie and Billy Jack got away because they were not in the hideout when we raided it."

The Rangers all agreed that it was too bad they weren't there and said they would do everything possible to help him get Charlie and Billy Jack.

This time they would make sure Charlie would never have a chance to get away again.

CHAPTER TWENTY-TWO

Playing the Waiting Game

Rocky found himself just sitting around Fort Worth waiting for Charlie Christian and Billy Jack Reynolds to hold up a bank somewhere in Texas so he had some idea of where he needed to look for them.

All the time he was waiting for them to make their move, he couldn't do anything but think about how Latesha was doing.

The one thing he could do was to keep praying for Latesha to fully recover from her ordeal, so he filled his days and nights doing that. He was sure God was tired of receiving prayers from him on the same subject every few minutes, but Rocky couldn't do anything else.

The days continued to go slowly by, and then the weeks went slowly by but still nothing about a bank robbery in Texas. Rocky found it to be unbelievable that Charlie hadn't robbed a bank in this amount of time.

Rocky wondered what Charlie was doing for money, then he began to think what if Charlie didn't return to Texas like he thought he would.

Where would he go? Maybe he got a ship bound for California, or maybe he went east to Mississippi or Georgia?

No, if Charlie was anything, he was a creature of habit. He would return to Texas and start robbing banks again just like he had been doing for so many years.

Rocky said out loud, "No way, Charlie, you've got to come back to Texas and pick up right where you left off, robbing banks!"

The five Texas Rangers working in the Fort Worth Texas Rangers office, where Rocky was waiting to hear about a bank robbery in Texas, all looked up from their work at Rocky's sudden outburst but said nothing.

Three of the rangers used to work for Rocky, and they knew sometimes when he was trying to solve a case in his head, he would all of a sudden make a statement that just seemed to come out of nowhere, like he just did.

The two new men looked to see how the other men reacted to Rocky's outburst, and when they saw, they just shook their heads and went back to work; they didn't say anything either.

Patience was a quality that Rocky had in short supply, as Latesha was so quick to remind him. Latesha's words came back to him like she was saying them to him right now, "Patience, patience, Rocky."

This always reminded Rocky of an old joke he remembered about two vultures sitting in a tree waiting to find something dead to eat, and then one vulture said to the other one, "Patience, hell. I'm hungry, let's kill something!"

Yes, Rocky wasn't a patient man; he was used to acting and getting things done. Yeah, Rocky wanted to kill someone by the name of Charlie Christian.

This sitting around waiting was killing him, and being away from Latesha and knowing he should be with her was only making it worse because he knew he wasn't there for her in her time of need. He should be with her no matter what.

Rocky decided he would find his way to Mayo Clinic in Rochester, Minnesota, to be with Latesha as soon as he could get there.

Rocky was getting up from his chair on his way to Minnesota when a ranger came into the room where Rocky and the five rangers were working and said, "We got a telegram from the sheriff in Jasper, Texas, telling us two men just robbed the Bank of Jasper this morning. He said the men left town headed northwest out of Jasper. He and his deputies chased them until the men shot one of his deputies in the chest and they had to take him back into town to a doctor. However, they were too late getting him help, and the deputy died."

Rocky asked, "What's the closest ranger station to Jasper, and how long will it take me to get to Jasper?"

The ranger replied, "Nacogdoches is going to be the closest rangers' station we have to Jasper. Nacogdoches is northwest of Jasper, so the bank robbers are headed in the right direction for us to find them."

Rocky said, "That would be nice if the bank robbers continue riding in that direction."

One of the rangers who had been assigned to the rangers' office in Nacogdoches told him to get a train going toward Houston and get off in Huntsville. "Then you're going to have a pretty long ride from Huntsville to Jasper."

Another ranger suggested it might be quicker if Rocky took a train to Kilgore and then headed southeast since the bank robbers were going northwest when they left Jasper.

Also, that way he could meet up with the rangers in Nacogdoches, who would already be looking for the bank robbers.

Rocky said, "I think I'm going to go to Kilgore and then try to catch up with the rangers from Nacogdoches to see if they've had any luck finding these two men."

The ranger who had come in with the telegram said, "I'll let the rangers' office in Nacogdoches know you are on your way there so they will be expecting to see you."

Rocky thanked him and picked up his things, and he and Nick left and went out to where Spring Rain was tied. Rocky mounted, and they soon made their way to the railroad depot in Fort Worth.

Arriving at the railroad depot, Rocky tied Spring Rain to the hitching post, and he and Nick made their way to the ticket counter.

Rocky asked when the next train to Kilgore would be leaving and was told, "Tomorrow morning at 5:00 a.m."

Rocky began explaining to the ticket agent he was on a mission with the Texas Rangers to try to catch two bank robbers who had robbed the Bank of Jasper, Texas, this morning and killed a deputy making their getaway.

The agent said, "Just a moment, I have an idea for you. We've got a freight train getting ready to leave the yard in a few minutes headed toward Shreveport. Let me see if they might be able to take you."

The agent left the window and walked back to the office of the depot manager and was gone for several minutes, and when he returned he had another man with him.

The agent said, "This is the depot manger, Samuel Baxter."

Mr. Baxter said, "I understand you are with the Texas Rangers and trying to get to Kilgore as soon as you can because you're trying to catch up with a couple of bank robbers that robbed a bank this morning and killed a deputy making their getaway."

Rocky replied, "Yes, sir."

Rocky took out his Texas Rangers Captain's badge and showed it the Mr. Baxter.

Mr. Baxter said, "We're going to get you on our freight train leaving here in about fifteen minutes, if you're ready to go."

"Yes, sir, I'm ready, just one more thing, can I get my horse on the train too?"

"Okay, Captain, I'll get our people to load your horse, and you can ride in the caboose with the conductor."

It didn't take but a few minutes before Mr. Baxter had everything taken care of.

Spring Rain was loaded into a cattle car, Rocky and Nick boarded the caboose, and the freight train was on its way to Shreveport, and they would make a special stop in Kilgore, Texas, for him.

It took the freight train a little over three hours to arrive in Kilgore and about thirty minutes to find a location to be able to unload Spring Rain.

As soon as they had Spring Rain off the train, it was on its way to Shreveport, and Rocky, Nick, and Spring Rain were on their way to Nacogdoches.

Rocky knew they wouldn't be making the same number of miles in an hour as they did on the train, and they still had a long way to go before they got to Nacogdoches.

Rocky rode his horse for over four hours before he found a place for them to bed down for the night. By the time he unsaddled Spring

Rain, rubbed him down, gave him some grain, and gave some food to Nick and made something for himself to eat, it was past midnight.

By the time Rocky unrolled his bedroll and found a spot that was cleared off enough for him to lie down, he felt like he had a full day.

Nick curled up next to his bedroll, and Spring Rain seemed to be standing guard over both of them only a few feet away.

Rocky said his prayers before going to sleep and asked God to please help Latesha to totally recover from her ordeal.

Lastly, he asked God to let him find Charlie Christian and let him send Charlie to hell for all the evil things he had done to people and for all the ones he had killed.

Rocky thought about what he had just asked God to help him do and realized he was asking God to let him kill somebody, which was against one of the Ten Commandments God had given Moses, "You shall not kill."

Maybe God would forgive him for wanting to kill Charlie Christian for all the people Charlie killed, and maybe Charlie had even killed Latesha. She certainly wasn't doing well the last time he saw her.

Rocky was up at daybreak and was soon saddling Spring Rain. Rocky asked him, "Are you ready to take me a lot of miles today?"

Spring Rain raised up his head and gave a little snort, like he was telling Rocky, "Okay, I'm ready."

Rocky gave Spring Rain a pat on his neck and said, "Okay, boy, let's get going."

Rocky climbed up in the saddle and asked Nick, "Are you ready to go, Nick?"

Nick looked up at Rocky and gave a very quiet bark, one of the few times Rocky had ever heard Nick bark.

"Okay, Nick, if you're ready and Spring Rain is ready, I guess we're off to Nacogdoches."

It took Rocky another two days of riding twelve hours a day to reach Nacogdoches, arriving there about eleven o'clock the third day of travel.

He located a small saloon that was open and found they had rooms available. The bartender told Rocky he could put Spring Rain in the barn behind the saloon for the night.

After Rocky unsaddled Spring Rain and gave him some oats and water, he and Nick made their way back inside the saloon and got a key for their room on the second floor.

By the time Rocky laid down on his bed, it was well past midnight.

Rocky had forgotten how hard it was riding that many hours a day for several days. It had been too many years since he had done it.

He was asleep almost before his head hit the pillow and wouldn't wake up until Nick roused him sometime around noon the next day.

Rocky reluctantly made himself get out of bed, and when he saw what time it was, he hurried dressing so he could take Nick outside to relieve himself.

After Rocky had taken care of Nick's need to go outside, he asked the bartender if he could get something to eat and for his dog, too.

The bartender asked Rocky what he would like to have to eat.

Rocky told him he would love to have three eggs, some bacon if he had some, and bread and butter, and for Nick, his favorite was a big juicy, raw steak.

The bartender told him to have a seat at one of the tables, and he would have his cook fix him and Nick up with their food.

It didn't take the cook long to come out from the kitchen carrying Rocky's food, and on the next trip from the kitchen, he came back with a plate with a nice juicy raw steak for Nick.

After Rocky finished eating and Nick consumed his steak and was chewing on the steak bone, Rocky said, "Bartender, please tell your cook how much I enjoyed my breakfast, and it looks like Nick appreciated his steak as well."

The bartender replied, "Yes, sir. I'll be happy to tell him, and I'm sure he will be happy to hear it since he normally only hears somebody complaining about their food."

Rocky kind of smiled and said, "Yeah, too many of us are way too quick to criticize and way too slow to compliment people."

The bartender replied, "You sure got that right, cowboy. Are you staying over another night, or do you have to push on?"

"Right now, I don't know what I'm doing. I have to go over to the Texas Rangers' office and talk with them about a matter."

"No problem, cowboy, we'll hold your room for you. Just let me know when you can."

"Thank you, I'm going over to the rangers' office right now. See you soon."

Rocky walked across the street to the rangers' office and found there was only one ranger there, and he was busy with a man who was telling him two men stole a couple of horses out of his corral.

Rocky listened closely to what the man had to say, wondering if it was Charlie Christian and Billy Jack Reynolds who stole his two horses.

The ranger was busy writing down the information about the two horses and what the men looked like and paid no attention to Rocky, and when Rocky heard the man's description of the two men, he knew it was his prey.

Rocky let the ranger complete his report before Rocky asked the man, "What direction did the men ride off in?"

The ranger looked at Rocky and asked, "Excuse me, sir, but what's your interest in these men?"

Rocky replied, "I'm Captain Rocky Stone with the Texas Rangers. I'm pretty sure the men who stole this man's horses are the two men who robbed the Bank of Jasper a few days ago and kidnapped my wife and killed two other women in New Orleans. They are the ones I'm after."

The ranger said, "I'm sorry, Captain, I hadn't met you before, but we did get a telegram from Fort Worth that you were coming."

Rocky asked the man, "Did you try to stop these men from taking your horses?"

"No, sir, I was in bed with my wife, and it was very early in the morning when I heard a big commotion outside and saw these two men as they were riding away from the corral on my two horses. By the time I could get dressed and get my rifle, they were just going over the top of a little hill away from my ranch, riding east."

Rocky said, "You were probably lucky you didn't get out there too soon because I'm pretty sure they would have killed you. You're lucky they just took your horses. I understand it's bad enough to lose your two horses, but it would have been a lot worse to lose your life. I'm going after these men myself. If I have any luck, I'll get your horses back to you. At least, we're going to do everything we can to get them back for you."

"Thank you, Captain."

The man left the office and Rocky asked the only ranger in the office "Where are the other rangers in your company?"

The ranger said, "They left to go to Jasper about two days ago to see if they could pick up the bank robbers' trail."

Rocky asked the ranger, "Can you tell me where the ranch is where the man who reported his horses being stolen lives?"

The ranger said, "His ranch is about halfway between Nacogdoches and San Augustine."

Then Rocky said, "When the rest of the ranger company gets back from Jasper, tell them to meet me in San Augustine. I have a hunch that's where I'm going to find the men I'm searching for. Their names are Charlie Christian and Billy Jack Reynolds. Thank you for your help, ranger. By the way, what's the brand on those two stolen horses?"

"The rancher's brand is triple X."

Rocky went back to the saloon and told the bartender he was going to stay again tonight and would be leaving at first light tomorrow morning.

CHAPTER TWENTY-THREE

All Hell's Broken Lose in New Orleans

Henry had everything arranged for his private train car to leave New Orleans for Rochester, Minnesota, and he had hired Nurse Susan Ray to look after Latesha during their trip.

Chuck Carson and his men would accompany Henry and Latesha during their trip to Rochester and stay with them to provide protection for them at all times, including when Latesha was at Mayo Clinic.

Captain Leon Cooper and his platoon of Federal soldiers would be traveling on the same train as Henry Hudson's private train car as far as Chicago, and from there they would take another train from Chicago to New York City.

Captain Robert Lawrence, the chief marshal, had made plans for his men and himself to do the same as the army troops, but the day before they were to leave, Doc Knox asked him to come to police headquarters to have a private meeting about another problem in New Orleans that he had been working on.

Captain Lawrence was rather anxious to get home to his family, and all his men were ready to go home.

Captain Lawrence arrived at the police department headquarters to meet with Captain Doc Knox and thought he could take care of whatever little problem he was having in a few minutes.

When Captain Lawrence arrived at the police headquarters, he was taken to a large conference room where Doc Knox and several other detectives were waiting for him.

Captain Lawrence was surprised to see several large boxes of files had been brought into the conference room, and when Doc Knox began his presentation, Lawrence was shocked.

Doc said, "Captain Lawrence, my men and I have been investigating Mayor Henri Rousseau and his top administration officials for several years, and we have found they head up the major crime organization in New Orleans. These boxes contain the information about the extent of their crimes and how they are organized. Each member of the mayor's top officials has their own organization for their criminal activities.

"Detective Smith, if you would put up the organization chart for Captain Lawrence to see, I think it would be helpful to him to understand the full extent of how their organization operates."

Detective Smith went to the front of the conference room and unrolled a large organizational chart and hung it up at the front of the room.

At the head of the organizational chart was Mayor Henri Rousseau, followed by his six top city officials, their names, their city job titles, and next to their titles what their jobs really were:

> Louis Delcour, Commissioner of Public Safety: collection of police protection payoffs, aided by Chief of Police Fred Johnson and Lieutenant Toby Chambers and his squad.
>
> James Froelich, Commissioner of Finance: take 10 percent of all taxes and fees paid to the city, using fraudulent purchases of city equipment and supplies, aided by the purchasing director, Charles Kerby and city clerk, Bob Brady.
>
> Nichols Keesling, Commissioner of Streets and Sanitation: collection of payoffs from potential

suppliers and from companies already selling products or supplies to the city.

Jeff Micorore, Commissioner of City Utilities: provider of protection for any organized gangs operating in New Orleans for 10 percent of their take of all jobs performed in the city.

David Joeckel, Commissioner of Parks: in charge of enforcement of anyone who threatens the mayor or his organization, without any limit to what they will do to keep everyone in line, including murder.

Sam Sweany, Commissioner of Building and Development: collects a 10 percent fee for every building permit issued and each violation, and in charge of vote counting for the city.

Captain Lawrence listened to the three-hour presentation Doc Knox and his team of detectives made about all the illegal doings of the mayor and his people. He examined the boxes of evidence they had compiled over several years of work and asked, "Why don't you take all this to the district attorney or the Louisiana Attorney General?"

Doc replied, "We would be laughed out of their office. They all know, or suspect, all of these wrongdoings, but they're afraid to try to do anything about it. No, our only hope is to have Federal prosecutors and Federal protection for all of us and our families, or we would all be dead before any trials were ever started here in New Orleans.

"Captain Lawrence, you are our only hope of cleaning up this city once and for all. If you won't or can't help us, then all of our work is for nothing. The mayor already suspects me of digging into all of his rackets, and if we don't get the Federal government's help, we're all going to be dead, and maybe our families, if they find out what we have done."

"Okay, Captain Knox, I'll contact the attorney general's office and tell him what we have uncovered here in New Orleans and see what he has to say. One thing I will promise you is I won't leave or let the platoon of Federal troops leave until I know what the attorney general wants me to do."

Doc said, "Thank you, Captain Lawrence."

Captain Lawrence told Doc he would go back to his hotel and contact the attorney general's office and see what they could do.

Two hours later Captain Lawrence and his men came back to the police headquarters and asked for Captain Knox. When he met with him, Captain Lawrence said, "Effective right now, all the boxes of evidence you have in your possession in the case that you presented to me this morning will be taken by my men and held for the attorney general's office. A representative of the attorney general will be here tomorrow from St. Louis, and as of this moment, you and all of your men involved in this case are under house arrest."

Doc Knox stared at Captain Lawrence like, what have I done?

Captain Lawrence's men picked up all the boxes of evidence that Doc and his people shared with him that morning and loaded them into a wagon in front of police headquarters.

After all the boxes of evidence were safely loaded onto the wagon, Captain Lawrence told Captain Knox and his men they would be coming with him and his men.

The desk sergeant called the police chief and told him what was going on, and when Chief of Police Johnson came out where Captain Lawrence was, he demanded to know what was going on. Captain Lawrence said, "My name is Captain Robert Lawrence, Chief Federal Marshal, and we're involved in a federal investigation, and we believe these men are involved in our case. As of right now, we will be holding them and their families under house arrest until further notice from the attorney general's office."

Chief Johnson said, "I demand to know what case you are talking about, Captain Lawrence."

"Chief Johnson, you can demand all you want, but I'm not at liberty to discuss the case with you. However, I believe you are aware that we have been in New Orleans on a kidnapping of a very important person, and that's all I'm going to tell you."

Captain Lawrence and his men took Captain Knox and all his men out of police headquarters, and when they got outside, the chief of police could see six Federal troops take each one of his officers and start walking them to waiting buggies.

As soon as the men were in a buggy, the troops drove off, taking each police officer to their home, where they would remain under house arrest.

Captain Lawrence had Captain Knox placed in his buggy, and when they were out of sight of police headquarters, Captain Lawrence said, "Sorry, Doc, that was the only way we could figure out how to get you and your men and the evidence out of police headquarters. It's also a way we can protect you until we can make an arrest of all of the suspects in this case. I tried to give the impression to your chief of police that this had to do with Latesha Stone's kidnapping, or at least I hope that's what he thinking."

"Well, Captain Lawrence, you sure as the hell confused me. I thought you must have gone over to the mayor's side when you started taking our evidence files out and saying we and are families were under house arrest."

"Doc, I'll take you by each one of your men's home so you can tell them what's going on, okay?

"Great, I'll certainly be happy to let all of my people know what's going on. I'm pretty sure they're all as confused as I was."

"Well, Doc, I would certainly think they would be."

When they arrived at Doc's home, Captain Lawrence had soldiers posted at the front and the rear of the house so there would be no doubt that it would appear as if Doc and his family were under house arrest.

Doc went inside the house, and Sarah said, "Doc, it's about time you came home. You haven't been here for three days—or is it four days now?"

"I don't know, Sarah, I've lost track of days. I've got something I have to tell you. For a while, we're going to be having soldiers guarding our house twenty-four hours a day."

"Doc, what in the world did we do to have soldiers guarding our house?"

"Because we have just turned all the evidence we have been gathering about the mayor and his people's crooked dealings and rackets to the US marshals. The soldiers are here to protect us, even though the police chief thinks we are under house arrest for something about the kidnapping of Latesha Stone."

"Well, Doc, why in the world would he think that?"

"Because, my lovely wife, that's the impression Chief US Marshal, Captain Lawrence, hinted was why he was taking all of the evidence and my men out of police headquarters."

"What in the world are our neighbors going to think?"

"I'm fairly sure they're going to think your husband is some kind of a crooked cop and the Federal Government has us under house arrest for my misdeeds."

"Oh, Doc, that's awful!"

"Well, Sarah, it's not as awful as all of us being killed by some of the mayor's henchmen, is it?"

"No, it's not, but how long is this going to last?"

"Sarah, I don't have any idea, but right now I have to go with Captain Lawrence and let my men know what's going on. They have no idea of why they were taken out of police headquarters and taken home and now have soldiers guarding their homes."

Sarah laughed and said, "I can tell you it's a heck of a surprise to me, and I know some of those men's wives are not going to be talking nicely about you getting them into something like this."

Two days later, Attorney John Upshaw from the US Attorney General's Office in St. Louis and five other attorneys arrived in New Orleans and opened an office in the US Customs Building in New Orleans.

After they set up their office, they had Captain Lawrence's men bring over all the boxes of evidence compiled by Captain Knox and his men on the wrongdoings of the mayor and his henchmen.

Soon after the office was open, they began to look over the material gathered by Captain Knox and his men.

Attorney Upshaw requested Captain Lawrence to have Knox and all his men brought to the offices.

On their arrival, they were invited to come into a very large conference room where they were given coffee and chairs at the conference table. A few minutes later Attorney Upshaw and the other five government attorneys joined them.

Upshaw said, "My name is John Upshaw. I'm the chief attorney for the third district of the United States Attorney General's Office in St. Louis, Missouri, and the city of New Orleans is located in my district. After my associates and I have had a chance to review of the evidence you men have collected regarding the illegal activities of your mayor and his men, we are ready to file federal charges against all of them.

"At this point, I would like to offer each of you men appointments as Federal investigating agents of the attorney general's office, with Captain Knox being in charge of the investigation. He would be the one who would coordinate everything with my attorneys and me and also be the one to provide any news releases to the local newspapers regarding this case.

"If you men agree to join us, we will swear you in this morning and put you on the payroll effective today. Your salaries will be at the Federal government's standard rates for the position you would be holding, which I can say is higher than what you have been paid for your current jobs with the city of New Orleans. Also, you don't have to kick back a percentage of your salary to anyone as you have been required to do when you were working for the city. Let me have a show of hands of any of you men who agree to join our team."

All the detectives and Captain Knox raised their hands, and Attorney Upshaw said, "Congratulations, and welcome to the United States Attorney General's Department."

A short time later, all the men were sworn in as Federal agents and given badges reading "Federal Agent, Department of Justice."

Each of the new Federal agents was assigned to work with an attorney from St. Louis, and each of these new teams began going through one of the boxes of evidence brought from the police headquarters and compiling charges against one or more of the mayor's henchmen.

Where's My Wife?

Attorney Upshaw had Captain Knox working with him and devising plans as to when and how they would make an arrest of the mayor and his men.

Upshaw asked Doc if he knew a newspaper man he could trust to keep information to himself until they were ready to make these arrests and make the announcement of the arrests and charges against each of the men involved.

Doc told him he knew of two men with the major newspaper in New Orleans they could trust, the publisher, Mr. Zwald, and his star reporter, Buddy Larson.

Upshaw said, "I want to you go over to the newspaper and ask these two men to come over to our office and meet with us as soon as they can. One more thing, Doc…it's okay if I call you Doc, isn't it?"

"No problem, Mr. Upshaw. I know how to answer to that name."

"Okay, Doc, please call me John."

"Great, John, what's the other thing you want me to do?"

"Doc, what was the man's name who was running for mayor against Mayor Rousseau in the last election?"

"He's a very good man by the name of Gary Armstrong. He's from one of the oldest families in New Orleans, educated as a lawyer at Harvard, and spends a lot of his time raising money for all kinds of charities."

"Doc, we'll also need to meet with Mr. Armstrong because if we don't have someone that's qualified and ready to take over as mayor of this city, it could be a real disaster for the city government and its residents."

"Okay, John, that not a problem. I'll make arrangements to have Mr. Armstrong come here to meet with us whenever you're ready."

"Doc, let's meet with the newspaper people first."

"Okay, I'll go over to the *Picayune Daily News* and see if I can get Mr. Zwald and Buddy Larson to come here right now."

"Great, I'll see you when you return."

Doc left the Custom House Building and walked the few blocks over to the *Picayune Daily News* and met with Mr. Zwald and Buddy

Larson. He told them he needed them to come with him and meet a very important visitor to New Orleans.

Although they were both busy, they agreed to go with Doc because they trusted him, unlike most of the members of the police department.

They walked over to the Custom House Building and made their way back into the offices being used by the Federal attorneys. Arriving there, Doc introduced them to John Upshaw, chief attorney of the attorney general's office in St. Louis.

Mr. Zwald asked, "So, Mr. Upshaw, what brings you to New Orleans, and why did you want to meet with us?"

"Gentleman, Captain Knox brought to the attention of the US Chief Marshal, Robert Lawrence, who was in your city due to the kidnapping of Latesha Stone, certain information about crimes being committed by your mayor and his commissioners. We are in New Orleans to begin making arrests of these men and will be prosecuting them for their crimes."

Mr. Zwald said, "Wow, somebody who's willing to do something about that nest of crooks! It's about time. Frankly, I never thought I would live long enough to ever see it."

John replied, "Yes, sir, you're going to see it very soon thanks to the efforts of Captain Knox and his men. The reason I asked to see you is I want you to be ready to publish the story as soon as we are ready to make these arrests."

Mr. Zwald asked, "How soon do you think you will be ready?"

"Maybe as early as next week, and when we do, all hell is going to break loose here in New Orleans, and we want you to be ready for the story."

Zwald replied, "We'll be damn ready to break that story when you're ready."

John said, "Good, Captain Knox will be the spokesperson for the US Attorney General's Office since as of today Captain Knox and his detectives are now employed as Federal agents with the attorney general's office.

"I have one more question I want to ask you, gentlemen. Captain Knox seems to think a Mr. George Armstrong would be a good replacement for the mayor. Do you have anything comment about that?"

Mr. Zwald replied, "Other than the man's name is Gary Armstrong, not George, we think he would be a great leader for the city. The newspaper supported him in the last election, but Rousseau and his band of crooks could buy too many votes, and Gary lost the election by a few hundred votes.

"You can count on the *Picayune Daily News* supporting Gary Armstrong as our mayor, and what a breath of fresh air that would be. To have an honest citizen as our mayor would be something that hasn't happened in New Orleans for twenty years."

John replied, "I'm glad you know Mr. Armstrong's name and feel he would do a good job for the city and that your newspaper would support him.

"I appreciate you taking your time to come over and visit with us, and I want to ask that you not let any word of our operation out until we ready to move."

Mr. Zwald replied, "No problem, you can count on our full cooperation."

John said, "Thanks again, and, Doc, will you show these gentlemen out and see if you can locate Mr. Armstrong?"

"Yes, sir."

Doc went out of the Custom House Building with Mr. Zwald and Buddy Larson and headed out to see if he could find Gary Armstrong at his home in the Garden District.

Doc was in luck. He found Mr. Armstrong at home, and when he asked him to come to a meeting with Mr. John Upshaw of the US Attorney General's office, he agreed to come with him even if he didn't understand why he was meeting him.

Arriving at the Custom House Building, Doc introduced Gary Armstrong to John Upshaw, and after John told Mr. Armstrong what he was in the process of doing, he asked Gary if he would consider taking on the responsibility of the mayor's office.

Mr. Gary Armstrong said he would be glad to take the job as mayor of New Orleans, even on a temporary basis.

Two weeks passed, and everything was ready to make the arrests of Mayor Rousseau and his henchmen.

All the warrants were prepared with the various charges, and John Upshaw had requested a company of soldiers to come to New Orleans from Jefferson Barracks in St. Louis to help with the arrest of these men.

Captain Knox and ten soldiers went to City Hall and directly into the mayor's office, in spite of his secretary telling Doc he couldn't go in to see the mayor until the mayor was ready to see him.

The mayor looked up at Doc as he came into the office, and Mayor Rousseau said, "What in the hell do you mean coming into my office unannounced? I thought you and your men were all under house arrest for something you did during that Stone woman's kidnapping case."

Doc replied, "Not any longer. I'm here as a US Federal Agent to arrest you for so many crimes it will take your lawyer a week to read them all."

The mayor shouted, "Get the hell out of my office before I have you shot."

Doc replied, "Mr. Mayor, you've just added another charge against you, threatening a Federal Agent."

Four of the ten soldiers with Doc came into the mayor's office at the same time the mayor threatened Doc.

Captain Knox said, "Captain, put handcuffs on the mayor and take him down to the police wagon and over to the Custom House Building."

The captain walked over behind the mayor and took hold of his right hand as he was trying to reach inside his desk drawer to pick up a pistol. Another one of the soldiers grabbed his left hand and locked a handcuff onto the mayors left wrist, and the captain grabbed the right wrist and put the handcuff on it.

Captain Knox said, "Captain, the mayor is to be locked up in one of the rooms we have prepared for a jail cell there."

"No problem, Captain Knox, we'll take care of this man."

Out the office door the mayor went, along with the four soldiers who came in to take him to their new jail in the Custom House Building.

Captain Knox told the other six men to secure this office and all the mayor's files until they had time to pack up everything and bring every piece of paper in the mayor's office over to the Custom House Building. No one was to be allowed in the office or in the file room.

In addition to the mayor being arrested, the following men were also arrested on the same day: Louis Delcour, commissioner of public safety; the chief of police Fred Johnson; Lieutenant Toby Chambers; James Froelich, commissioner of finance; purchasing director Charles Kerby; city clerk Bob Brady; Nichols Keesling, commissioner of streets and sanitation; Jeff Micorore, commissioner of city utilities; David Joeckel, commissioner of parks; and Sam Sweany, commissioner of building and development

In addition to telling the story of these arrests, the *Picayune Daily News Extra* also ran the story that the Federal Judge in Baton Rouge declared the last election for the mayor of New Orleans was rigged in favor of Henri Rousseau, and he further declared that Mr. Gary Armstrong, a local lawyer in New Orleans, was the legally elected mayor of New Orleans, and he was to take office immediately.

Mayor Armstrong announced at his news conference that Captain Doc Knox, a Federal Agent with the US Department of Justice, would be appointed as the new chief of police for the city of New Orleans.

CHAPTER TWENTY-FOUR

Latesha's Progress at St. Mary's Hospital

Dr. Charles Mayo met the train when it arrived with Henry Hudson IV's private railcar in Rochester, Minnesota, because he wanted to see how Latesha had made the trip and check her over before moving her.

Henry met Charles at the door of his private railcar and said, "Dr. Mayo, I'm really glad to see you and have high hopes you will be able to help my daughter, Latesha."

"Well, Mr. Hudson, we are certainly going to try. I wanted to have a look at her before we moved her to the hospital."

Henry replied, "Great, her nurse, Susan Ray, is with her in the bedroom. Come right this way."

Henry led Dr. Mayo through the train car until he came to Latesha's bedroom, opened the door, and showed the doctor in.

Henry said, "Dr. Mayo, this is Susan Ray, Latesha's nurse, who's been looking after her since we got Latesha back from her kidnappers."

Dr. Mayo said, "Nurse Ray, how is your patient doing?"

"Well, sir, she's not doing very well since she continues to go in and out of consciousness, and when she is conscious, it's only for a brief amount of time."

"Has there been any sign she is getting any better since you first started taking care of her?"

"No, sir, I wouldn't say she has, but on the other hand, she hasn't got any worse either. The only thing I can say is by our getting some water down her, her vital signs have improved, and her color is much better."

Henry said, "She certainly looks better than when we first got her back."

Dr. Mayo said, "I want to examine her before we move her out of her bed and take her over to the hospital."

With that said, Dr. Mayo began a complete examination of Latesha, with Nurse Ray helping him.

When the examination was finished, Dr. Mayo said, "Mr. Hudson, we're going to take Latesha to St. Mary's Hospital now. It was opened by the Sisters of Saint Francis of Rochester, Minnesota, under the direction of Mother Alfred Moes. We have a twenty-seven-bed facility and a staff working twenty-four hours a day. We work closely with them with our patients who need to be hospitalized for some length of time.

"I'm afraid Latesha is going to be there for some time, and I can tell you we will do a good job looking after Latesha. One more thing, Nurse Ray, are you planning on staying in Rochester or returning to New Orleans?"

"Sir, I was planning on going back to New Orleans. Why do you ask?"

"I think it would be a very good idea if you could stay and help the sisters care for Latesha, and when we have her back in good health, I believe you might be a great help to our hospital as well. We certainly need good people to accomplish what we are trying to do."

"Thank you, sir, I would be honored to stay with Latesha to see her nursed back to health, and I will certainly think about staying and working with you at the clinic."

Henry said, "Susan, I think Dr. Mayo has a great idea, and I would certainly continue paying you for staying and working with Latesha until you get her back on her feet."

Dr. Mayo said, "Fine, that's all settled. I'll get my people to move Latesha to St. Mary's Hospital, and I'll look in on her later this evening."

Henry replied, "Thank you, Dr. Mayo, for taking your time to come to the train station and taking a look at my daughter."

Dr. Mayo answered, "Looking after our patients is what we do here, and I'll see you this evening."

Dr. Mayo left the train car, and a few minutes later two burly-looking men, dressed in white uniforms, came into the train car and said, "We're here to pick up Latesha Stone and transport her to the hospital."

Seeing the size of these men, Henry wondered if he should be concerned that they might hurt his daughter by picking her up and carrying her.

But he decided if Dr. Mayo trusted these men to look after his daughter, then he guessed he should, too.

Henry showed the men where Latesha was lying in bed and watched carefully as these two burly men picked up his daughter and placed her onto a stretcher and carried her as gently as if they were carrying priceless crystal.

A few minutes later they placed his daughter's stretcher onto a cot in a special carriage made to transport patients.

One of the men stayed by Latesha's side, and the other man drove the carriage.

Henry and Susan Ray watched as the carriage pulled away from the station, and then a man said, "Are you Mr. Henry Hudson?"

Henry replied, "Yes, I'm Hudson."

The man said, "Dr. Mayo asked me to take you to St. Mary's Hospital after your daughter was picked up by his men to take her to the hospital."

"Fine, yes, I'm ready to go, and can you take Nurse Ray with us as well?"

"Yes, sir, no problem. Just follow me to my carriage and I will take both of you to the hospital right away."

Henry and Susan Ray followed the man to his carriage, got inside, and were soon on their way to the hospital.

It only took about fifteen minutes for the trip to St. Mary's Hospital, and the man told them to go on inside, and there would be someone inside that could direct them to Mrs. Stone's room. He said he would be waiting outside the hospital for them if they wanted to go anywhere else.

He also told Mr. Hudson if he wasn't in his carriage, he would leave word where he was or when he would be back with the lady who worked at the front desk of the hospital.

Henry thanked him and told him he appreciated him taking care of his transportation needs.

The man replied, "No problem, sir."

Henry and Susan Ray went inside St. Mary's Hospital, and Henry went directly to the front desk and told the lady working there that his name was Henry Hudson and his daughter had just been brought to the hospital by two hospital attendants, and he wanted to know which room had been assigned to Mrs. Latesha Stone.

The woman working at the front desk looked on a chart and told Henry his daughter was in room number 27.

Henry and Susan Ray were directed down a hallway by the desk clerk and said, "Mrs. Stone is in the last room on the right."

When they arrived at room 27, the door was closed. Henry knocked on the door, and it took some time before a nun opened the door and asked who he was and the lady with him.

Henry replied, "I'm Henry Hudson, Latesha's father, and this lady is Nurse Susan Ray, my daughter's private nurse from New Orleans."

The nun said, "How do you do? My name is Sister Margaret, and I have just been checking Latesha over after she arrived at the hospital. She seems like she would like to wake up but just doesn't seem to be able to do it. I understand she has been in a stressful situation that caused her to be in this condition."

Henry replied, "You could say that, since she was kidnapped for a long time and deprived of food and water. I would describe that as a stressful situation."

Sister Margaret said, "I would certainly think so. I can assure you, Mr. Hudson, we at St. Mary's and our doctors will do everything possible to help her have a full recovery."

Henry answered, "That will be wonderful, and Nurse Ray has come here to help you look after my daughter."

Sister Margaret said, "I certainly look forward to working with Nurse Ray and looking after your daughter during her stay here at St. Mary's. I am required to ask if you or your daughter is a member of the Catholic Church?"

"No, sister, we are members of the Episcopal Church."

Susan Ray spoke up and said, "I'm a member of the Catholic Church."

Sister Margaret replied, "The reason I asked is that the sisters have a daily mass, and I wanted to offer you the opportunity to attend our service."

Susan said, "I would love to attend your service every day if I could."

Sister Margaret replied, "Nurse Ray, we would be delighted to have you with us."

A doctor came into the room just as Sister Margaret finished her statement.

The doctor said, "My name is Dr. Samuels, and I work with Dr. Mayo. He asked me to examine Mrs. Stone."

Henry said, "Dr. Samuels, I'm Henry Hudson, Latesha's father, and this lady with me is Nurse Susan Ray from New Orleans."

Dr. Samuels replied, "I'm very glad to meet you, Mr. Hudson and Nurse Ray, and look forward to visiting with both of you later. Right now I need to take a peek at Mrs. Stone, and I'd ask you, Mr. Hudson, if you would mind stepping out to the waiting room while I'm checking over Mrs. Stone.

"Nurse Ray, I would like for you to stay with me during the examination since I understand you have been with Mrs. Stone since she was first rescued from her kidnappers."

Henry turned to go out the door when Sister Margaret said, "Mr. Hudson, I would be glad to show you to our waiting room and get you some tea or coffee, if you don't need me, Dr. Samuels?"

Henry replied, "Thank you, Sister Margaret. I would appreciate a cup of tea."

Dr. Samuels said, Thank you, Sister Margaret, since we have Nurse Ray with us now, she can assist me during my examination of Mrs. Stone."

Henry and Sister Margaret left the room and walked back to the front of the hospital. Sister Margaret led Henry into a small dining room and set about preparing both of them cups of tea.

Henry watched Sister Margaret as she was making their tea and wondered what made her to decide to become a nun. He could tell she was a very beautiful young woman, even dressed in her habit. Henry thought surely some man must have caused her to become a nun.

As Henry and Sister Margaret sipped their tea, Dr. Samuels did a complete physical examination of Latesha, with Nurse Ray's help.

After Dr. Samuels completed his examination, he said, "Physically, Mrs. Stone seems to be in fairly good condition except she has obviously lost a lot of weight since she's down to nothing more than skin and bones.

"I would say the lack of food and enough water seems to be the major problem with her health. She doesn't seem to have any bruises except a very small one on her head, where she had been hit some time ago.

"She shows no sign of rape or sexual abuse, which was one of Dr. Mayo's and my thoughts that might be causing her not to be able to regain consciousness."

Susan Ray replied, "Dr. Johnson and I examined Latesha Stone when she was first rescued from the kidnappers. Dr. Johnson checked her at that time for any sign of rape or sexual abuse and found nothing.

"She was in need of water when she first arrived at the hospital. Dr. Johnson came up with this idea of using a hollowed out reed to get some water down her throat. I can tell you it took a lot of time, but at least we began to get her some water."

Dr. Samuels said, "Dr. Johnson had a great idea. Did he have any other ideas that might help her?"

"Dr. Johnson told us to keep talking to Latesha so she knew someone was with her. He thought it might wake her up and keep her here with us."

"You know, Nurse Susan, I think your Dr. Johnson may have a really great idea, so I would say you and her father and anyone else working in her room should keep talking to her."

"Yes, sir, we'll keep talking to Latesha, and I'll keep giving her water using the hollowed out reed."

"Nurse Susan, may I just call you Susan?"

"Certainly, that's not a problem for me."

"Great, Susan, Dr. Mayo and I talked about some ideas to try on Latesha to see if we can get her out of her unconscious state, and I want you to try something we've thought about."

"What's that, Doctor?"

"I'm going to have a large bathtub brought into Mrs. Stone's room. I want you to fill the tub with very warm water, and with some help place Mrs. Stone in the water. Let her stay there for a long time by adding more warm water to the tub when it starts to cool."

"Doctor, how long, are you thinking about keeping her in the warm water?"

"At least an hour and doing it, say, three times a day."

"What do you think that's going to do to help her stay awake?"

"Dr. Mayo thinks it might create the feeling of her being back in the womb, and when you take her out of the water, perhaps she will feel like she's been born again."

"Well, Dr. Samuels, I think it's the craziest idea in medicine I've ever heard, but if you and Dr. Mayo think it's worth a try, I'll do it."

"Good, Susan, let's see if we have any other results other than having one very waterlogged patient."

Both Dr. Samuels and Susan began laughing pretty hard, and when they did, Latesha laughed out loud.

Dr. Samuels and Susan quickly looked down at Latesha, but she had quit laughing and still appeared to be completely unconscious.

Dr. Samuels said, "Well, maybe we should try laughing to get Mrs. Stone to wake up and be with us, so she knows what we're laughing about."

"Sounds like a good plan, Doctor."

As Dr. Samuels was preparing to leave, they heard a knock at the door, and Dr. Mayo came into the room and asked, "Dr. Samuels, have you had a chance to examine Mrs. Stone yet?"

"Yes, sir, I have with, Nurse Ray's assistance."

"So what do you think, Doctor?"

"I have to think Mrs. Stone suffered a tremendous fright while being kidnapped, followed by a lack of food and water, and her brain has tried to shut down as much of her bodily functions as possible to help keep her alive.

"I believe she is going in and out of consciousness because her brain is not certain that she is now safe and away from her kidnappers. In other words, she's too afraid to wake up or that her body is still too much in shock."

Dr. Mayo said, "In my examination of her, I couldn't see any type of physical wound that should be keeping her unconscious. Her body is certainly down to nothing much more than skin and bones from lack of enough water and food, but I believe, like you do, it's all mental at this point.

"It's too bad we can't operate on her brain and tell it, 'It's okay, you're safe now, you can wake up and go on with your life.' So the best we can do for her is to try to show her she's safe and try to convince her brain it's safe enough for her to come out of this unconsciousness and stay out."

Dr. Samuels replied, "Nurse Ray is ready to start getting her in a warm bath three times a day and will continue talking with her all the time she's in the room. Her father has been doing that as well."

Dr. Mayo added, "That all sounds good, but I think we need to add one more step, and that is to have whoever is in the room to keep touching her. Humans respond to being touched, and I think that might help her as well."

Nurse Ray replied, "I believe that, sir. I will certainly keep a hand on her all of the time I can when I'm not doing something else for her."

Dr. Mayo said, "I'll talk to our other doctors to see if any of them has any other idea on how to get someone out of a coma. We also need to try to find ways to get more water and food in her."

As Dr. Mayo was leaving Latesha's room, he met Henry Hudson, who asked the doctor what he thought Latesha's chances of recovering were.

Dr. Mayo said, "I'm afraid to answer that question right now. I think we'll have a better idea after we have a chance to try some of the ideas to get Latesha out of her coma."

Henry thanked him and continued into Latesha room. He met Dr. Samuels, who was just leaving Latesha's room, and Henry got the same answer from him as he had gotten from Dr. Mayo.

When Henry was back in Latesha's room, Nurse Ray said, "We have some new things to try on Latesha to see if we can get her out of her coma. Dr. Mayo and Dr. Samuels suggested that when we're talking to Latesha, we should also be touching her. They think that may help her regain consciousness. They also told me to give her a warm bath three times a day for an hour each time. The one good or bad thing both doctors said? They thought she was afraid to wake up, and we had to convince her brain it would be all right for her to wake up."

Henry replied, "Well, I guess we'll do whatever they ask and pray that it helps."

Henry sat down on Latesha's bed and started talking to her about when she was a little girl growing up in New York, and while he was talking, he took her left hand into his right hand.

Three days later, after Latesha had nine warm baths and some seventy-eight hours of people touching and talking to her, and as her dad was holding her hand and finishing reading the story of *Peter Rabbit* to her, Latesha suddenly opened her eyes and said in a whisper, "Daddy, could you read me *Peter Rabbit* again?"

Henry pulled her up into his arms and said, "My darling girl, I'd read *Peter Rabbit* to you a hundred times if you'll just keep those eyes open for me."

Latesha replied in a stronger voice, "I will, Daddy, I will. Can I have something to eat? I'm hungry."

Nurse Ray said, "Miss Latesha, I'll get you something to eat right now."

Latesha asked, "Can I have some coffee, too?"

Nurse Ray answered, "You sure can, my love. You can have anything you want to eat and drink."

Then Latesha asked, "Daddy, where's Rocky?"

Henry replied, "Sweetheart, he's in Texas trying to find your kidnappers. I'm sure he will be here as soon as he can."

"Oh, Daddy, don't let anything happen to him, I love him so much."

"Don't you be worrying about Rocky. You know he can take care of himself. He doesn't want that man who kidnapped you to be able to come back and do it again or hurt you."

A few minutes later, both Dr. Mayo and Samuels came to see Latesha, and Nurse Ray arrived with her eggs, bacon, and some bread, as well as her coffee.

Dr. Mayo said, "Latesha, you have something to eat and we'll come back later to see you."

Latesha ate both of her eggs, a piece of bacon, and a little bit of bread and said, "I can't eat anymore."

Nurse Ray said, "It's okay, you haven't had anything to eat for a long time, and your stomach will have to get used to working again. You just let me know when you feel like having something else."

Henry said, "Baby, you've had a lot of people really worried about you. We didn't think you were ever going to regain consciousness. It's been a long time since you were awake for any length of time."

Latesha asked, "I know I'm must be in a hospital, but where am I?"

"You are in St. Mary's Hospital in Rochester, Minnesota, under the care of Dr. Charles W. Mayo and Dr. Samuels."

"How did I get here?"

"I brought you on my railcar. I know you must have a lot of questions, but for right now you probably need to rest before the doctors come back in wanting to check you over again."

Dr. Mayo came back in to Latesha's room and thoroughly checked her over, and when he was finished he said, "Latesha, you are going to be all right but you need to stay here with us for a while until we can get your strength built back up and to be sure you don't develop some type of problem that we don't know about yet, okay?"

"Since I don't think I have anything to say about it right now. I'll stay."

CHAPTER TWENTY-FIVE

We Gotta Git Home

As soon as Tom and Sandy Barr were released by the New Orleans Police Department, Tom said, "Sandy, we gotta git home as fast as we can to protect Ma and Pa and the kids."

"Tom, do you think Charlie is really going to try to kill our ma and pa?"

"I believe it as sure as I know we're sitting here in New Orleans. You know Charlie Christian hates me as much as he hated Rocky Stone, and look what he done to Rocky's wife."

"Well, you didn't send him to prison two times like Rocky did."

"No, but he knows we gave Rocky and the police information as to where they were holding Mrs. Stone. Plus you heard what Ronnie Barnhill told the police: that the reason Charlie and Billy Jack weren't at the hideout was because they were waiting for us to get off of the ferryboat and they were going to shoot us down.

"The only reason they didn't kill us then was because we came back to Algiers with the police, and when they saw the police, they got away. So what do you think? You think ole Charlie is just going to forget us? No, sir, he's going to be coming after us, and he'll kill Ma and Pa and the kids just for spite."

"Okay, Tom, I guess you're right. I just didn't think about all of that."

"Sandy, you better let me do the thinking for us. You keep thinking about marrying Julie Crockett and building Ma and Pa a new home with the money Rocky Stone is going to pay us."

"Okay, so when is he going to give us all of that money? I haven't seen any money yet?"

"Sandy, don't worry about Mr. Stone paying us the money. People like him honor what they tell people. He said we would git the money, and we'll git it. Right now we need horses and some money to be able to make it back home. Sandy, I still have three hundred dollars that Charlie paid us. That should git us home."

"You're right, Tommy, and I still have some money in my boot."

Sandy took off his boot and found he had almost four hundred dollars, so between them they had almost seven hundred dollars.

Tom said, "Since we have this much money, we'll take a train from here to Tyler and git us horses when we git there. That should save a lot of time traveling, and then we can ride from Tyler out to Pa's ranch."

"Okay, Tommy, let's git started."

Tom and Sandy gathered up their few belongings and asked directions to the New Orleans train station.

It took them about twenty minutes to walk to the train station, and arriving there, they approached the ticket counter and told the clerk they wanted two tickets to Tyler, Texas.

The clerk told them a train would be leaving in about an hour for Shreveport, and when they arrived in Shreveport, they would have to change trains to the Fort Worth train.

Tom said, "Sir, we don't want to go to Fort Worth, we want to go to Tyler, Texas."

The railroad clerk looked at Tom for a second and replied, "Son, I know you want to go to Tyler, but the Fort Worth train will be the one taking you to Tyler, and when you get to Tyler, the train will stop and you can get off."

"Thank you, sir, my brother and I have never been on a train before."

"It's okay. I understand not too many people have ridden trains before, but it will be okay. The man working on the train is called the conductor, and he will make sure you get off the train where you are supposed to.

"When you get to Shreveport, the people working at the station will see that you get on the right train going to Tyler. Then the conductor on the train going to Fort Worth will be sure to help you get off the train when it gets to Tyler."

"Thank you, sir, we appreciate your help."

Tommy paid for their tickets, and Tom and Sandy sat down to wait for the train going to Shreveport.

Sure enough, about thirty minutes later the man who sold them their tickets came out and shouted out, "Train to Chicago now boarding on track 2, with stops in Shreveport, Memphis, and all points along the way."

Tom and Sandy got up to go outside to board the train, and the railroad clerk Tom had been talking to while buying their tickets showed Tom the car they were to get on and how to find the train car number on their tickets.

Tom and Sandy thanked the man again for all his help.

They found seats and sat down and were startled when the train started moving; it jerked them forward in their seats, then kind of stopped, then jerked them forward again.

Tom said, "Man, this thing is worse than my horse."

Then the train began to smooth out as it began picking up speed, and Tom and Sandy could see they were going past buildings at a speed their horses could never take them.

Sandy said, "Man, this train can really move. I think we may get home a lot quicker than we ever thought we could."

Tom replied, "I sure hope Charlie and Billy Jack didn't take a train, or we will never make it home before they get there."

"Tom, I doubt they took a train with everybody looking for them because of posters up all around New Orleans offering a big reward for their capture."

"I think you're right. Charlie was always pretty careful, so I doubt he would go to a train station where the police might be looking for him."

The trip to Shreveport took several hours, with the train stopping at several stations on the way. They finally arrived in Shreveport, and by this time, Tom and Sandy were used to the conductor walking through the car yelling the name of the next station.

So when the conductor announced Shreveport, they began gathering up all their things to be ready to get off of the train.

The two men got off the train and went inside the station and asked when the train for Fort Worth would arrive and when would it leave.

The man at the ticket counter told them it would be about four hours before the westbound train would arrive. Then they would have to service the train before it left, and that would take about an hour before their train would be leaving.

Tom asked the clerk if there was some place they could get something to eat that was near the station; he was told the hotel down the street had a restaurant.

Tom thanked the clerk, and then Tom and Sandy made their way to the hotel and had something to eat.

After they returned to the station and had time to look around, Sandy found that the telegram operator had Elgin pocket watches for sale and told Tom they should buy one for Pa.

Tom asked the telegram operator how much it cost for one of the pocket watches and was told they had different models; the least expensive one was twenty dollars, and the nicer gold watch was fifty dollars.

Tom and Sandy talked about which one they should buy, and Tom said, "I think our pa deserves to have the gold watch even though it costs fifty dollars. Look at all the things he has done for our family, and he's never bought anything for himself."

Sandy agreed, so Tom counted out fifty dollars and paid the man. The telegram operator started to put the gold watch in a special watch box, but before he did, he said, "You really should get your pa a gold chain to go with his watch. It will keep him from losing it and make it easy for him to get it out of his pocket."

Sandy agreed, so Tom paid the man another ten dollars.

The telegram operator attached the chain to the watch and then placed the watch in its special box.

Where's My Wife?

As the man was handing Tom the box, Tom said, "It's kind of unusual for telegram operators to be selling watches, isn't it?"

The operator replied, "No, since the railroad works on close time schedules on all the trains, people have to have a watch to be sure they are where they're supposed to be according to their schedules. One of our telegram operators in Illinois made a deal with the watchmakers to allow us to sell the watches, and it lets us make a little extra money."

Tom thanked the man, put the box with Pa's new watch in his pocket, and he and Sandy found a place to sit down and wait for their train.

After the hours passed slowly by, their westbound train finally arrived at the station.

Tom and Sandy walked outside to see what all the men had to do to service the train.

They found they had to load on coal and water, and some men went around checking the wheels of the train. They told Tom they were checking for hotspots, and if they found any they had to do something with the wheels.

The agent in the station had told them right; it was just about an hour when the conductor shouted, "All aboard."

Tom and Sandy found their car and got aboard; they were now experienced train riders.

When the train started up, they waited for the jerk the train seemed to go through each time it started moving, and this time they were ready for it.

It took the train only about two and half hours to go from Shreveport to Tyler, even after making two stops in between.

They heard the conductor shout out, "Tyler, Texas, next stop," and they gathered up their things once more and were the only two passengers getting off the train in Tyler.

As soon as they were off the train, the conductor climbed back on board, and the train began moving on toward Fort Worth.

Tom said, "Sandy, I think we better stay the rest of the night here in Tyler and get an early start in the morning. I don't know about you, but I'm pretty tuckered out."

"Sounds like a really good idea. I'm certain I could use some sleep."

The two of them walked across the street to a small hotel, opened the door, and walked up to the counter. Tom saw a bell to ring for service and began ringing the bell.

A few minutes passed before an elderly man came through a door located behind the counter and asked if he could help them.

Sandy asked, "We need a room for the night, if you've got one?"

The old man retorted, "Sonny, we got a room, if you got the money."

Sandy said, "I reckon we got enough money, if the room don't cost too much."

"The room will cost you two dollars for one night."

Tom said, "Okay, we'll take it," as he reached into his pocket and pulled out two silver dollars and put them on the counter.

The old man took a key off a nail behind him and handed it to Sandy and said, "Thank you, it's room number 7."

Then the old man said, "We have breakfast served in the morning from six to eight o'clock. If you're interested, it's twenty-five cents."

Sandy replied, "Thank you, that sounds good. Good night, sir."

The old man looked at Tom and Sandy and said, "Good night, men."

They went to their room on the second floor of the hotel. Opening the door they found two beds, and it didn't take them long before they were in those two beds and quickly fast asleep.

It didn't seem like they were in their beds very long until the sunlight started dancing off the wall and into their eyes.

Sandy said, "Tom, you said you wanted to get an early start home, but does it have to be this early?"

Tom reached over to the little table next to his bed where he had placed the little box that contained Pa's new watch and saw it was only a few minutes after five.

Tom said, "Sandy, it's only a few minutes after five. I think we could get another hour and half of bedtime. Okay?"

"Okay."

Where's My Wife?

Sandy rolled over on his left side and went right back to sleep, and Tom wasn't very many minutes behind him going back to sleep.

They both stayed asleep until Tom woke up and saw it was now seven thirty and shouted to Sandy, "Sandy, we have to get up. It's seven thirty and we're going to miss breakfast."

It took the boys only about ten minutes to get their boots back on and down the stairs to get their breakfast.

A young woman showed them to a table, and the boys took seats, and Tom asked, "Are we too late for breakfast?"

The young woman replied, "It's not eight o'clock, so we're still serving breakfast. What would you like to have?"

Sandy answered, "Eggs, bacon, and some bread and butter."

Tom said, "I'll have the same."

The waitress replied, "Two regular breakfasts: eggs, bacon, and bread."

Tom said, "If you have some jam, I'd sure like to have that too."

Sandy added, "Me too, if you got some."

The waitress answered, "We've got some wonderful strawberry jam. I'll bring you some with your order."

Tom thought their waitress was very pretty. She looked to be about his age, and she had long black hair with a little curl that fell down on her forehead. She had beautiful dark brown eyes and a very nice smile.

Tom guessed she must be about as tall as his mother, which was about five foot five. He even liked the way she walked; she kind of swayed from side to side.

Tom thought it was a little like watching wheat moving in the wind when it was golden brown, gently swaying with the wind.

It took almost thirty minutes before their waitress brought their orders along with a large bowl of strawberry jam.

It only took about ten minutes for Tom and Sandy to empty their plates and finish off the strawberry jam.

Tom paid the bill and left the waitress a twenty-five-cent tip, which was a lot since she never had a tip before.

Tipping just wasn't done in Tyler, Texas, no one ever thought about leaving a tip for somebody for just bringing them their food.

The next thing they needed to do was find a couple of horses to ride back home.

As they were leaving the hotel, suddenly their waitress came up to them and said, "Sir, you forgot your money. It was lying on the table, and she reached out her hand to Tom with the change.

Tom said, "No, ma'am. I didn't forget it. I was leaving it for you for serving us so well. It's called a tip."

"Well, whatever you call it, I can't take it. They don't do things like that here in Tyler."

Tom replied, "Okay, ma'am, I didn't mean to cause you any trouble."

As the waitress handed Tom back his change, their hands touched, and Tom felt like he never felt before.

Her touch was wonderful, and he asked, "What's your name, miss? It is *miss*, isn't it?"

The young woman stopped and took a really good look at Tom and said, "Yes, it's *miss*, Miss Jane Jones, and my grandpa owns the hotel."

"Miss Jane Jones, my name is Tom Barr, and this is my brother, Sandy. Our folks have a ranch near Chandler."

Jane said, "I'm glad to know both of you. Your folks' ranch is near Chandler? That's not too far from Tyler."

Sandy said, "Actually, our ranch is about halfway between Tyler and Chandler. It's just a little bit closer to Chandler."

Jane replied, "Oh, then you're not too far away from Tyler."

Tom said, "No, it's not that far away. I could ride here in a couple of hours or so."

Jane asked, "You could do it in a couple of hours?"

Tom said, "I could do it if I had a good reason to do it, like I was coming to see you."

Jane said, "Coming to see me would be a good reason?"

Tom replied, "It'd be a damn good reason, sorry, ma'am."

Jane just smiled and said, "Like some Sunday afternoon you might be able to come?"

Tom answered, "Maybe like next Sunday afternoon?"

Jane said, "That would be great. I don't live at the hotel though, my folks' house is the big white house at the end of the street. I'm sure looking forward to seeing you next Sunday, Mr. Tom Barr."

Tom replied, "I'll see you next Sunday afternoon, Miss Jane Jones."

Sandy said, "Okay, Tom, now that you folks have a date. We need to buy a couple of horses so we can get back home."

Tom said, "You're right, Sandy, we need to find some horses."

Jane said, "Try the livery stable down the street."

Tom replied, "Thank you, Miss Jane Jones, I'm sure looking forward to Sunday."

With that, Sandy grabbed his brother's arm and said, "Come on, Tom, we've got to get going, or it's going to be Sunday before we get out of here."

Jane laughed and turned to go back into the dining room, and Tom and Sandy left on their way to the livery stable.

They were able to buy two very nice-looking horses for eighty dollars and spent another hundred dollars for two saddles, bridles, and blankets.

The livery stable had their new horses saddled up and made ready for them while Tom went into the office to pay and get a bill of sale.

One of their new horses was a beautiful pinto gelding, and the other was a big white stallion with blaze that looked like lightning on his forehead.

After he collected their money for the horses and as they were about ready to mount up, the livery owner said, "That stallion is a little wild, he's just green broke, but I figure you boys, growing up on a horse ranch like you said you did, could handle him all right."

Sandy looked at Tom as he was mounting on the pinto and said, "Big brother, it looks like you drew the stallion."

Tom replied, "Thank you, my little brother."

As Tom took the reins from the stableboy and started to mount up on the stallion, he asked, "What did you say this horse's name is?"

The stable boy said, "Lightning."

Tom stepped his foot in the stirrup, and before he could get his leg slung over the saddle, Lightning took off like he had been struck by lightning.

Tom was hanging on to the saddle horn for dear life, but he finally got his right leg over the saddle and his butt down on it.

When Sandy saw what happened, he tried to catch up with Tom and his horse, but he soon saw it was useless, so he slowed the pinto down and just tried to keep Tom and his horse in sight.

Tom decided if the stallion wanted to run, he'd let him, but after about an hour of running as fast as his steed could go, Tom pulled back on the reins, and the stallion slowed down to a trot. Then Tom pulled the reins back again, and the stallion slowed down to a walk.

He let his horse walk for a while, then pulled back on the reins and said, "Whoa, Lightning," and his horse stopped.

Tom got off his horse and dropped the reins to the ground to see if Lightning would stay.

Tom was happy to see the stallion stayed where he was.

Several minutes later Sandy and the pinto caught up to where Tom and Lightning were.

When Sandy got up to Tom, he asked, "Did you have a nice ride, big brother?"

"Well, I can tell you the beginning of my ride was pretty exciting. I didn't get my butt in the saddle before Lightning took off running. After that it was a pretty nice ride. So how did you make out with your new pinto, little brother?"

"It was smooth as silk, or at least as smooth as I heard silk was."

"Good for you, it was sure nice of you to let me have this nice gentle stallion."

"No problem, Tom, I know you're so much better than me that you would be able to handle a horse that was little wild."

"Don't say I'm better than you. You're a much better person than I am."

"Sure, everybody knows that."

Tom got back on Lightning and said, "Let's go home and see the folks."

An hour later they rode up to the front of the house and saw their mother sweeping off the front porch. She looked up at them but couldn't see who it was because the sun was in her eyes.

Tom got off his horse and shouted, "Ma, it's Tom and Sandy. We're home."

Their mother stood there for a moment, then rushed as fast as she could to Tom, and he took her in his arms and hugged and kissed her.

His mother said, "Oh, Tom, I prayed so hard and so long that you boys would come home to us. We've been so afraid you would be getting into trouble riding off with a bunch of men. Oh, son, you have no idea how happy Pa will be that you've come home."

Sandy had been standing by Tom and his ma waiting for a chance to give her a hug and a kiss.

Finally, Tom said, "Ma, Sandy's here, too."

Tom released her, and she turned to Sandy, and he took her in his arms and gave her a hug and a kiss and his ma said, "It's about time your brother brought you back home. We've all been missing you both so much."

Sandy said, "We've sure been missing you, Ma, and Pa, and the kids. We're glad to be home."

Ma said, "I hope you had enough of running around the country now. Julie Crockett keeps asking about you every time I see her at church. I think she's sweet on you, that's what I think. I can't stand here talking all day. I've got to fix Pa some dinner now before he gets back from the south field. He's going to be hungry."

Tom asked, "Where are the kids?"

"Your three brothers are with Pa, and the girls are staying over at the Crocketts' with their two girls."

Ma went on into the house and started fixing dinner, and Tom could hear her, thanking the Lord for bring her babies safely back home.

Pa and their three brothers returned to the house a few hours later, and he was so happy his oldest sons had returned home safely.

Ma had dinner ready and had asked Tom and Sandy to help her set the table so everything was ready for the family to sit down for dinner.

Pa said a special thank-you to the Lord for bringing his two oldest sons back home and asked the Lord to keep all his children close to home from now on.

After everyone finished eating their dinner, Tom said, "Pa, Sandy and I brought you a small present to let you know how much we appreciated you being our pa and raising us. We just want to say thank you so much."

Sandy handed their pa the little box with the gold pocket watch in it, and when he opened the box, he couldn't believe what was inside. He had never seen anything like it. It was so beautiful.

Pa didn't know what to say, but finally said, "Thank you, my sons, I'm so proud of you, and thank you for coming back home to Ma and me."

Tom had one more surprise and said, "Ma, we didn't know what you would like, so we wanted to give you something that we know our family always needs."

Than Tom handed her an envelope he picked up at the hotel, and when she opened it, she found three hundred dollars.

She nor Pa had never had that much money at one time in their lives.

Ma began to cry and could only say, "Thank you, boys, I love you."

The family all left the table, and Ma asked two of the younger boys to help her clean the table, and Tom told his pa he needed to talk with him by himself.

The two of them went out to the barn, and Tom said, "Pa, Sandy and I got ourselves mixed up with some really bad men, and we even were involved in kidnapping a woman."

Pa sat down on a bale of hay and shook his head and said, "What made you do it, son? I don't understand."

"Pa, I don't understand it either, but when these men came and bought the horses from us, they asked Sandy and me to go with them. They said they robbed banks, and we thought it sounded so exciting, so we went with them.

"We were never involved in actually robbing any bank, but we were involved in kidnapping a woman in New Orleans, and when we found out the leader of the gang planned to kill her even if the ransom was paid, we turned them in, and the police and her husband saved the lady, but the leader of the gang, Charlie Christian, and another man, Billy Jack Reynolds, got away.

"Pa, Sandy and me are afraid these men may be coming to try to kill you and all of our family. That's why we came home to try to help keep our family alive."

"Tom, is that the only reason you boys came home?"

"No, Pa, we came home because we learned our lesson about being away from the people we loved, and we were coming home anyway. But when we found out these men escaped capture, we knew we had to come home and help protect our loved ones."

"Thank you for that. I don't know how much of this I can tell your ma 'cause she thinks the sun rises and sets 'cause of you. We'll never understand why you would go off with people who told you they robbed banks. Beats the hell out of me."

"Pa, we were just young and stupid. That's my only excuse, and I wouldn't blame you for asking us to leave."

"Son, your ma and I would love you no matter what you done, but I still will never understand why you would go off with such men."

"Neither would I now, Pa."

CHAPTER TWENTY-SIX

Ride, Rangers, Ride

Rocky awoke early the next morning, and as soon as he and Nick had something to eat, they were on their way to San Augustine, Texas.

Spring Rain was rested and was moving along very well after a day or so of rest and some extra grain. Rocky thought they were making very good time.

About noon they came upon a nice little creek, and Rocky thought this would be a good place to stop and let Spring Rain get a drink and eat a little bit of grass before they pushed on.

Rocky knew it was about forty miles to San Augustine, so they should be able to make it in two days easy enough.

Rocky sat down beside the creek, pulled off his boots and socks, and cooled his feet in the fast-moving water.

Rocky would have been content sitting here with his feet in the water and Nick's head resting on his lap the rest of the day, but he knew he had to get back on his way to try to catch up with Charlie and Billy Jack before they had a chance to rob another bank.

Rocky climbed back up on Spring Rain and pushed on toward San Augustine, hoping to get there before Charlie got away or killed another bar girl.

Rocky knew Charlie loved to kill women, and for some reason it seemed to give him great pleasure. He only hoped that he found him before he killed another one in San Augustine.

Rocky had never been too concerned about being able to take care of himself in a gunfight, but he had no idea what Billy Jack Reynolds looked like.

He knew by his reputation that he had killed several men, but he didn't know how he killed them. In other words, was he a fast-draw gunslinger or just some guy who could kill people when they were not really engaged in protecting themselves?

Rocky knew there was a big difference between shooting someone who was facing you with his gun in his holster and shooting someone in the back.

Rocky knew he wasn't as fast a draw as he used to be, but he still kept his fast-draw practice up. Even being a little slower than he used to be meant he would still be one of the fastest draws in Texas.

The other thing about being fast was whether you could hit something you aimed at when you pulled your Colt. Recently in New Orleans, he had proved again that he could pull his weapon and hit what he was shooting at.

The one advantage Billy Jack had was he knew what Rocky Stone looked like from seeing his pictures in the newspaper in New Orleans, and Rocky had no idea of what Billy Jack looked like.

Rocky couldn't worry about that. He had to let his training and instinct take charge of whatever situation he faced with Charlie Christian and Billy Jack Reynolds.

After riding for another five hours, it was time for Rocky to call it a day and get something to eat for himself and Nick and give some grain to Spring Rain.

He needed some rest before he rode into San Augustine and faced his foes.

Rocky got up early the next morning, and Nick lay next to his bedroll for a while after Rocky was up.

Rocky said, "What's the matter, Nick? Up too early for you this morning?"

Nick continued to lay there, but he did wag his tail a little and raised his head up to look at Rocky and then put his head back down on the bedroll.

Rocky fixed himself some coffee and got out some hardtack and dried beef and ate it for his breakfast.

By the time Rocky finished his breakfast, Nick was ready for his.

Rocky gave Nick some of his hardtack and dried beef. Nick sniffed the hardtack and left it lying in the dirt but quickly ate all the dried beef offered to him.

Rocky said, "You're pretty damn particular about your food, Nick. Hardtack's not good enough for you? I know you like your big steak twice a day, well, some days you just can't have what you want. This is one of those days."

Nick rubbed up against Rocky's leg and looked up at him, like, it's okay.

"Nick, you're going to have to be my backup today because I don't know when the rangers can get here to back me up. I don't want to wait for them and let Charlie kill another girl. He's killed enough of them already."

Rocky saddled Spring Rain, picked up his bedroll, tied it on behind his saddle, and they were off to San Augustine.

Rocky decided since they didn't have too many miles to go, he was going to push Spring Rain to get him into town as early this morning as possible.

They made it to town about ten thirty, and Rocky went directly to the only saloon he saw in town. The bartender was just opening the place up when Rocky arrived.

Rocky and Nick went inside and quickly surveyed the saloon and saw they had only about four rooms upstairs. Rocky thought Charlie and Billy Jack must have two of those rooms.

The bartender said, "Looks like you have been riding pretty hard this morning. If you need a drink that bad, you came to the right place."

"Why do you say that?"

"Well, as I was opening the doors, I saw your horse, and he looked like he was sweating quite a bit for so early in the morning."

"Yes, he was, I was pushing him to get in to town as early as I could before there were too many people in town." He gave a rueful smile. "I'd have a cup of coffee if you have some made. I'd like to talk with you where I'm not standing next to the bar where people on the second floor can look down and see me."

"Okay, mister, come with me and I'll get you your cup of coffee, and we can sit down over at one of the tables that's under the balcony."

"Thanks."

The bartender walked over to a door leading into a kitchen located behind the tables and went inside and brought back two cups of steaming coffee.

Rocky sat down, and Nick lay down next to him at one of the tables where Rocky had a good view of the stairs coming down from the balcony by looking into the big mirror behind the bar.

The bartender sat down and asked, "So what's the problem with you standing at the bar to have your coffee?"

"My name is Rocky Stone, Captain of the Texas Rangers, and I believe you may have two men staying here that are wanted for bank robbery, kidnapping, and the murder of several women."

"You don't say. I don't see you wearing a badge."

Rocky took out his badge that read "Captain Texas Rangers" and showed it to the bartender.

Rocky asked, "Do you have two men staying in your rooms upstairs?"

"Yes, in fact, we have all four of our rooms filled right now."

"The men I'm looking for probably have been here for two or three days."

"Yeah, two of the men have been staying here for the last three days, and one of the men has had one of my girls, Tess Brown, with him for the past three days."

"How about the other man? Does he have a girl with him?"

"No, he acts like he doesn't have much interest in the ladies."

"What does that fellow look like?"

"Oh, I don't know. I guess he must be about thirty years old, about five foot six tall, doesn't carry much weight on him. His gun is about the biggest thing about him. It's some kind of a long barrel looking thing. It looks like it's way too big for him.

"He's got a big scar on his right cheek, and if he has his hat off, he's only got a little bit of black hair left on the top of his head. One thing about him, he gives you the impression that he thinks he's a pretty tough hombre."

"Well, he may be. I understand he's a killer. What about the other fellow with him. What does he look like?"

"Totally different. He's about six foot tall, loves the women. He must be over forty years old and not a bad-looking guy. Anyway, the women seem to like him. He's got a couple of guns, one you can see in a holster hanging on his belt and one you can't see. He's got some kind of a rig with a derringer up his right sleeve."

"How do you know that?"

"My girl told me about it. She saw him take it off when they were going to bed."

"What's your name, bartender?"

"Tony Martin."

"Tony, I want to thank you for all the information you've given me, and the last thing you told me may save my life. Tony, do you know what time these guys usually come downstairs?"

"Well, it varies, but I would say the little guy comes down about this time and the tall one comes down around one or one thirty in the afternoon."

Tony had just finished saying that when Rocky saw someone coming down the stairs in the mirror.

Tony glanced at the mirror and said, "That's him."

Rocky took out his badge and pinned it on his shirt. He got up from his chair and watched until Billy Jack was all the way down the stairs and beginning to walk over to the bar.

Rocky said, "Billy Jack Reynolds, you're under arrest for bank robbery and kidnapping. Walk over to the bar and put your gun on the bar with your left hand, then put your hands up over your head and step three paces away from the bar."

Billy Jack started to turn around to face whoever was talking to him, and Rocky calmly said, "I'm a Texas Ranger. Don't turn around. Just keep walking to the bar and put your gun on the bar, like I told you to before."

Billy Jack didn't keep walking as he had been told to do. Instead he began turning his body around to the left so the gun in his holster on the right side was hidden by his body.

As Billy Jack turned, Rocky could see he was reaching to pull his gun out of its holster, so he pulled his .44 and fired one shot just as Billy Jack's gun was being pulled out of his holster.

The bullet hit Billy Jack in the left side of his chest, and it must have gone straight into his heart as he fell hard and now lay crumpled up on the floor with his gun falling out of his hand.

Rocky walked to where Billy Jack's body lay, picked up Billy Jack's gun, and handed it to Tony and said, "Here, Tony, you can have this to display in your saloon. It's the gun belonging to the famous gunman and killer, Billy Jack Reynolds, killed here by a Texas Ranger."

Rocky wasn't sure if Charlie Christian would be concerned if he heard the shot or if he would think it was only some cowboy shooting his gun off for the fun of it. Rocky only knew he would have to be ready for whatever came next.

Several minutes passed and there wasn't any stirring around upstairs, so Rocky wondered if Charlie had even heard the shot that killed his cohort.

Suddenly, Rocky heard a scream from upstairs. It was a woman's voice, and the next thing he saw was a naked woman come running down the stairs holding the right side of her neck. Rocky could see blood spilling out from between her fingers.

Rocky started up the stairs to help her when he heard the sound of the gunshot and felt a pain in his right side.

Rocky fell down on the stairs, and then slowly his body began falling down the stairs, one at a time, until he was lying on the bar room floor.

The woman made it past Rocky, and Tony took a bar towel, folded it, and placed it over the knife cut on the woman's neck.

Charlie Christian started coming down the stairs cautiously, trying to see if he could see anybody else in the saloon other than the bar girl, the bartender, and the two men lying on the floor.

The bartender was busy as he had the bar girl lying down on the bar and was trying his best to stop the bleeding from the cut on her neck.

Charlie went over to where Billy Jack lay and checked to see if he was still alive. He wasn't.

Charlie started walking over to where Rocky was lying; however, he didn't recognize who it was.

When Charlie got close to where Rocky was lying, suddenly Nick jumped on him, knocking Charlie to the floor with Nick on top of him, trying to bite Charlie's neck.

Charlie swung his pistol as hard as he could and hit Nick in the head, knocking him unconscious.

Charlie got up and kicked Nick in the ribs as hard as he could, then made his way over to where Rocky was lying.

Charlie leaned down to turn the man over to see if he had killed him, and when he turned him, he found he had the business end of a gun barrel pointed directly in his face.

Rocky said, "Drop your gun and step back away from me before I pull the trigger on this .44."

Charlie dropped his gun to the floor and stepped back, away from Rocky.

Rocky used the stair railing to help him get up off the floor as Charlie stood there watching to see if he would pass out or something.

After Charlie realized it was his hated enemy, Rocky Stone, he asked, "How's your wife, Rocky?"

"She's in a coma and not expected to live, thanks to you."

"Oh, that's too bad, I really feel bad about that. She was such a pretty little thing, too. You're sure going to miss her."

"Charlie, you make one wrong move and you can be in hell before Latesha's in heaven."

Rocky said, "Tony, can you bring me a chair so I can sit down? Then I want you to put my handcuffs on Charlie Christian for me. Can you do that for me?"

Tony put another bar towel around the bar girl's neck and tied it on with some string.

Tony picked up a chair and started over to where Rocky was leaning against the banister.

Before Tony could get to Rocky, Charlie activated the device on his derringer, and it popped out of Charlie's sleeve, but before he could pull the trigger on the derringer, Rocky shot him right between his eyes, and he dropped the derringer and fell backward to the floor with his head hitting the floor in a thump.

Rocky sat down on the chair Tony brought him, and Rocky said, "You don't have to put the handcuffs on Charlie now.

"Tony, would you see if my dog is all right?"

Then Rocky fell off the chair and back onto the floor.

The saloon doors opened, and in rushed four Texas Rangers with guns drawn.

Tony said, "You fellows can put your guns away. Your captain has already killed the two outlaws you fellows were looking for, but he needs a doctor because he's been shot. One of you needs to go over to Dr. Dodge's office across the street and see if he can come over as soon as possible. We've got two people wounded here and a hurt dog."

One of the rangers turned and ran across the street.

Tony quickly found a sheet and spread it over his naked bar girl. The cut on her neck had almost quit bleeding now.

A few minutes passed as the rangers checked over the two dead outlaws, and Tony said, "Captain Stone told me I could have the two guns that tall fellow had so I could display them in my saloon. I plan to put a plaque under the case saying, 'Charlie Christian, outlaw, was killed on this date by Captain Rocky Stone of the Texas Rangers in the Last Chance Saloon.'"

The ranger in charge, Ben Elliott, said, "It looks like it was certainly the last chance for Charlie Christian and Billy Jack Reynolds."

The ranger who went to the doctor's office came back in a few minutes with Dr. Dodge.

Dr. Dodge looked over the bar girl and said, "I'm going to have to put in some stitches in your neck to completely stop the bleeding."

The girl spoke for the first time and said, "Doc, I need a drink before you start sewing on me."

Tony asked, "If she has a drink, it's not going to be spilling out of the cut on her neck, is it?"

The doctor laughed and said, "Not unless that cut's a lot deeper than I think. Go ahead and give the girl a stiff drink, Tony."

Tony poured out a water glass full of whiskey and handed it to her, and she said, "Tony, you're going to have to hold it for me. I don't have enough strength to hold the glass."

"Okay, I'll do it for you."

Tony carefully lifted up the girl's head, held the glass up to her lips, tipped the glass up, and she got a small amount of whiskey down her throat and promptly passed out.

Dr. Dodge said, "That worked just fine. Now I can get that wound stitched up and she won't even know it."

It took the doctor a short time to put twenty-eight stitches in her neck, and he told Tony, "The best thing you can do for her now is to put her to bed and let her get some rest.

"She should be all right in a few days. Thank goodness, the cut wasn't too deep so she didn't lose too much blood."

By this time two other bar girls had come into the saloon, and Tony said, "Beth, I want you to stay with Peggy. Some damn outlaw tried to kill her and cut her neck."

Tony picked the girl up and wrapped the sheet around her so her bottom wasn't hanging out and took her upstairs to one of the rooms. He put her to bed, and Beth stayed with her.

When Tony returned downstairs, the rangers had picked Rocky up from the floor and placed him on the bar, and the doctor had Rocky's shirt off and was looking at his wound.

Dr. Dodge said, "Well, the bullet is still in there. I'm going to have to get it out before it causes him an infection. It's just as well he's already passed out. It doesn't look like the bullet struck any organs, but it's lodged up next to his rib, so it doesn't look like it's going to be too hard to get out. He has lost quite of bit of blood, which is going to leave him pretty weak for a while, so he's not going to be able to travel."

The doctor opened up his bag and began to lay out several instruments and asked the rangers to help hold Rocky down in case he started to try to get up.

The doctor had one man on each leg, one holding each arm and shoulder and Tony holding down his head.

The doctor took a scalpel and cut a small incision into Rocky's right side and wiped the blood away from the cut and then took a small probe and pried on the bullet to loosen the bullet from around the rib; then he took a large tweezers device and grabbed the bullet with it and pulled it out of Rocky's side.

The doctor took some whiskey and poured it into Rocky's wound. Rocky tried to rise up from the bar, but the rangers and Tony were able to hold him down.

Then Rocky settled back down, and the doctor said, "He will be okay now."

The doctor cleaned the wound and stitched it up.

"Tony, you're going to have to find a room for Rocky because he's going to need several days' rest before he can travel. I'll come back and check on both of my patients before I go home tonight."

Tony said, "Just a minute, Doc, you've got one more patient."

"Who else got hurt? Did you get hurt Tony?"

"No, Doc, it's the German shepherd lying over there by the back wall."

"Tony, I'm not a horse doctor. What do you think I can do?"

"Doc, in case you hadn't noticed, he's a dog, not a horse."

"Okay, I'll take a look at him, but he better not bite me."

Dr. Dodge walked over to where Nick was lying and leaned over to check Nick and found he had a wound on his head.

The doctor took some whiskey, cleaned up the wound, and tried to put a small bandage on Nick's wound, but Nick wouldn't keep his head still long enough for Doc to put a bandage on.

Dr. Dodge said, "You know, don't you, you're not the best patient I've ever had, but if you don't want a bandage on your head, okay. I'll leave it off."

Nick got up off the floor and went over to where Rocky was and lay down next to him.

Tony said, "Rangers, if you can take Rocky up to room number 1, I'll have my cleaning lady get the room cleaned up and you can put him in bed."

Tony's cleaning woman came into the saloon and saw the two bodies lying on the floor and Rocky lying on the bar and said, "Looks like you had a busy morning."

Tony replied, "You could say that. Can you get room 1 cleaned up and put on some clean bedding so we can move this Texas Ranger upstairs and put him in a bed and let me have my bar back in case we get a customer in here today?"

The cleaning woman replied, "I'll get the bed and the room ready."

It didn't take her long to have the room ready, and four of the rangers took Rocky upstairs and put him in bed, with Nick following along right behind them.

Once the rangers had Rocky in bed, Nick lay down right next to his bed.

Tony said, "One of you rangers needs to take Rocky's horse down to the livery stable. It's tied up in front of the saloon."

Ben Elliott told one of his rangers to take Rocky's horse to the stable and explain that his owner, Captain Rocky Stone of the Texas Rangers, had been shot and was resting at the Last Chance Saloon and would come and get him as soon as he able.

Then Ben said, "Tony, when Rocky is alert enough to know what you're telling him, please tell him that Ben Elliott with the Texas Rangers will send a telegram to his father-in-law, Henry Hudson, letting him know that Rocky killed Charlie Christian and Billy Jack Reynolds, and although he was wounded, he will be all right."

"No problem, I'll tell him as soon as I know he'll understands it."

CHAPTER TWENTY-SEVEN

Reunion and the Mission

Dr. Dodge stopped by the Last Chance Saloon to check on his three patients on his way home for the evening.

First, he checked on the bar girl, Tess Brown, and found she was doing very well and was well enough already to be worrying about how bad the scar on her neck was going to be.

Dr. Dodge said, "I wouldn't be worried about the scar. You're lucky to be alive. If he'd cut you a little lower and a little deeper, you wouldn't be here with us tonight. You might want to think about doing sometime else with your life."

Tess said, "Thanks for the advice, Doctor. It would be good if I could find something else."

"Tess, I'll tell you what, if you decide you want a different kind of life, you let me know, and maybe you could come to work for me. I could use a smart girl like you and one that didn't faint at the sight of blood."

"Dr. Dodge, what would your patients think about you letting a bar girl work in your office?"

"That's not my worry, like what are they going to do, go to some other doctor? The closest doctor from here is forty mile away. I don't think it's a problem. Besides, people have short memories. They would soon forget you ever worked in a saloon if they ever even knew you did."

Dr. Dodge left Tess's room and went down to Rocky's room and found Ben Elliott had one of his rangers, Randy Hughes, staying with Rocky.

Randy introduced himself to Dr. Dodge and said, "Rocky hasn't roused up at all since we brought him upstairs."

Dr. Dodge checked Rocky's bandage and found it looked all right and then said, "Randy, I don't think we want to try to wake him up. Let's let him get as much rest as he can, and I'll check back on him in the morning. I guess I better see how his dog is doing."

Dr. Dodge walked to the other side of Rocky's bed and found Nick lying next to Rocky's bed. When the doctor reached down to touch Nick, he got up and rubbed against the doctor's pant leg.

Dr. Dodge rubbed his hand down the side of Nick's neck and could see his head was looking better.

The doctor said, "Okay, boy, I think you're going to be all right."

Randy asked, "Dr. Dodge, do you think it would be all right if I took the dog outside and then got him some water and something to eat?"

"I think you would become a good friend by doing that. I'm sure he needs to go outside, and I'm pretty sure he would like to have some water and something to eat."

"What do you think he would like to eat, Doctor?"

"After what he's been through today, I would say a nice big raw steak would do him very well."

"Okay, Doctor, I'll tell Tony that the doctor ordered a big steak for him."

Randy took Nick outside and then came back into the saloon and told Tony the doctor said the dog needed a nice big steak.

Nick soon had his steak and a large bowl of water, both of which he finished in short order. Then Nick went back next to Rocky's bed and lay down and promptly went to sleep.

The next morning when Dr. Dodge came to see how Rocky was doing, he was surprised to find Rocky sitting up on the edge of the bed asking Randy where his clothes were.

Dr. Dodge said, "Hold on a few minutes, ranger. I'm Dr. Dodge, and I'm the one who dug a bullet out of you yesterday afternoon, and

I don't think you're ready for your clothes just yet. I think you're going to need some more bed rest. Let's take a look at your wound so I can see how you are coming along. Please lay back down so I can check you over."

Rocky laid back down on the bed and his head told him maybe he wasn't ready to get up and get dressed yet. Rocky felt like he was going to pass out.

Dr. Dodge checked the wound and found the bandage was spotted with blood. The doctor put on a clean bandage and said, "Rocky, I would be a lot happier if you didn't try to get out of bed yet. At least try to stay in bed as much as you can today, and then I'll check you in the morning to see how you're doing."

Rocky nodded his head okay without saying a word.

The following morning Rocky was feeling much better, and after Dr. Dodge changed his bandage he said, "Rocky, you're healing up very well. I would say if you can take it easy for another week, I would be willing to tell you that you can get out of San Augustine."

"Okay, Doctor, we'll see, but I have to tell you if I get to feeling a lot better before then, I'm on my way to see how my wife is.

"She in St. Mary's Hospital in Rochester, Minnesota, and I don't know if she's ever going to recover from being in a coma or not."

"Okay, Rocky, but it won't do much good if she recovers and you die, will it?"

"I guess not, Doc."

"Good, I'll see you in the morning. Take it easy and look after your dog. I understand he may have saved your life by attacking that fellow when you were down on the floor. He sure took a nasty blow to his head for doing it and several kicks in the ribs. What's your dog's name anyway?"

"It's Nick. He's a good dog, but I didn't know he attacked Charlie Christian after I'd been shot."

"You can talk to Tony, He can tell you all about it."

"Thanks, Doctor, I will."

The very next morning when Dr. Dodge came to see Rocky, he found Rocky dressed, sitting on the bed, and Rocky said, "I'm okay, Doctor, I'm on my way to Minnesota today."

"Well, before you go, let me take a look at my handiwork one more time."

"Okay, Doctor."

Rocky lay back down on the bed and let the doctor check his wound one more time.

After Dr. Dodge dressed the wound again, he said, "You're healing up very well, but I want you to take along some bandages so you can change the dressing daily.

"Don't do anything that might tear those stitches, and when you get completely healed up, go to a doctor and have him take the stitches out."

"Okay, thank you, Doctor, for looking after me."

After the doctor left Rocky, Nick and Randy stopped downstairs to thank Tony for all his help.

Tony told Rocky all about how Nick jumped Charlie Christian, which allowed Rocky time to get his gun out when Charlie was coming over to finish him off.

Randy went to the livery stable and got their horses for them, and when he came back to the saloon, Rocky and Nick were waiting outside for him.

Two days later they rode into Nacogdoches and stopped at the rangers' station. Ben Elliott handed Rocky a telegram from Henry Hudson they had been holding for him.

Rocky's hands were shaking as he opened the envelope and read the telegram that said Latesha had regained consciousness and was improving daily and that Henry planned to take her to Boonville as soon as Dr. Mayo released her to travel.

Tears were falling down Rocky's cheeks, and Ben said, "I'm sorry it was bad news about your wife."

Rocky said, "On the contrary, my friend, my wife is doing well and will soon be on her way home to Boonville, Missouri. I hope to be home to meet her."

The following day Rocky sent a telegram to Henry telling him that he was on his way to Boonville and hoped to see him soon.

Randy rode along with Rocky to Tyler to be certain he didn't have a relapse from his gunshot wound.

Where's My Wife?

Rocky thanked Randy and asked him to tell all the rangers in Nacogdoches again how much he appreciated their help.

Rocky and Nick boarded the train to Shreveport with Spring Rain riding in a cattle car. From Shreveport they would transfer to a train to Kansas City, then on to Boonville by another train.

Three days later they arrived in Boonville, and as he was waiting for Spring Rain to be unloaded, he saw Henry's private railcar parked on the siding.

As soon as Rocky had Spring Rain saddled up, he was on his way home that overlooked the Missouri River and to see his sweet wife.

As Rocky rode through the streets of Boonville, he saw several people he knew, and they shouted and asked how come he'd been gone so long.

Rocky shouted back, "You'll have to buy my new book. It will tell you all about it."

The people all laughed, and all Rocky could do was smile.

When he got home, he flew off Spring Rain and into his house with Nick right by his side. Rocky was shouting, "Latesha," and, of course, she didn't answer.

So through the house he went, then out to the backyard, and there he saw Latesha and Henry watching traffic on the big muddy Missouri River below them.

When Latesha saw Rocky, she ran directly into his arms. He picked her up and gave her the biggest, longest kiss they had ever had in their lives.

The kiss ended only when they needed to take a breath, and Latesha said, "Rocky, are you sure it's all right for you to be picking me up?"

"Hell no, I'm not sure, but I'm picking you up anyway. Oh God, how I've missed you. I love you so much, and I thought I'd lost you forever. Gosh, you look wonderful, Latesha. Dr. Mayo and his people did a great job getting you well."

Latesha looked Rocky up and down and said, "Cowboy, you look pretty good to me too."

Henry walked up to where they were holding each other and said, "Rocky, son, you look good, and you look even better in my girl's arms."

Rocky said, "Henry, I'll never be able to repay you for doing such a great job of taking care of Latesha for me."

"I didn't just do it for you. She's my girl, too, you know."

"Of course I do, she has always been your girl, from the day she was born."

During all this, Nick stood next to Rocky watching every move the three of them made.

Latesha asked, "Rocky when did we get a dog, and what's his name?"

Rocky said, "It's a long story, but he's been with me for so long now. To think I never thought of having a dog before. His name is Nick. He's a great dog, and he helped save my life. I'll tell you all about it later."

Nick seemed to take up with Latesha and her to him, as Nick went up to her and rubbed against her skirt, and she gently petted him behind his ear.

They spent the rest of the day talking about everything each one of them had been through since the last time they were together.

Latesha said, "Okay, Rocky, we've talked about lots of things, but you have to show me where you were shot."

Rocky answered, "Okay, but it's a long way to the Last Chance Saloon in San Augustine, Texas."

Latesha shouted, "Rocky, you smart-ass, I'm talking about where the bullet hit you!"

Rocky answered, "Okay, you don't have to get riled up about it."

"Yes, I do, I care about you, and I want to see where a bullet went in you."

Rocky didn't say another word. He pulled his shirt out of his of his pants and pointed to the bandage on the right side of his body just above his pants.

Latesha said, "Well, it doesn't look like it's too big of a hole in your side, judging by your bandage."

Rocky replied, "Well, it was a small bullet, but believe me, it didn't feel too small when it hit me. The local doctor, Dr. Dodge, did a good job of removing the bullet that was pressing against a rib. So now I'm getting all healed up, and all I have to do is to have a doctor take my stitches out. Then I'll be through with everything about my gunshot wound."

Latesha said, "I'm glad you are okay. I was really worried about you going after those men."

"It's all right now. These men will never be coming after you or me again because I killed both of them. You know, I'm getting hungry. Do we have anything to eat in this house?"

Henry replied, "As a matter of fact we do have food here, and I'll ask my cook to make you a banquet to celebrate both of you recovering from your ordeals."

Henry's cook, John Paul, fixed them a wonderful dinner, and they had a bottle of champagne, well, maybe two. It was a wonderful homecoming for Latesha and Rocky, and they were both so pleased Latesha's father, Henry Hudson, was there to share it with them.

Henry told them over their last glass of champagne that the next day he had to go back to New York City. He said, "Children, I've been away for much too long, and there are several new projects that need my personal attention. I would like for both of you to come to New York as soon as you can so you can begin to understand the projects and the people we are working with.

"I think you will find it fascinating to see all the new inventions coming in this new century. Just think of it, we'll soon be in the twentieth century. Our world will change so much you will never believe it, and you can have a big part in making these changes and making our world a better place for all of our people."

Rocky replied, "Henry, I really appreciate you wanting me to come to be a part of all of these projects, but basically, I'm nothing more than a nineteenth-century lawman and have been lucky enough to write a few stories that made a little money. Besides, it's Latesha that has the business sense because you've been training her to take over your business since she was a little girl. She's got the education and the knowledge about what you are doing.

"I would be just in the way. It's Latesha that you need, and I'm willing to not only come to see you in New York but for us to move there so Latesha can be a part of this new twentieth century, with you standing right by her side."

Henry listened closely to each of Rocky's words and said, "Rocky, I've liked you since you and Latesha were married, but I didn't know your character or the drive you have, and certainly not your intelligence.

"You have a native ability to judge people, which you need when you're deciding if you could trust them with your money to make a project successful. You can't learn that lesson from any book. I think it's not only Latesha who needs you. I need you too, to help build this twentieth century. In fact, we both need you."

Latesha added, "I'm glad father sees all of the qualities you have that I've known about since I first met you. I couldn't take on father's work without your help."

Rocky replied, "Sorry, folks, with all this talk about how wonderful I am and how much you both need me, I'm going to have to go to bed right now because tomorrow I'm going to have such a busy day. I'll have to spend all day looking for a bigger hat because my poor head is swelling so much tonight. "

Latesha and Henry both started laughing so hard that they couldn't stop for several minutes, and then Latesha said, "I can see if we don't need you for anything else, we'll have to keep you around so we can have a good laugh."

Henry added, "Rocky, Latesha's right, we always need a good laugh, but you are way more than someone to provide us with a laugh. You are able to provide us with real common sense knowledge because you weren't brought up where you had people to do everything for you. You were never like Latesha and I, who never had to worry about if you could afford something you wanted.

"Rocky, you've learned and earned everything you've ever had and have belonged in the so-called *real world* that Latesha and I haven't. You can be a real asset to not only us, but to the *masses* of people living in America."

Rocky sat there and didn't say anything for several minutes. The three of them sat in silence for several minutes before Rocky finally said, "Henry, Latesha, I've heard what you both said, and although I'm not as sure that I can be as much help to you as both of you think, I can tell you there is no way I can say to you I won't do it.

"I will do my best to help you with whatever you are trying to accomplish. About these new inventions coming in the twentieth century that you think will help these *masses* of people, I will also help you with that, not because I think I can but because I love both of you."

Latesha and Henry both put their arms around him and told him they loved him, too.

After the hugs, Rocky said, "Latesha, you and I have one more thing we have to do before we go to New York, and that is we have to go to Texas and pay Tom and Sandy Barr their reward of $250,000 for helping us set you free."

Latesha said, "Of course we do, but are you sure I'm worth all that money?"

Rocky and Henry both said, "Yes, we do."

Henry said, "Now that our future is settled, I'm going to bed, and you two should do the same. It's getting late."

Latesha answered, "Yes, Father."

Rocky piped up and said, "Yes, Dad, we're on our way."

Henry smiled and went upstairs to his bedroom, and Rocky and Latesha soon followed to their bedroom.

When they got into their bedroom Rocky said, "It's been a long time since we've been in this bedroom together, and I've had a lot of dreams about us being together here. I spent a long time wondering if we would ever be in bed together again. Now here we are. God, I missed you so much, my love, and I'm sorry I wasn't with you when you were in the hospital in Rochester."

Latesha said, "The only thing important now is you're here and I'm here."

Rocky reached for Latesha, and they held each other a long time, telling each other how much they loved and missed each other.

The next morning came much too quickly for Latesha and Rocky. They didn't want to leave the confines of their bed or bedroom. They just wanted to be with each other and let the world go its own way.

They stayed in their bedroom until almost eleven o'clock, and when they went downstairs, they discovered Henry and his people had already left for New York.

Latesha found a note from her father which read, "Dear Latesha and Rocky, I look forward to you joining me in New York as soon as you finish your mission and have a chance to enjoy each other's company. Love, Dad."

Latesha handed the note to Rocky, and after he read it, he said, "We need to get started, as your dad said, on our mission of taking the reward money to Tom and Sandy Barr and telling them how much we appreciated their help in setting you free."

"Can we have breakfast first? I'm still trying to catch up on all of the meals I was deprived of when I was kidnapped."

"Of course you can, my love. You can have two breakfasts if you want to, as long as you fix them yourself."

Latesha said, "Damn, why don't we have a cook?"

"Sorry, love, we're just one of those *masses* that have to cook for themselves. However, I'll help you if you would like me to."

"I can't have that, since I'm just one of those poor Missouri housewives who have to do all the cooking, scrubbing, and taking the laundry down to the creek to wash up our few clothes."

Breakfast would have to wait a little longer since the poor housewife and the master of the house found they had something more important to do with their morning than making breakfast.

Five days later, Rocky, Latesha, and Nick were pulling up in front of the Barrs' ranch house in Texas with a rented team and buggy.

Tom Barr was working out near the barn when he saw them pull up at the house and came over to where Rocky stopped the buggy.

Tom said, "Mr. Stone, is that you?"

Rocky replied, "Yes, Tom, it's me and my wife, Latesha, and we came to thank you for your and Sandy's help freeing Latesha."

Tom said, "Mrs. Stone, I'm so happy to see you looking so well. I was afraid you were not going to make it. The last time I saw you, you were in really bad condition. I've said a lot of prayers for you."

Latesha said, "You know, Tom, now I remember you. You were the only one who tried to help me when I was kidnapped. You even gave me more water than what Charlie wanted me to have."

"Mrs. Stone, I wanted to do a lot more to help you, but I was too afraid of Charlie and Billy Jack Reynolds because I knew they would kill me and my brother if I did. I'm still afraid Charlie and Billy Jack will ride up to our ranch and kill my whole family. He hated me that much."

By this time, all of Tom's family had gathered around the buggy, and Mr. Barr said, "Won't you folks step down and come into the house?"

Rocky replied, "Yes, sir, we would be honored to."

Rocky got out of the buggy as Tom helped Latesha out.

Once inside, Tom said, "Folks, this is Rocky and Latesha Stone. He's a famous writer and a retired Texas Ranger. I'm sorry to say that Mrs. Stone was the lady that Sandy and I helped some very bad men kidnap.

"I know you all didn't know anything about Sandy and me being involved in something like that, but I think all of you need to know we made a big mistake by getting involved with the wrong kind of men.

"Ma, I know Sandy and I are awfully ashamed to tell you and the kids we did something like that, but we did."

Sandy was standing back away from the rest of the family and looking very distraught at what Tom had just told his family.

Rocky spoke up then and said, "Tom and Sandy made a mistake, but they stepped up and did something to make up for it. They helped us save my wife, Latesha, from been killed by these men.

"The reason we're here today is to say thank you personally to both Tom and Sandy. Otherwise, my wife would have died at the hands of these men. We're also here today to give them a reward for helping us capture these men and freeing Latesha."

Latesha said, "Tom, Sandy, would you come here by me? I want to give each one of you a cashier's check for one hundred and twenty-five thousand dollars, along with a big kiss for saving my life."

Tom came up to Latesha first, and she handed him his check and planted a kiss right on his lips.

Next Sandy came, and Latesha and gave him his check and kissed him on his lips.

Rocky said, "I hope this money will help all of your family and give all of them a better life. I would like to give Tom and Sandy each a big kiss myself, but instead, I'll give them a warm handshake."

All of the family laughed at Rocky's statement.

Rocky said, "One more thing I would like to do, and that is to speak to Tom and Sandy by myself before Latesha and I have to leave, if that's okay."

No one had any problem with that, and Rocky, Latesha, Nick, Tom, and Sandy walked out to the buggy.

When they got there, Rocky said, "I want you to know you don't have to worry anymore about Charlie Christian or Billy Jack Reynolds coming here trying to kill you and your family. An ex-Texas Ranger killed both of them in San Augustine, Texas, a little over two weeks ago."

Tom asked, "Was that ex-Texas Ranger's name Rocky Stone?"

Latesha answered, "Yes, that's his name."

Sandy said, "Thank you. We really appreciate that, Mr. Stone."

Tom added, "Life for us will be a lot better knowing that. Thank you, Mr. Stone."

Tom helped Latesha into the buggy and got in, and Rocky said, "I never want to ever hear about either one of you ever getting in trouble again."

Tom and Sandy both said, "Don't worry, Mr. Stone, we won't."

Tom and Sandy went back in the house and told their folks they planned to divide the money up so that their folks had enough money to pay off the loan on the ranch and enough money so they could add on more land to the ranch.

They also told their folks they planned to put money aside for each of their brothers and sisters, so when they were eighteen years old, they could draw their money and use it for whatever they needed it for.

Both of them planned to buy their own ranch and hoped they would be getting married very soon.

On the way back to town to make arrangements for their trip to New York to begin their new life working with Henry Hudson IV, Rocky said, "Latesha, I promise you I will never write another book where the wife gets kidnapped or murdered."

"Rocky, you'll never know how happy that makes me feel."

THE END

CLARK SELBY
"SELBY MASTER OF MAYHEM"

Clark Selby was born in 1936 in Miami, Oklahoma, and attended school in Kansas and Oklahoma. He and his wife, Karen Serene Selby, live in Springfield, Missouri.

He spent over forty-five years in the parking industry. Clark's work in the parking industry took him to over sixty countries on six continents.

During his years in the parking industry he served as Director of Parking for the City of Hutchinson, Kansas; Assistant Director of Transportation and Parking for the University of Iowa; Parking Consultant with De Leuw Cather & Company, a Transportation Engineering Company in Chicago and Project Manager for a parking study in Perth, Western Australia.

He worked for several years for Duncan Industries, as a Sales and Service Engineer; Director of Manufacturing, then was promoted to Vice President of International Sales and President of the company.

As Vice President of International Sales for Duncan Industries, he won the *President of the United States Excellence in Exporting Award*.

Clark last position in the parking industry was President of Worldwide Parking Corporation, before he retired to care for his first wife, Patricia after she became paralyzed and he continued to care for her until she passed away.

Clark served in the Kansas Army and Air Force National Guard for more than six years before he began traveling in the parking industry and was a Sergeant in radio communications.

Clark and his wife, Karen spend as much time as possible traveling and exploring places they haven't been and plan to keep doing it as long as their health allows them to.

Clark loves writing new novels and plans to keep doing it, as he says, *"I always hope my books tell a good story."*